Iris:
Queen of the Partially Redeemed

(Persephone, Book #2)

Regan Wolfrom

1

NOT EXACTLY SILVER LINING FRIDAY

Things got worse before they… well, they haven't gotten better yet, actually.

I mean, things are a little better with Iris not being a zombie anymore, but given that the rest of the world seems headed in the opposite direction she is, it's not exactly Silver Lining Friday here in the Red River Valley.

But we'll make do, because somewhere in our blood is the blood of hard-nosed European farmers who were used to things like cold and damp sod houses and every second infant going blind or dying off altogether.

Errol's Dad had reached a country radio station in Winnipeg, and told them about the outbreak and the cure, and in response they'd just assumed he was trying to troll them.

And about a minute and thirty of trying to convince them, the signal went dead.

The sat phone wasn't dead.

But it couldn't make any more calls.

So that's a crap sandwich with a side of… more crap.

It had taken Dad and Beth and Kellen some time to fully recover from being carved up like prime cuts of meat, longer than I would have expected for magical manic pixie dreambots, but obviously less time than most people would need if they'd had their frickin tongues lopped off.

And all the while, the three of them had needed way more food and water than you'd expect, probably five times what a normal NDSU lineback would need, enough that I'd wondered more than once if we'd actually remembered to cure them after we'd got them out of Fargo.

But we had, using the same handful of syringes we'd used on

3

everyone else, drawn directly from me and Iris.

It didn't take more than ten mL of blood to kill off the parasite, we'd deduced, so it hadn't been particularly taxing on our nubile young *bothot* bodies. But I'll definitely feel like some kind of dairy cow for vampires if we have to do the rest of the frickin human race.

I know that Iris had been all hot for angsty vampires when she was just discovering the joys of male six-packs, but I doubt she's big on spending the next ten years of her life being milked for her bot blood.

I'm sure there's someone out there who's into that kind of thing, but I doubt that weirdo happens to have the cure *slash* vaccine pumping through their pervy veins.

Kellen showed us quite early on that he had a serious broken-brain problem that the bots can't fix. He took the magic minivan we'd gotten from the cannibal wannabes — still one of the only ones we'd seen that hadn't been shut down by big brother — and drove before sunrise into the megalopolis of Moorhead, to join in with the zombie looters in seeing what they could grab from the nearest sporting goods store.

We almost placed bets on it, but while Iris and Dad and I were standing out on the driveway of our temporary headquarters, still stuck debating the ethics — and giving Fender friendly pats on that black patch on his otherwise brown head — when Kellen and his scraggly goatee came back.

Dad wasn't pleased when he saw what the minivan was holding, a little bottled water and beef jerky, along with several compound bows and a buttload of arrows.

"Guns were too hard to get," Kellen said. "And these are better."

"Have you ever shot an arrow?" Dad asked him.

"Nope. Haven't shot a gun, either."

"The arrows are perfect," Iris said. "Thank you, Kellen."

He smiled at her. I mean, he gave her *the smile*.

And with that a short-lived period came to a close, the one in which it hadn't been proven beyond a doubt which of the Schmidt sisters Kellen would choose to fawn over. No bets had been placed on that, either. Especially since Iris is currently winning against me by around 130,000 to zip. Or 130,000 to Errol Kimmern. So I guess that's slightly better?

"So why are arrows perfect, anyway?" I asked.

"For the blood," Iris said.

"It's an arrow, not a straw. And I don't think you should be drinking that stuff."

"You want to bite every person we come across, Seffy? Or strap them down for a hot bot injection?"

Now I understood. It's been a long month.

I took an arrow out through the sidedoor of the minivan.

I passed it to Iris.

She took the arrow and sliced the tip into her hand. "So we scrape the arrow across our palm," she said. "Get a little bit of supergirl blood on it. Then we shoot it into our friends and neighbours, and voila! No more zombies. Assuming that it's enough blood to do the job."

"Better than biting," I said.

"Less homoerotic," Dad said.

Iris and I both gave him *the glare*.

"Seriously, Dad?" I said.

"So where do we go?" Kellen asked. "What do we do next?"

"What was it like out there?" Dad asked him.

"They assumed I was infected," he said. "I think we seem that way if we don't get too close. Because they can sense the bots, but I don't know if they can read them."

"But they can read them if you get close," I said. "And I'm probably a shining beacon of botless wonder."

"Yeah."

"We can't just drive straight into town and start slinging bloody arrows at large crowds of people," Iris said. "We're bound to pick up a few bullets in our brains. And that makes it kinda hard not to die, bots or no bots."

"We should focus on survival," Dad said. "First and foremost. We find a place farther out, and we gather supplies."

"We can't be wasting that kind of time," I said. "My mom is still out there. And how many other people we care about?"

"Once we know we're okay, we can try going into the city. Try to bring people over."

"Bring people over?" Kellen said. "So we pick them off one by one?"

Dad nodded. "Exactly. Find a way to isolate them, small groups at most."

"Mom first," I said. "That's who we need to find. And Aunt Callie."

Dad gave another nod. But it felt like he was just patronizing me. Like he wasn't particularly invested in tracking down his ex-wife and her sister. Not a huge surprise, actually.

But it's not really up to him, is it?

I realized that I hadn't mentioned Iris' boyfriend David, or his busy tongue. I wondered if Iris would mention him...

"We'll find them, Seffy," Iris said. "Don't worry."

Maybe David was becoming the afterthought he so rightly deserved to be.

"It sounds like a tall order," Kellen said. "Really risky."

"It's important," I said.

"To you."

I nodded. "To pretty much everyone who isn't you."

Not that I believed that. Mom and Aunt Callie were my family. No one else's.

Iris walked over and started inspecting the rest of the bows. She took out one that was almost a dead ringer for the classic "lady bow" I'd shot her with, back when I'd convinced myself that she was a particularly lithe-yet-buxom turkey.

"So it'll be like picking teams for dodgeball," Iris said. "So, first off: no fat chicks."

"Not funny," I said. "Even with the bots, I still got an intense food baby A-T-M."

Along with a surprisingly large list of things I still want to change about myself. Bots don't make you perfect, really, as I've happened to notice quite clearly by looking in the mirror; they're just as good as you can get, which for me, means not as good as I want to be. Because let's face it, if you could choose between my winning personality and Iris' long legs, goddess nose, and sheer Iris-ness, you'd take the hot blonde in a nanosecond.

And let's face it... bots were never going to fix whatever the frick is going on with my hair... I mean... it's like the world's creepiest-looking octopus mated with a bowl of moldy spaghetti.

Iris reached out and patted my little paunch. "It's so adorable," she said with a grin. "Like you swallowed the world's cutest pot-bellied pig."

I punched her on the shoulder.

"Unwanted weight comes from all that gluten in your diet," Kellen said. "Oh, and GMOs. *Especially* if there are GMOs in any of it."

Iris and I stared at him.

Dad laughed.

"What?" Kellen said.

"These girls are going to tear you to shreds," Dad said. "And I think it'll be good fun for all of us."

So I've made a decision, to give my father the rest of the day. Just Friday, to find a home base and get done what he needs to, before I bring whoever I can with me, to head into downtown Fargo, to get Mom and Aunt Callie. Assuming they hadn't gotten blown apart by the bombing run, they were still trapped in a city filled with over-clocked zombies.

A city where the food would run out at any point, now, and once that happens, the zombies will turn on each other. Those messed-up cannibals with a taste for Daddy-thigh were only the start of it.

And... I love my mom, but I know that with everything else she's going through, she wouldn't have any chance of being the last zombie standing. And she'd cause more than enough trouble to drag Aunt Callie down with her.

I know we don't have much time. Assuming we have any left at all.

So, unrelated, but it's no surprise that Dad still hasn't told Iris who her real father was; apparently his *t. gondii* infection managed to render him *permanently gutless*.

He'll have today for that, too.

I'm going to tell her on Saturday, if he hasn't done it by then. I'm going to tell Iris that somehow she and I are actually related to each other. That whatever is in her that makes every man swoon is stuffed deep down inside of me, too.

I guess maybe David's slimy tongue had found it, and that's why it went in for the kiss.

I know I'll have to save David if I see him.

And then I'll have to tell Iris what he did.

So either way — and I know this sounds really effing harsh — whatever's left of David will still end up as a hunk of dead meat.

We'd discussed sticking it out where we were, but where we were was a house that was just too small. We were already ten people and the world's cutest effing dog, and on top of Mom and Aunt Callie, we wanted to bring in even more people as we went, at least until it was safe enough to try and get our lives back on track... not that I think we can go back to something... it's more like we'll move on to something new.

I still wonder what will happen with Jetta and Leona; I know Leona wants to get north to Canada as soon as possible, but I think Jetta's torn. I think she doesn't want to leave us.

But since we have one van with precious little gas at the moment, those stinky-bottomed Canadian girls aren't going anywhere yet.

I know we'll find fuel for that minivan soon; most farms have gas and/or diesel for their machinery, so it's just a matter of time before we stumble on the right stuff.

It's quiet out here, quieter than usual, which is usually pretty quiet... *did I mention the quiet?*

I think a good number of farmers were already in the city, since the fields were done for the season, and you'd be surprised how many farmers have part time work in town during the winter. Maybe some of the others are still hunkered down in the farmhouses, waiting for the crapstorm to pass.

Maybe some are like us; maybe they saw what happened to Fargo, and they're well on their way to the quietest corner of Minnesota. I *think* that bit's a little to the north of us, north of Grand Forks and Highway 2, close to the Canadian border.

Heading north would be good for all of us, I think, assuming we don't hit some new isolation line. From what we've seen, people who show up on the edges of our little asylum aren't being greeted with warm cups of cocoa.

The network is still down, obviously — as well as the sat phone connection or whatever, not that I know how it could help for navigation — so we're relying on paper maps to figure things out. Dad thinks we should cross Highway 75, to try and find a quiet corner away from major transportation links.

Pat is arguing for crossing back into North Dakota, since we all know it better than the Minnesota Gopher side of the valley.

Iris thinks we shouldn't be so damned ambitious, that we should just find the closest big farmhouse we can find, and move in.

I think I agree with her.

And it won't be hard to get Jetta on board, no matter what Leona says.

So that's what we'll do.

Occam's razor. No assumptions about less people or fewer roads.

The closest bed is the best bed, assuming it isn't already in use.

Kellen drove us north along the river, Dad in the passenger seat with Dan's rifle and Pat toting his own gun at the far back, all of us keeping an eye out for anything bigger than our last stop. Two miles up we found a nice yardsite, but the ranch house wasn't big enough.

And we saw what could be signs of life, an SUV with the back hatch open, and what looked like supplies inside.

"Could be another group of survivors," Errol said.

"Could be bloodthirsty zombies," Iris said.

"High risk, little reward," Dad said, twisting his body around to face the peanut gallery.

Iris groaned. "*Frick,* Dad. What does that even mean?"

"It means that either they're zombies and will want to hurt us, or they're not zombies and still might want to hurt us. Did you not hear what happened to your sister in Enderlin?"

"They wanted my girl parts," I said.

It's funny that a girl like me seems to only get noticed when it's time for the guys to get all skeevy. Like I have a sign on my ass that says "EZ-tap".

"We won't save anyone by hiding out," Iris said.

Dad shook his head. "We won't save anyone by dying, either." He looked over to me, twisting back a little further. "Head shots will kill us, won't they?"

"Probably," I said. What am I, a brain scientist?

"Your father's right," Errol said.

"Someone's a kiss-up," Iris said.

Kellen kept driving north, the gravel road curving around a bend of the Red River.

He reached a sign along the road and slowed the minivan.

"Gaia's Point B&B," Kellen said, reading it out loud for some reason, as if any of us wouldn't have locked our eyes onto the frickin thing.

"I've heard of it," Leona said, from the row behind me.

"*You've* heard of it?" Dad asked.

"We were looking for a place to stay. This one was way over-priced, but they had space."

"How much space?"

"I'm not a tour guide," she said with a smirk.

"You'd make a great one, Leona," Jetta said. "A perfect combo of know-it-all and excellent cleavage."

I laughed. And felt Jetta's hand squeeze my shoulder.

I turned to look at her.

"You all have good cleavage," she said. "Erm… maybe not Fen-der… or Mr. Schmidt…"

"You really don't need to talk, Jetta," Leona said.

Kellen turned down the long driveway, passing through a large garden with wilted flowers and vegetable stalks. Not spooky wilted, just end of the season wilted.

"Don't see any vehicles," Dad said. "Maybe they bugged out."

"I like it," Iris said. "Persephone and Iris, two botshot goddesses, hanging with an Ancient Greek Mother Earth."

"I want to be a goddess," Jetta said.

"It's a highly-sought position," I said. "And I'm not sure you can get there being named after a rusted-out Volkswagen."

"Then I'll change my name. I'll be Gaia."

"You just want top bunk," Iris said. "Assuming they have bunks."

"It's not a summer camp," I said.

"No," Leona said, "somehow it's even worse."

We all followed her jutted-out finger and matching chin.

A big handpainted sign in cutesy lettering.

GMO and Toxin Free Reffuge

I looked over at Kellen.

He smiled at me.

And pulled the car up in front of a very large two-and-a-half story farmhouse. Custom-built to look a lot older than it was.

For ambience, I guess.

"You know they spelt that wrong, right?" I asked him. "Too many Fs?"

"And they should probably have hyphens on 'GMO' and 'Toxin'," he said with a grin. "But we all have our blind spots. Some of us are a little too hooked on science. Know what I mean?"

"*Too* hooked?" Iris said. "Maybe like being too healthy? Or too well-adjusted?"

"I happen to like a little woo with my coffee," I said.

"What's woo?" Jetta asked.

"It's how they minimize opposing viewpoints," Kellen said.

"OMFG," Iris said. "Are you for real? I mean, seriously?"

"Oh, I'm for real." He honestly sounded like he was trying to be flirty.

Talk about your cognitive dissonance.

And now *I'm* starting to sound like an ass.

"They call us 'deniers'," Kellen said, apparently not done talking. "To lump us in with the kind of people who deny the Holocaust."

"The Holocaust must have happened," Jetta said. "I hear jokes about it all the time."

Iris laughed.

Dad glared. But *at me*, for some reason.

We climbed out of the minivan, Dad and Dan moving toward the house, while Pat and Errol stayed at the back of our group. We *little ladies* were left standing outside by the front door, along with Kellen and the demonstrably more lovable Fender.

There was a definite vibe of misogyny in the air, including Pat's watchful gaze, which was directed more at the comely shapes of some of the girls' asses, and not any external threats… but I wasn't going to focus on that.

I was more worried about a house full of who the *hurr* knows what. Seriously. It's a long list of the terrible things that *could* be in there.

One of these days I'm going to have to write out that list.

Let's see… you got your opportunist bullies like Lucas, or like that grotty cop who'd unzipped his pants two inches from my mouth, or whoever had taken shots at David and me and our two pretty horses when we posed little to no threat…

Those people are all still across the Red in North Dakota, from what I know, but that doesn't make me feel any better. You'd have to be an idiot to believe that "Minnesota Nice" is anything more than less-jerky-than-Wisconsin. If anything, what we'd seen in North Dakota had established a certain baseline of incredibly poor behavior. Out of all the strangers we've run into, I can't think of a single one who'd had our best interests at heart.

But, then again…

Jetta had been a stranger, just a few days ago.

And now she was an honorary sister. How's that for not trying to kill us?

Not too shabby.

We waited for Dad and Dan to come back out.

It took three very long minutes before they did.

"Unoccupied," Dad said. "And pretty well-stocked."

"Thank Lucifer," Iris said.

That got her the next dad glare. "That's not funny," he said.

Iris nodded. "It's more of a mood-setter. Most of today's jokes will revolve around the Holocaust."

"I don't remember any of them," Jetta said.

We all went inside, all of us except Errol's creepy uncle Pat, who was still standing watch outside.

Maybe it did seem too perfect… the big house full of supplies, the half-packed SUV that someone had decided to leave behind…

Won't we feel silly when we're viciously attacked and possibly murdered. I'd die of embarrassment… or maybe just from massive blood loss.

Certainly not ideal.

∽

But there didn't seem to be a trap.

No one came back for the SUV or the oversized farmhouse. So we brought in what little we had, mostly the bows and arrows and dried strips of dead cow.

Everything a frizzy-haired vegetarian needs.

Kellen moved the van behind the house, to hide it from the road.

He couldn't do the same with the SUV, since we didn't have any way of getting the effing thing to move. Maybe if we found a tractor to pull it around back... but that wasn't the priority.

We had the move-in complete by just after one o'clock, based on our motley collection of non-networked electronics and a large grandfather clock right at the back of the entryway.

There was time to go into town; the sun wouldn't set until around five. Or at least I thought there was time, not that anyone agreed with me.

They'd been unanimous in it. That we should wait until morning. Even Errol wanted to wait, no matter what I said to try and persuade him. The only one who hadn't told me no was Kellen, but only because he wasn't in the house at the time.

But it didn't matter, I didn't care.

I had to try to find my family. The part that wasn't related to dear old Dad. The part that no one else had a vested interest in finding.

It wasn't up to any of them.

I grabbed the best-suited compound bow and a pack of arrows. I found Kellen outside, checking the garden for remainders.

"You gonna drive me in?" I asked him.

"Yeah," he said. "Who's coming?"

"Me and you."

"What about your Dad?"

"He's busy," I said.

Kellen nodded. "And you don't see a problem with this?"

"So I need to drive myself."

"I didn't say that," he said.

"You kinda inferred it, actually. Passive-aggressively, I'd say."

"Do you want my help or not?"

I nodded.

"I think we need one more person," he said. "Another set of

13

eyes."

"I can handle that myself. Got two of 'em."

"You can't look in front and behind at the same time, Seffy."

"I think I can," I said. I guess I was just being ornery. I'm allowed to be ornery.

"Did you ask Errol?"

"What?"

"Errol. Your boyfriend."

"He's not my boyfriend," I said. "Who told you he was?"

"I just assumed. So who is your boyfriend?"

"I need a boyfriend now?"

"Girlfriend?"

"I'm focusing on my career," I said. "You know, shooting zombies with blood-soaked arrows."

"Yeah, about that…"

"Come on, Kellen. We haven't even left and you're already pissing me off."

"We need someone with a gun," he said. "Arrows aren't good enough."

"Did you forget what we're supposed to be doing?"

He shook his head. "Here's what needs to happen, Seffy. You bring someone with a gun or we don't go."

"Then I'll go by myself."

"Why?"

"What?"

"Why do you want to go by yourself?" he asked.

I groaned. "I asked you to drive me, remember? But you were being a toolbag about it."

"They don't want you to go. Because it's a bad idea. But you want to go anyway."

"Thank you Captain Play-by-Play."

"I'm not driving you," he said. "And I'm not giving you the key."

"Seriously, Kellen. I need to go into town."

"Sorry, Seffy."

I rolled my eyes at him.

What the *hurr* else could I do?

I felt like such a teenager.

I heard something.

A vehicle.

Coming from the north, I thought.

Kellen looked over at me.

"I hear it," I said.

"We should keep low," he said. "Maybe they won't be looking too closely."

I nodded.

And lowered myself down, using a bank of shriveled corn stalks for cover.

I watched as the vehicle drove by, kicking up heaps of gravel dust.

From what I could make out through the gravelly haze, it was a long, white bus, resembling a stretched-out ambulance, complete with what looked to me the blue and white snake-on-a-staff symbol.

A mass evacuation bus. Like you'd use to move hospital patients, and in a big hurry.

"We should signal it," Kellen said.

But by then it had already driven past.

"They dropped bombs on us," I said. "And now you want to tell them we're here?"

"That wasn't the military. Those buses are for helping people. And we're people."

"You really believe they're driving into Fargo to evacuate the wounded?" I asked.

He nodded.

"On a gravel road," I said, "when there's a paved highway like two miles to the east."

"What else would they be doing, Seffy? Maybe the highway's blocked."

I didn't know what was happening.

But it didn't feel like some kind of salvation. Or good news of any kind, really.

"We need to tell everyone," I said.

I was still miffed about the severe number of completely unhelpful douches I now lived with, but I tried to tell them calmly enough what I'd seen.

"They're not evacuating a thing," Dad said. "No way."

"You're awfully sure, Dad," Iris said. "Doesn't that usually mean you're wrong?"

He glared at her. "Can you at least pretend to respect me?"

"Maybe they're looking for survivors," Beth said, rubbing my father's shoulder as she spoke. "Maybe we should try and catch up to them."

"Maybe they can get us back home," Leona said, looking over at Jetta and pretending that there was nothing selfish about wanting to leave us all behind. "We don't know what's going on in Winnipeg."

"No," Dan said, "I talked to Winnipeg. We know the infection is spreading."

"Has it reached them?" Jetta asked.

Dan sighed. "They weren't sure. But it was only a matter of time, because no one was trying to stop it."

"What do you mean?" I asked. "How could no one be trying to stop it?"

"I'm not saying no one," Dan said.

"You literally just said 'no one'," Iris said.

"I meant that there was no isolation line between here and Winnipeg. Not that I know where that line got moved to."

"They were using rivers before," I said. "On the quaint notion that zombies can't swim."

"Wrong kind of zombies," Iris said.

"And no one knows it can be cured," Jetta said.

"They didn't believe me," Dan said. "They thought it was just wishful thinking on my part. No one expects a cure from a random bunch of people in Fargo."

"Why not?" Beth asked.

"Because we have places like the CDC," I said. "People would just assume that they would be the ones with the best shot of figuring it out."

"But they didn't," Jetta said. "*You* figured it out, Curlicue."

"Are we still doing that?" I asked her.

"Until I get my goddess name."

"Can you girls focus, please?" Dad said. He sounded a lot angrier than I would have expected. It seemed like there was something about Jetta that just pissed him off. And Beth's furious shoulder-rubbing wasn't cooling him down. If anything it was doing the opposite.

Iris was glaring at him.

There's something nice about being the daughter who isn't giving your father the gears; I think Iris has taken the job from me, and I don't mind at all.

I still want my father to like me. But I'm not sure why he deserves so much consideration. Or why I even feel the need to convince him to see things our way; he shouldn't have any power over me and Iris.

But for some reason I keep trying to make peace.

"There's no harm in waiting this out," I said. "We have supplies, and we can defend ourselves."

"I thought you wanted to go into the city," Kellen said.

"I'm still going into the city," I said. I looked over to Errol. "First thing tomorrow morning."

Errol hesitated, but then he nodded.

"We can stay here a few days," Dad said. "We look for the people we're missing, and we keep an eye out for more signs that someone might be coming to help us."

"No one's coming to help us," Pat said, as he sat and stared out the window, his rifle beside his chair. "They decided to wipe us out. There's no coming back from that."

"I don't believe that," Beth said. "Not if they know there are survivors. That we aren't all infected."

"They think we are infected, Mom," Iris said. "First it was *zombies can't swim*. Now it's *zombies are like us*. They probably think we're all frickin zombies now. They're still gonna want to wipe us out. They're probably just resting up for the next bombing run."

Beth walked over to Iris. And there was more shoulder rubbing.

Sometimes I think of Beth as this completely ineffectual person, like she's just this saccharine blond seat-filler who has no real purpose beyond, well... rubbing people's shoulders. I'm sure she was always prettier than my mom, and now that she's edging close to forty — not that she isn't still way younger than anyone else's mom — she doesn't have much to fall back on.

Lately she hasn't done much to change my opinion.

"We have to assume the worst," Dad said. "There's no reason to be optimistic."

"My father, everyone," Iris said. "Mister Positivity."

"I'm being realistic, Iris."

She nodded. "I know, Dad. I just wish you were wrong."

❧

After we broke off the discussion with what I think was some kind of consensus that we're all screwed, Iris and I found a quiet place in the basement to talk.

It's not that we're avoiding anyone… it's just that Jetta tends to follow me around, and Leona tends to keep tabs on Jetta…

Sometimes you just need time to be sisters, you know?

We stood and sorted old cans and boxes of food as we talked, first by best before date and then by what we thought would be the closest to appetizing. There was an over-emphasis of lentils, in canned and dry form.

"I think you might be pushing Dad a little too hard," I said, as Iris started building a tower of corn niblet cans on our dusty sorting table.

"His bot-heart can't take it?" Iris said, rolling her eyes.

"I'm not sure I can take it."

"Come on, Seffy. You know he's dragging his feet. He doesn't want to save anyone else."

"That's his job," I said. "To keep us alive. That's what parents are about."

Iris steadied her leaning tower of aluminum tins.

I thought about pushing it over, but I knew the noise would attract any nearby Canadians.

"Don't you worry that he's trying to keep us from finding your mom?" Iris asked me.

I shook my head. "I don't think he cares about that. I think if Mom and Aunt Callie showed up right now, he'd be generally indiff-erent."

"That's not how love works, Seffy."

"Love? Are you serious?"

"He hates what happened to your mom. But he loves her."

"There's no way Dad's still in love with my mom."

She piled on another can, of peas, since she'd run out of corn. "Two different things, Seff. Two different things."

"I don't want to ever have that," I said.

"You're gonna want to eat the peas," she said. "Corn isn't even a vegetable."

I chuckled. "You're a vegetable."

"I was almost in love with David," Iris said. "Like I could almost feel it. Just out of my reach, you know?"

"No… I don't know, actually. Since I'm patently unlovable."

Iris rolled her eyes again. "They're pretty much lining up around the block for you now, Seff. Assuming the block is only like — let me do the math — half a person long."

"What the *hurr* are you talking about?"

"It sucks when they're not the people you want," Iris said. "But it's not the worst thing."

"And what's the worst thing?"

"When it's someone you want, and it still doesn't click."

"And that was David?" I asked.

She nodded. "Maybe this is the big game-changer. When I see him again… maybe I'll feel it."

"Yeah… maybe…"

I wasn't about to ruin that silver lining with something as unimportant as the truth about David and his wandering tongue.

"I'm glad we're sisters again," Iris said.

She put her cans aside and came in for a hug.

"We've always been sisters," I said.

But I didn't elaborate on that point.

2

HUNTING FOR BAD CHOICES

Kellen drove the van, and Errol took the passenger seat.

Iris, Jetta and I took the back.

A rifle for Errol, and bows for me and Iris. Maybe we'd go all blood-sister, slicing our palms open and dipping our arrow tips in our bloody bot-filled goop.

Or maybe we'd just watch as Errol shot people, since I couldn't exactly picture myself hanging out the window like a Mongol horse archer.

Although I can almost see Iris doing something like that.

Everyone else had chosen to stay back, to watch over our new home. I think most people would be all reluctant to call some random accommodations their new home; they'd be pining for wherever they'd lived before. I guess I'm awfully lucky that my home life was generally sucky.

Or that I'm slowly starting to think only in rhymes.

Multi-platinum hip hop career in my future?

Do people in North Dakota have to take sides in that East Coast - West Coast feud? Do I need to know what the B.I.G. stood for? Do I have to stop listening to soulful indie folk?

Kellen took us back to the bridge where we'd crossed, in Oakport, the one that becomes Broadway and takes you on a scenic drive past the picturesque waste treatment plant. I've never been to Manhattan, but I'm pretty sure their Broadway has more of an urban flair.

There were no vehicles on the road. We saw two people walking; or they had been walking, until they saw or heard the van and scurried behind a bank of trees. I had a feeling that everyone we would see would be infected, that everyone in Fargo was infected now, because it would be close to impossible to not be.

As we passed the houses south of 32nd Ave North, I could see every single one had either front windows smashed open or front doors knocked down. Every house ransacked by looters.

They'd already looted the supermarkets; that had happened before the bombing. I wasn't sure if these houses had stayed untouched that long, but I did know that the rest of the city would be the same… any parts that weren't bombed into oblivion.

Like the other side of Broadway Drive. Across from the broken-in houses was a huge apartment complex, Trollwood Village, which is only a ridiculously funny name if you haven't lived in Fargo for a while. It was the first building we'd saw in the daylight that had been bombed.

Obviously I knew there'd been bombs dropped… I'd felt them when we were at Sanford Biomedical Lab. And I'd seen the fires and the flashes on our way out of the city.

But this was something different.

Half of a building torn away, looking like a cross-section, rubble piling up in a hill.

And there was the smell.

Like corpseflowers in Indonesia.

I know what I'm saying.

I know we were all thinking about it, or at least Iris and I would be, about how many of the people under that rubble were infected, and how many were not. I remember Iris had been especially interested in that specific facet of the botshots; what would happen when the body they were maintaining died. Botshots couldn't prevent every cause of death, such as having several floors of a building land on your head.

She'd read that a man in Ireland had drowned in a river; his bots had managed to keep his braindead body close to pristine until long after they fished him out. A couple of doctors had claimed that the man could have been saved had he been found a few hours sooner.

And there'd been that woman in Hong Kong, who'd tried to hang herself from her closet rod; her bots had kept her alive and strangling for six hours, before she was discovered and "rescued". Six hours of strangling, but those little machines had managed to find enough oxygen to keep feeding her brain.

I know that the bots under that blown-up apartment building

would have done their best to stop the rot, even for people who could never be saved. But eventually they would run out of resources, and even the people who could have been dug out would be well beyond help.

There were probably still dozens of infected people under there, trapped in the rubble, their bodies mostly patched up by their bots, probably getting just enough air through the holes and cracks in the debris that they'd end up dying of thirst or starvation.

I'm guessing that's even worse than six hours of strangling. Especially at the end, when you still end up dead.

Maybe if the other "zombies" had stopped to think — because apparently zombies can think — they would have taken some time to try and dig out their neighbors. But they'd been too busy robbing and biting their *other* neighbours, the ones who'd still had something left to give up.

And that's what I didn't know, how long it had taken before the house-to-house attacks would have started, before or after the bombs, people turning from waiting-and-seeing to taking anything they thought they'd need.

I know the infected would be a hundred times worse than anyone else for that, since they'd need to keep feeding, either on their neighbor's collection of towering canned corn or on their neighbors themselves. Their bodies would have constantly fed them signals that they were starving, that they had to keep taking whatever they could get.

It would have been terrifying. For anyone who'd managed to avoid being infected. And for the real people still trapped inside those parasite-addled bodies.

I want to save them all. To redeem them. I know Iris feels the same way.

The closer we got to downtown, the quieter things became.

And the more rubble we found.

It seemed like the bombing run had followed up Broadway Drive, since any place that looked like it could house more than a single family had been targeted. And the high school, too... I guess that was part of the kill-everything doctrine, that a lot of people would probably crowd into a public space, hoping to find help.

"I don't know how many people could have survived this," Kellen said.

"People have survived," Iris said. "It's a lot harder to kill everyone than you'd think."

"Especially if they're infected," I said. "Whoever would have normally been killed by things like blood loss or organ damage would have recovered."

"Then where are they?" Jetta asked.

I didn't know.

And since Iris didn't reply either, I guess she had no idea, either.

"They've gone to ground," Errol said.

"What are you talking about?" I asked him.

"Low profiles, hiding out. Probably moving to the edge of the city, in case there's another bombing run. I think the only thing keeping us from being overrun where we're staying right now is the lack of cars that can drive anywhere."

"I don't think that will last forever," Kellen said.

"What do you mean?" Iris asked.

"Either the cars will get turned back on, or people will find another way to move out to the farms. You saw where we were. Almost untouched."

"I think he's got a point," I said. "I'd say it's only two or three hours of walking to reach that B&B. It only took a thousand years for people to move from Alaska down to the tip of South America. They didn't have cars, either."

I worried that I sounded like a kid in school, trying to impress people with what they saw TV the night before. But maybe it doesn't matter, since I don't really want to impress anyone.

"So it's only a matter of time," Errol said.

I nodded. And then I realized that not everyone would be wasting their time looking in my direction.

"We won't be able to spend much time searching for people," Iris said. "We need to focus on finding a way to defend ourselves."

"Or on moving farther away from the city," Jetta said.

"Somewhere with game to hunt," Kellen said.

"Not so great for us vegetarians," Iris said.

Kellen laughed. "Vegetarian? After all this? I think that's a luxury you're gonna have to give up."

"It's not a luxury," I said. "It's a belief system."

"Now that sounds like woo to me," Errol said. He started chuckling.

I rolled my eyes at him. The idiot was just trying to get a rise out of me.

I appreciated the sentiment.

"Oh no," Jetta said.

We all turned to look at her, even Kellen, who should have been sticking with eyes forward and hands at ten-and-two.

Jetta pointed out the window. Out my window.

I hadn't been paying attention.

A group of people. Maybe a dozen.

Probably infected.

A few armed with rifles.

For some reason, they were very interested in the one vehicle that still seemed to be driving around the city of Fargo.

Kellen stepped on the gas pedal.

The street itself was getting rough, debris from the bombings mixed with the large numbers of stalled vehicles; Broadway was generally wide enough to make a path through the dead cars, but not at the speed Kellen wanted to take us.

And the other streets, the side streets... they wouldn't have that kind of room, even if they had less stalled traffic.

"We need to make it to 19th Ave," Kellen said. "It should be wide enough. We get there and we find a way back out of the city."

"We've already blown past them," I said. "You can slow down now."

"No... it's not safe."

"Slow down," Iris said.

"Kellen's right," Errol said. "This was a bad idea. We're too much of a target."

"They can't keep up with us," I said.

"Someone will find a way to stop us," Kellen said. "It's not rocket science. And besides, we can't slow down enough for you guys to try saving anyone."

"Dangit," Jetta said. Probably her way of agreeing with Errol and Kellen... and of disagreeing with me.

"I need to find my mother," I said. "And my aunt. And then there's David..."

"Even if we find them," Kellen said, "which isn't likely at all... but even if we do..."

"We might not make it back out," Errol said.

"You guys are pansy-flowers," Iris said. "Long-stemmed."

"You should drop us off," I said. "We'll find my family and we'll find our own way back."

I heard Jetta groan.

I looked over to her. "What's your problem?" I asked her.

She shook her head.

"Tell me," I said.

She frowned. "You sound insane, Seffy."

"I didn't ask for a psychiatric work-up, thanks."

"You won't make it out of here," she said. "You or Iris. And I won't, either."

"You actually don't need to come with us," Iris said. "Since this is a family matter."

"You can't do it," Jetta said. "You can't."

"Don't tell me what I can't do," I said. "You don't even know me."

"I freaking know you well enough, Seffy. And you're my friend."

"And you can't stand seeing me like this, right? This is an intervention?"

"We go back to the B&B," Errol said. "We come up with a better plan... a better way to get back in and find them."

"There is no better plan," I said, basically floundering with my arguments. "This is all we've got. We need to save people, we need to keep pushing until we change this around. No more wasting time."

"This isn't the way to do it," Errol said. "I'm sorry, but it's just not."

"Drop us off," Iris said. "Just like Seffy told you to do. We'll take our bows and we'll figure it out."

"We're not dropping anyone off," Kellen said.

He hadn't slowed down. He was making his way to 19th Ave, as fast as he could. He was a pretty good driver, actually. You know, *for a moron.*

I knew I couldn't do anything. I wasn't going to jump out of a moving vehicle. I wasn't going to tuck and roll.

Just like I knew Kellen and Errol — and Jetta — were right.

That Iris and I couldn't do it on our own, on foot with two compound bows... and that if all of us did it... well, we couldn't risk losing our only ride.

And the dying part would be pretty crappy, too.

But... I didn't want to give in.

I couldn't give in.

Not because I was too proud, that I didn't want them to know that I had a basic understanding of common sense. It was because I didn't want to admit that I couldn't save my mother.

That I couldn't to it now, and maybe not *ever*.

So I didn't say anything else, and Kellen made his turn onto 19th Avenue North.

And Iris was keeping her eye on me. I had a feeling she understood. She'd been standing with me as I pushed on like an idiot. Because she knew what I was dealing with.

Kellen took us back out of the city, moving us north toward Gaia's Point B&B. As we hit the gravel road that would take us along the Red, I felt a hand reach for mine.

Jetta, who gave me a warm smile.

And I realized that all of us were going through something like that, not just me. It's not like anyone's sitting pretty, surrounded by everyone they love and care about.

Except maybe my father, if you go with my understanding of the man. He'd be happy enough with just Beth and Iris and me.

And probably even happier if Jetta and Leona headed north for home.

We arrived at Gaia's Point just after ten in the morning, our bold rescue plan having failed in less than an hour and a half.

We'd wasted more gas, too, and brought back nothing new that we could use.

I knew Dad would give us a hard time… not a yelling kind of hard time, but the kind where we can see just how disappointed he is, as he pretends that he isn't.

But Dad wasn't there.

No one was. Not even Fender.

"What the heck?" Jetta said, as we walked through the house. "They left us behind."

"The supplies are still here," I said, checking the pantry.

Still an overflowing pile of organic and GMO-free labelled products. And the selection of placebo meds, things like echinacea and valerian root.

They have a saying among skeptic jerks like me: there are plenty of herbal supplements that have been proven to work; it's just that we now call those ones *medicine*.

"The bus," Kellen said. "They must have come for them."

"That was for patient evacs," I said. "Not general evacuation."

"Maybe they're doing that, too," Iris said. "Evacuating everyone who isn't infected."

"Evacuating them where? Everywhere around here's infected."

Then I saw it. On the wide-doored stainless steel fridge.

A sticky note. I didn't recognize the handwriting.

Taken to FEMA camp. We're okay.

And then some directions. Around twenty five miles to the southeast.

I called everyone over.

We all crowded around the fridge, like it was a funny cat video.

"I think that's Leona's handwriting," Jetta said. "She really did leave without me."

"So we believe it?" Errol asked.

"What do you mean, believe it?" I said. "Believe that my father would just take off on us? Not that hard to believe…"

"Leona could have been coerced."

"Sounds a little far-fetched," Jetta said. "I think this is pretty straightforward. We said we'd wait and see if there was some kind of rescue mission happening. Well, someone came and got us. Most of us, anyway."

"But they didn't wait for us," Iris said. "Shouldn't they have waited?"

Jetta nodded. She looked like she couldn't decide how to feel.

Which is kind of my thing, actually.

"They should have waited," I said. But I couldn't say for sure that they *would* have waited. Okay, I would have thought my Dad would wait for his precious Iris, at least. But then again, maybe she'd have thought the same for me. It's funny how two people can see their shared corner of the world so very differently…

"This could be it," Jetta said. "They'll see that we've all been cured. That we're immune."

"We should take this one step at a time," Errol said. "We scope the place out, make sure it's what they say it is."

"I don't have a problem with being careful," Iris said. "As long as we go down there and find out."

"And find out if Fender is with them," I said.

"I don't want to go," Kellen said.

We all looked at him.

He was leaning against the kitchen counter, staring at the food on the shelves.

"You're not going to explain that to us?" Iris asked him.

"We have supplies," he said. "And they didn't even bother taking them. So I'm going to stay here, up until I can't."

"Why?"

"That's not my family out there. My family's in Fargo, like Seffy's mom. I have no reason to rush over to some overcrowded FEMA camp."

"Maybe because it's safer?" I said.

"I feel safe enough here," he said.

"You'll be on your own," Iris said. "No backup. No weapons and no vehicle."

He shook his head. "I'm the one who found this vehicle."

"You mean you told us about it while we were saving your miserable life," Errol said.

Kellen took a step back from the rest of us. Which was better than getting all up in Errol's face. "I didn't ask for your help," he said.

"So you were just waiting for the right moment to hatch your daring escape plan?" Iris asked.

Kellen shook his head at her. "You think you're so darned clever, huh?"

Iris smirked. "Reasonably, yeah."

"Just keep holding court, Iris. Just don't waste it on me. Because I'm not interested in what you have to say. And I'm not interested in wild goose chases."

"We're taking the van," Errol said.

"You don't need to fight my battles," Iris said, glaring at Errol.

"No one's fighting anything," I said. "We need the van to see what's happening." I looked over to Kellen. I gave him a smile. A paltry attempt at an Iris kind of smile.

Maybe I could sway him.

"You should come with us," I said.

For a moment he seemed to waver. A little.

Then he stuck out his chin. "I'm staying," he said.

"We're still taking the van," Errol said.

Kellen didn't bother to answer.

❧

We left all of the supplies back with Kellen, since FEMA had apparently seen no need for anyone else to bring them along, and we made our way toward what we assumed was the camp.

I regretted leaving the food behind, about two minutes down the road. Then I revised that opinion a few minutes later. I knew something didn't fit, and bringing our previous canned corn seemed a little premature for a recon mission.

I didn't know if I ought to speak out on that. I didn't want to drop a deuce all over Jetta's hopes and dreams. Not unless we're making some kind of amateur film for the German market.

"I only know FEMA from hurricanes on the news," Jetta said. "And never the best endorsements."

"They only bring them out when something goes wrong," Errol said, still on lookout in the passenger side, as Iris drove. "Most of the time I'm sure they're doing a perfectly close-to-adequate job."

"You used to say that about my job," I said, with a smirk.

He turned around and smiled at me.

"This is pretty good odds for you, Errol," Jetta said. "Three girls and one close-to-adequate sausage."

He blushed.

"I can see you've thought about it," Iris said.

"Come on, guys," I said. "Take it easy on him. He's squeamish."

"I'm not squeamish," Errol said. "I just don't want to make anyone all green-eyed with envy."

"I'm already envious," Iris said. "Of Kellen and his alone time."

"So what are supposed to do when we get there?" I asked. "It's not like they won't see us coming from a mile away. Literally."

"They'll see the dust off the gravel, at least," Errol said. "So we can't just drive up."

"You want us to walk the last mile on foot?" Jetta said.

"Mile wouldn't be far enough back. Probably five miles, at least." He was punching something onto the console screen. "I don't see any trees on sat view."

"The network's back?" Iris asked.

"No... I guess the local area is saved in."

"This place doesn't feel that local," I said.

"I don't know how it works," he said.

"I don't think I can do five miles," Jetta said. "I'm not what you'd call country strong."

"I don't know what that means," Iris said.

"We don't all need to walk in," I said. "Just a couple of us, to see what we can see."

"We shouldn't split up," Errol said.

"We shouldn't just leave the van behind. So someone needs to stay back with it."

"Seffy's right," Iris said.

"About so many things," I said, with a grin.

"Who's our best shot?" Errol asked. "Gun or arrows."

"I've never shot anything," Jetta said.

"I'd say it's Seffy," Iris said. "She's really good at shooting people in the lung."

"*Oooh*... I know," Jetta said. "Maybe pretend the zombie heads are all just lungs with hair on the top."

"You guys are *hi*larious," I said.

"I'm okay with a rifle," Errol said.

I nodded. "So you're thinking you and I should go..."

"No. I think I should go, and you should stay behind."

"I should go if I'm the best shot," I said. "Seriously. I'm pretty sure I'm better at it than you."

Errol gave me a nod. "You're right... in that you'd be better at it. But I don't want you to go. In case it's some kind of trap."

"I think we're all hooped if it's a trap," Iris said.

"So let's just drive up, then," Jetta said. "Maybe we can get de-loused before lunch."

I'm not sure any of us knew if she was serious.

"I'm going on foot," I said. "If someone comes for me, I'll get them with an arrow. A lot quieter than shooting off a gun."

"Someone should go with you," Iris said.

"I don't see what good that does."

"I have a bow, too," she said. "Just not as many confirmed maim-ings."

I rolled my eyes.

And waited, for Errol to drive close enough to the supposed camp for us to start walking.

❧

Iris and I walked along the road for the first four miles, the first three paved and the last one gravel. We had our bowhunting packs, from Kellen's adventures in Moorhead, complete with eight arrows a piece.

And oodles of parasite-killing blood in our veins.

Not that there were supposed to be any infected people there... or at least I didn't think so.

Unless the FEMA workers had all been infected.

Unless we were walking back into the same kind of trap we'd run into on our way out of Fargo, when Iris and I ended up duct taped on a cold garage floor.

What a fanfabulous *time that was.*

We had a mile or so to go on our trip, after crossing a drainage ditch and cutting across the first quarter-section of harvested crops, toward where the FEMA camp was supposed to be. It looked like it had on the tablet, like a large meat producer with dozens of out-buildings.

I used a pair of binoculars we'd brought with us to take a closer look.

"It's a Hutterite Colony," Iris said. "Guess they don't put that part on the map."

"What?"

"Hutterites. Weird German accents, weirder homemade cloth-ing..."

"I know what Hutterites are."

We live in North Dakota. Or did. And there was one near Ender-lin that I'd seen more than once. Sundale, I think it was called.

I'd never liked the idea of communal religious communities. It was hard not to just assume it was some kind of cult. I remembered a story that Errol had told me, one that he'd heard from a friend of a friend, someone who probably lived a life that was filled to the brim of made-up crap.

The story was that this random friend-of-a-friend had been out drinking one night, and as he left the bar to drunk-drive his way home, he was stopped by an old man in suspenders, who was flanked by two somewhat homely young women.

According to the story, the old man had asked for a sperm sample, to be deposited into an empty milk jug with its top cut open. To add new blood to the gene pool.

I know that's bunk.

But I guess that tells you what people think of Hutterites. That they're backwards, that they probably are some kind of cult.

I'm not sure I disagree; to be honest, I'd never given it enough thought to form a firm conclusion. I'm not sure if that's intellectual honesty of sheer laziness on my part.

But either way, it didn't make sense for their colony to be used as a FEMA camp.

So I said something.

"This doesn't make sense," I said. "There's definitely something wrong with this."

"Pass me the binoculars," Iris said.

Once she had them, she spent a couple of minutes surveying the colony.

"No Hutterites that I can see," she said. "Just tents."

"Tents?"

"You didn't see them? Behind that row of trees, in front of the dorms."

She passed the binoculars back to me and pointed.

I saw the tents. They looked like what you'd see for a backyard wedding, white canvas with multiple triangular peaks. I could also see a row of small white trailers.

I'd seen photos like that. From Hurricane Fiona, outside Jacksonville, Florida.

It looked like a FEMA camp.

At a Hutterite colony.

"I don't know," I said.

"The Hutterites might still be there," Iris said. "I just don't see any, you know?"

"Assuming they dress like we think they do. We're basing it off of what, exactly?"

"Dark patterned dresses and kerchiefs for the ladies, then overalls for the gents. True-to-life stereotypes."

"So what do we do?" I asked.

"I guess we go back to the van and tell them what we've seen. I don't see a reason why we should think it's some kind of trap."

I shook my head. "We have no way of knowing. Like Dad said, there might be no way for the authorities to come back from what they did here. They tried to bomb out an entire city."

"So they set up a death camp?" she said. "Mass graves out the other side? Sounds a little overwrought, slightly-bigger sister."

"It does sound ridiculous."

"Then we don't need to worry, right?"

I shrugged.

And then we made our way back toward the van.

Iris had parked the van on the side of the asphalt-paved street, just north of a corner with a collection of four somewhat identical — and recently abandoned — yardsites. It took us a full half hour for the round trip.

Even with the bots and their continual fight against sour milk muscles, my legs were feeling it by the time we made it back to where we'd left the van.

And of course, to go along with the rest of my absolutely fabulous day, the van wasn't where we'd left it.

And there was no sign of Errol or Jetta.

"They might have been in danger of being spotted," Iris said. "We should wait here."

"Uh… okay… so we'll just wait here and hope they come back."

"You have a better idea?"

"Not really."

She nodded. "Look, Seffy, if they'd driven to the camp, we'd have seen them. We'd have seen any sign of them once they hit gravel, some kind of dust cloud."

"So they drove somewhere else, on the paved road," I said. "That doesn't make me feel any better."

"I guess we shouldn't have split up."

"Thanks for the advice. Any warnings for Franz Ferdinand while you're at it?"

"We could keep walking," she said, "but we wouldn't know the right direction."

"Can't really make out the tracks in the gravel," I said. "I mean... maybe they were looking to turn around, but those tracks might be from someone else."

"You're not a tracker, Seffy."

"Neither are you."

"So we wait. We can check out those houses we passed. They looked *desocupado*, but they might have supplies."

"*Desocupado?*" I asked.

"Unoccupied."

"Then why didn't you just say unoccupied?"

"Because this is more fun. It's like... it's like we're an old married couple."

"I don't think sisters can marry each other," I said.

She grinned. "We're stepsisters, so I'm pretty sure we can do all kinds of nasty things together. Things that would make Jetta pretty frickin jealous."

"What?"

"She likes you."

"Uh... okay..."

"Like *likes you*, likes you."

"I don't think she's... um..."

She laughed. "Dad's worried you'll take a lesbian lover."

"Almost makes it worth it," I said.

"So you're not...?"

"What?"

"Well, I don't know, Seffy. You certainly haven't done much of anything with the patently unfairer sex."

"Being unlovable by a man doesn't make me a lesbian."

"Well, I think you're lovable," Iris said. "Maybe Jetta will soon have a reason to be jealous of me." She started making kissy noises.

So she was having a grand old time.

As we sat abandoned on the side of the road during the zombie apocalypse.

I wanted to give in to that, to take a left turn into *Irisworld*, where anything, no matter how bad, is always worth a few jokes.

But that's... it's not really me.

"So Dad was supposed to tell you something," I said.

She nodded. "Don't eat yellow snow. Should have told that one to Franz Ferdinand."

"That makes no sense."

"You make no sense," she said, sticking her tongue out immediately afterward.

"He's your Dad, too, Iris."

"So I *can* eat yellow snow? In moderation?"

"No, I'm serious," I said. "My father is also your father. Biologically."

"Shut your sexy snout," she said.

"I'm not joking."

"So the mysterious and decidedly skeevy perv who got with my Mom was... *your Dad*."

"Yeah."

"While he was married to your Mom."

"Yeah."

"And he told you but never bothered to tell me," she said.

"You were *ocupado*," I said. "Infected, actually."

"My father's a two-timing crapmonkey."

"Hey, hey... my father's a jerk, too."

She laughed.

And then she gave me a hug.

"You wanted him to tell me," she said. "But he kept dragging his feet."

"Sounds like you know the man."

"Apparently I've known him my whole life." She smiled. "So now you're stuck with me. Poor Seffy Schmidt."

"Poor Iris Schmidt. Finding out you really are one of us."

She nodded. "We should check out those yardsites. Look for canned corn and/or clues."

"Okay," I said.

And then I followed my sister, who had already started walking down the road.

3

SHOULD OLD ACQUAINTANCE BE BUCKSHOT...

The first house had almost as many supplies as the bed and breakfast, with food, water, medicine, and a stockpile of batteries, both the little guys for small appliances and two mainline backups for the electrical panel itself.

We didn't really know what to do with any of it; not only did we not have the van at the moment, we also didn't know where we'd end up by the end of the day.

Let's not forget that there was still no answer on what kind of camp was up the road.

And no sign of Errol and Jetta.

So we made our mental notes of what the first yardsite had, and then we moved on to the second one, with two more to go after that.

I guess it was more a way to pass the time and not worry as much. It wasn't like we were expecting to find any answers.

"I feel like there are too many empty houses," Iris said, as we walked up to the front porch of farmhouse *número dos*. "Makes it all the more likely that people really are being evacuated."

"Moving five miles away isn't really being evacuated," I said.

And that brought up a good point.

It wasn't like we were dealing with a hurricane, where you were just moving people away from the affected areas, to somewhere outside the path of the storm.

They were moving people from one plot of land to another, all within the burgeoning Republic of Zombieland. There was nothing at that Hutterite colony slash FEMA camp to keep people safe from some hungry horde of infected psychopaths. It wasn't like there was a line of tanks or armor-clad marines. Or if there was, we certainly haven't seen it.

"They're not expecting to have to defend themselves," I said.

"Who?"

"Those FEMA people, or whoever they are."

"Because there aren't any zombies out here," Iris said.

She opened the front door and stepped inside.

I followed her.

"But there should be, right?" I said. "There were zombies in Fargo, zombies at Dad's farm…"

"So why no zombies here?"

"I don't know. I remember that they were doing bombing runs along the isolation lines. Probably mowing down anyone trying to cross out of our little petri dish."

We walked into the kitchen.

More supplies.

"So they could have done that here?" she asked. "People were making for some isolation line, and they stopped them with *redonkulously* extreme prejudice?"

"I don't know. That would still make them seem overconfident. It's not like they could expect to have killed every last zombie between here and I-94."

"They didn't kill us," Iris said.

"Exactly. So it's gotta be something else."

I heard a noise.

From the basement.

"Someone's down there," Iris said. "And I think they're asking for help."

I recognized the sound. I *remembered* that sound. *Muffled.*

Like I'd had done to me at that ag yard, outside Enderlin. Latex gloves shoved halfway down my throat.

Dad had done something similar to Iris. With a purple sock.

Someone was tied up in that basement. And gagged.

"Stay up here," I said, whispering now that it was probably way too late to keep quiet. "I'll go down. Keep an eye out… in case they know we're here."

"Who?"

"Whoever tied that person up."

I found the basement door.

I opened it.

No lights on. I flicked the switch, and the room below lit up.

I couldn't see anyone.

But the muffled noise got louder. More excited.

Like they knew I was coming. And that I wasn't one of the bad guys.

I walked down the stairs.

I saw her, tied to a chair with what looked like clothesline, a strip of duct tape hanging somewhat loosely off her lips.

A blond woman.

Petite. Pretty.

I felt like I recognized her.

I heard footsteps upstairs.

"Motherlover," Iris said.

More footsteps.

I saw Iris coming down the stairs.

She had her hands on her head. And she didn't have her pack.

Someone was behind her.

Lucas Berg. Carrying a small pistol, pointed at Iris.

I realized that the blond woman was the one Lucas had taken from Dad's farm. To be his own little toy zombie.

"I see they conned you, too," he said.

"The camp," I said.

"Not really FEMA."

"Then who? And how do you know, anyway?"

"They've been collecting zombies since Thursday. I followed them to find out."

"Then how do you know they aren't FEMA?" Iris said.

He smirked. "So I'm guessing your sister's not a zombie anymore..."

"Nope," I said.

"Any scars from that little stabby-time fun she had with me?"

"I'm completely healed," Iris said. "Aside from the gaping emotional wounds, jackass."

"I need to untie this woman," I said, motioning to the blonde tied to the chair.

"She's not really tied that well," Lucas said.

I watched as the woman started pulling against the rope.

Her hands came free after a few seconds.

She pulled the duct tape off her mouth. I could see it wouldn't have been enough to actually muffle her calls.

"I'm sorry," she said. I saw a weird necklace around her neck. A plastic ring, smaller than a donut, but not by much. Hanging by a leather strap. Another bit of deja vue...

"What has he done to you?" I asked her.

"I'm infected, remember? And... well, Lucas feeds me, keeps me alive. And one day you know I'll bite his ass."

"We can fix you," Iris said, still halfway up the stairs.

"Shut up," Lucas said. "I still don't like either of you girls."

"You don't like anyone," the blond woman said.

"Why are you here?" I asked, looking to Lucas. "So close to this camp. If they're not who they say they are..."

"This area's already clear," he said. "So they won't be wasting any time checking on these houses. And you may have noticed all the supplies. Now Seffy, I need you to get down on your knees and put your hands behind your back."

"You're kidding me," Iris said. "You really think you can just tie us up?" She'd stopped where she was, on the stairs. Trying to look defiant.

"I don't trust you," Lucas said. "Either of you. So if you're going to be here with us, you're going to be restrained. For all our safety."

"We don't want to stay," I said. "So we'll just be on our way."

"Doesn't work like that, sweetheart. When they find you guys you'll tell them all about us."

"Why the heck would we do that?" Iris said. "Sure, you happen to suck donkey nuts, but your Stockholm Syndrome girlfriend seems nice enough."

He shook his head. "You're staying here. Now on your knees."

"It's a bluff," I said. "What's he going to do, shoot us? That should draw some attention."

"Good point," Lucas said.

He gave Iris a shove.

She tumbled down the stairs, her head slamming hard against the concrete wall.

She wasn't moving.

I tried not to panic.

But trying wasn't really stopping it.

Lucas rushed down to the basement.

He put the gun to the side.

The blond woman had finished untying her legs. She stood up from the chair.

I tried to calm myself. I focused on my breathing.

I needed to figure things out. Find a way to beat him.

The blond woman was started walking toward me.

"Put the ring in," Lucas said.

The blond woman grabbed the ring and put it in her mouth, like a giant hollow pacifier. She pulled the leather strap tight.

She kept walking toward me. Lucas started over, too.

They were closing in, to pin me against the wall.

"I won't kill you," Lucas said. "But I've got absolutely no problem with hurting you. *Bad.*"

"I'm sure as frick not going to let you tie me up," I said. "And I know how to disable an attacker."

"You see that I've gotten Anna Louise to put in her ring... so she doesn't bite you."

"So that's what it's for."

"Keeps her from biting down."

"I saw that before," I said. "At your place. You had it before any of this even started."

"You've got me, sweetheart. I'm a friggin boy scout. Always prepared."

"For hot zombies."

"We won't make you a zombie if we don't have to," he said. "That's the deal, alright? You let us tie you up, no trouble, and we let you *be you.*"

"And you save on supplies."

He hesitated for a moment, then nodded. "I see you've got a handle on this."

"You can't make me a zombie," I said.

"Not me, dummy. Anna Louise will do it."

"Go ahead."

"She's immune," Iris said.

I looked over to her. She was sitting upright, against the wall, her forehead bloody. But I could tell that the wound itself had started to close.

"No one's immune," Lucas said.

"I'm pretty sure you're not really a trained immunologist," I said.

"So maybe don't make unfounded assumptions. An acquired immunity. Vaccination, you could call it."

"Anna Louise," Lucas said. "Take out the ring."

The blond woman did as he instructed, loosening the leather strap behind her head and pulling the plastic ring out of her mouth.

She stepped closer to me.

I didn't try to get away.

She leaned in by my neck.

"There's something wrong," she said. "I…"

I grabbed her shoulders.

I dug my mouth into her neck.

It tasted like a mix of uncooked fish and thick rusted water.

Not appealing in the least, though I'm sure she's a lovely person.

She fell back. I tried to stop her from falling, but she slipped out of my hands. She dropped down to her knees, clutching at the wound in her neck.

"W-What did you just do?" Lucas stammered.

"I just gave her the cure," I said. "She doesn't actually need you anymore, Lucas."

"You'll have to go back to sexually assaulting your left hand," Iris said. "Assuming we don't just kill you right here."

He turned and start toward Iris.

I went for the rifle.

I had it before he realized.

"You're not going to shoot me, either," he said.

"You're right," I said.

I swung the barrel at his chest, hitting him hard.

He fell back against the stairs.

"Now we tie you up," I said. I looked over to the blond woman. "Anna Louise… can you help us with that?"

She slowly pulled her hands away from her neck.

The wound had closed. Even faster work than I'd just seen with Iris.

"I don't know what you've done," Anna Louise said. "I don't understand."

She walked over to the chair and picked up the length of clothesline.

She brought the rope over to Lucas.

He quietly turned around, putting his hands behind his back.

She tied his wrists.

Iris stood up, and helped Anna Louise move Lucas up and off the stairs, and over to the wall.

They sat him down and tied his ankles.

"No need for this frickin ring gag," Iris said to Lucas, as she passed the rubber ring to me, for some reason. "But I would *love* to stick a broom handle down your throat."

"I didn't think she was human," he said. "Not anymore."

"But then she started talking," I said.

"She started talking."

"And you didn't let her go."

He nodded. "I'd... I'd already done it to her."

I put the weird rubber gag into my pants pocket. The last thing I wanted to do was leave it there for Lucas to use again, on someone else.

Not that he couldn't find some other thing to jam into his next victim's mouth. So far I've seen socks and tasted a plastic glove, so I'm getting to be a bit of a subject matter expert.

"So now what?" Iris asked me.

"I don't know what to do with him," I said.

"Honestly... we should just kill him."

"I don't think we can do that."

"You can't," Anna Louise said. "I can't let you do that."

"But after what he's done," Iris said.

Anna Louise shook her head. "It should be my decision, shouldn't it?"

Iris looked at me.

I gave her a nod.

"It's your decision," Iris said to Anna Louise.

"Thank you," Anna Louise said.

"You can come with us," I told her. "If you'd like."

"I'd like to," she said. She tried out a little smile. "Since I'm pretty short on options right now."

We left Lucas tied up in the basement, loose duct tape gag not included. We took both the pistol and the rifle, which Iris had inspected and found to be loaded with buckshot.

Anna Louise made it clear that she wasn't a big fan of guns, but that she was willing to make an exception, considering the circumstance. Not that we had time to give her a lesson in shooting a rifle, or that we were really the ones to teach something like that.

But she carried it anyway, and that looked menacing enough, assuming anyone could even see us out there.

More important than the rifle or the cute little blonde was Lucas' hot red SUV. Just like our long-lost van, it still ran despite the Homeland Security shutdown of pretty much everything else.

We had wheels all over again.

We just had to figure out what had happened to Errol and Jetta.

And we still needed to know what was happening at the so-called FEMA camp. I don't know how I got appointed to this job; I'm really more of a follower. Not a camp follower, mind you. Not unless we're filming that kind of raunchy commerce for our German porn project.

But now I have to figure out exactly what we're supposed to do. All over again.

$$\backsim$$

I decided that we needed to go back for another look at the camp. Iris agreed, and Anna Louise didn't seem too confident, though I wasn't sure if that was in giving us her opinion, or a lack of confidence in our abilities in general.

We'll mark it down as an abstention.

After moving Lucas' SUV somewhere where hopefully he wouldn't find it, we made our way back up the road, and onto the gravel, and into the fields.

We walked along a machinery road, moving closer than we had on our last approach, trying to keep our heads low.

We reached another drainage ditch; this one seemed to be headed where we needed to go, so we climbed down and walked through the two inches of cloudy water, which brought us low enough with our heads bent that we hopefully wouldn't be seen.

"Did Lucas make any trips up this close?" I asked Anna Louise.

She shook her head. "Not *this* close, no. We mostly watched the buses from the south side of the camp. That was all we needed to see."

"What do you mean?"

"There are charter buses and ambulance buses. Can't see what's in the ambulances, but the other buses are filled up with people. I don't know if they're infected or not."

"So they are evacuating people?"

"Lucas doesn't think so," she said. "Because the buses fill up at the camp and head out."

"That doesn't tell us anything," Iris said.

"Lucas thought it did," Anna Louise said. "He thought that the buses ought to be heading away from the isolation zone."

"Maybe they were heading toward the Twin Cities," I said. "That's probably outside the isolation zone."

"They turned right on Highway 10. Towards Fargo."

"And there is no isolation zone," Iris said. "They couldn't hold the line, remember?"

I shook my head. "All we know is that they fell back. Doesn't mean there isn't a new line somewhere else."

Anna Louise shushed us.

She pointed toward the camp.

Movement.

Two women in long floral dresses — one navy blue and one forest green — their heads covered with kerchiefs. They didn't look any older than us.

They were walking toward the drainage ditch. To where they would have no trouble seeing us.

"There are your Hutterites," Iris whispered.

We didn't move.

Trying to turn back would have made it even likelier that they'd spot us. Our best bet was to sit and wait, and hope that they weren't planning on coming out much farther into the field of canola.

So naturally, they kept coming.

One of them saw us. The woman in dark blue turned and said something to the other.

They walked up to our cruddy little ditch.

"We're hooped," Iris said, a bit too loudly.

"What else is new?" I said.

We were shushed again.

Not by Anna Louise.

"You don't want them to hear you," the Hutterite women in the blue dress said.

"Who?" I asked, quietly.

"The people who are running our colony now."

"Why are you out here?" Iris asked.

"We were looking for her," the other Hutterite woman said, nodding to Anna Louise. "We saw her out here yesterday. Well... not this close."

"Just her?" I asked.

Both women nodded.

"Lucas sent me to look," Anna Louise said. "Thought I'd be seen as less of a threat."

"Quite the gentleman," Iris said.

"You need to get far away from here," the first Hutterite woman said. "Are you infected?"

"No," I said. "We're immune, actually."

The woman nodded. "So are we."

"That's not possible," Iris said. "You'd need a vaccine."

"We don't have one," the woman said. "But there were infected brought into our colony, and they don't bite us."

Iris nodded. "Climb down here. I can tell you if you're immune."

Both Hutterite women took a step back.

"My sister was infected," I said. "So was Anna Louise, here. We found a way to cure it. But there's something... I don't know... there's a way for Iris to know if you've got the bots, and if those bots are being controlled by the parasite."

"They talk to me," Iris said. "I'm the zombie whisperer."

"Just go," the other Hutterite woman said. "Please."

"What do they do to the people on those buses?" Anna Louise asked. "You need you to tell us that much."

"We don't know," the first woman said. "But they're locked up, and they aren't... normal."

"What's normal?" Iris asked.

The woman in the blue dress shrugged. "They're not like you."

"Thanks," I said. "For the help."

The woman nodded.

She and the other woman started walking again, following along the drainage ditch, farther away from the colony.

Acting like they hadn't found anything of importance at that *random spot* where they'd stopped for a minute. In case they were being watched, I guess.

"Do you think they're telling us the truth?" Iris asked me.

"I doubt they'd make that up," I said.

"We should leave," Anna Louise said. "Get as far away as we can."

"With or without Lucas?" Iris asked.

"We can't leave," I said. "You know that, Iris."

"We can't stay here," she said. "Strategic withdrawal, Seffy."

"And then what?"

"I don't know? Do you?"

"We need to know more," I said. "We need to find out."

"Those Hutterite girls know more," Iris said. "But I don't know how we'll get them to tell us."

"I can pass for Hutterite."

"What?"

"I put on one of those dresses and cover my hair, and I can get inside."

"That's a bad plan," Iris said. "*Bad Seffy.* Bad plan."

I climbed up out of the ditch.

"Seffy," Iris said. "Don't get us killed. Not today."

I ran up behind the Hutterite women.

"What are you doing?" the woman in the blue dress asked me. "They'll see you."

"We need to switch places," I said.

"You need to leave." She started to hurry away.

I grabbed her shoulder. "We need your help."

"They killed the men," she said.

"What?"

"The people who came to our colony. They separated us and took the men away. I think they killed them."

"We don't know that," the woman in the forest green dress said. "We don't know what happened to them."

"I need to get in there," I said. "They took my family. I just need your clothes. You can stay with my sister until I get back."

"You won't get back," the woman in blue said. "They'll figure it out. They'll know you aren't part of the colony, and then they'll kill you."

"I'll give you my clothes," the other Hutterite woman said.

The woman in blue shook her head. "No, Claudia," she said. "It won't work."

"I want to know what's going on. This might be a way to find out."

"This doesn't involve us."

"You know that it does."

The other Hutterite woman shook her head. "It's not... it's not who we are, Claudia. Not what we believe."

"I've made up my mind," Claudia said.

"Thank you," I said to her. I motioned to the ditch. Trying to be subtle... the woman needed to get *nekkid*.

"We'll find some trees," Claudia said. "There's a shelter belt to the north."

The other Hutterite woman glared at me.

"She'll be okay," I said. "Iris... my sister... she'll keep her safe."

"You're going to get us all killed," the woman in blue said. "You may kill every woman and child at our colony."

"You'll be okay," I said.

Not that I sounded particularly convincing.

Since I think she might be dead right.

The five of us followed our original trail in, back to the road.

Claudia led us across to the line of trees, all of which had lost their leaves.

Not the best cover, actually.

I went first, taking off my shirt and then my pants, standing in my underwear and feeling especially happy that we'd left Lucas trussed up in a basement.

"You'll need my rubber boots," Claudia said.

"My shoes are soaked," I said. "Sorry."

"We won't lie for you," the other Hutterite woman said. "We can't lie for you."

"You're going to tell on me?" I asked her.

"I won't lie. So we should all hope that they don't ask."

"They don't know all of us," Claudia said. "Forty women and

forty-five children. They just assume you belong, as long as you don't stand out."

"She does stand out," the woman in blue said.

"I'm German," I said. "*Ish*. And you're German, aren't you? We have the same square head."

"It'll be fine," Iris said.

"As long as they haven't noticed we're gone," Claudia said. "They assume we won't run because we've got nowhere to go. But they do work to keep count."

I handed her my shirt and pants.

She walked behind the best cover she could find, and started to undress.

"I'm Persephone, by the way," I said, to the woman in blue, who was giving me a less-than-friendly look.

"My name is Ruth," she replied.

"I'm sorry we're not really hitting it off."

"They'll expect you to know your way around the colony. We all have jobs to do. There's always work."

I nodded.

Claudia held out her dress, out the side of a tree trunk.

I walked over and took it.

Then she handed me the rubber ring gag that I'd still had in my pants pocket.

"I don't want to know what this is for," she said.

"You definitely do not," Iris said. "My sister has certain... predilections."

"Seriously?" I said, glaring at her.

She giggled.

I handed the offending rubber object to my sister. But she didn't have any pockets, so she did the most obvious thing you'd do if you weren't trying to play nice with the local Hutterites: she hung it around her neck like some kind of diamond pendant.

"I'll hold on to this for you, dear sister," she said, trying not to laugh. "Even if I disapprove of your sinful lifestyle."

I heard Ruth take a deep sigh. One of those ones where it's definitely a statement — or judgment — and not some kind of involuntary response.

There was really no way for me to try and explain myself to her. I can imagine that there was only one word she'd use to describe me to her church elders, and I'll bet it rhymes with "scarlet".

I *squeezed* myself into the dress. It barely fit. Okay… it didn't really fit at all. And needless to say, it wasn't flattering.

"You might need to steal a different dress when you get there," Ruth said. "I'm sure you're okay with stealing."

I smiled.

Ruth didn't.

Once Claudia had put on my clothes, which were correspondingly loose on her, she took off her rubber boots and handed me her kerchief.

I completed my ensemble.

Claudia looked rather fetching.

And I was Seffy Schmidt the Hutterite Woman. The Exceptionally Frumpy Hutterite Woman.

Iris was trying extremely hard not to laugh.

"Ruth and I are sisters," Claudia said. "We lived with our father and mother and three brothers. With only my mother, now. Don't expect her to lie for you, either."

"This won't work if someone rats me out," I said.

"They'll chime for the noon meal soon," Ruth said. "Less than an hour."

"And I'll be outed by then."

"I think so."

"You'd better hurry," Iris said. "We'll wait here."

"I don't think that's enough time," I said.

"It needs to be," Claudia said. "Because I can't give you any more time than that."

4

PERSEPHONE SCHMIDT, POTENTIAL DITCH PIG

Ruth led me back to outside where she and Claudia had been working, in the chicken sheds.

"Last week was the slaughter," she said. "We do one every five weeks. Or we did."

"You've still got chickens," I said.

"Yeah. Still have chickens."

As Ruth walked back inside the long chicken coop building, I made my way toward the tents.

I kept my head low as I walked by three of the other women; they stared at me as a I went by, but didn't say anything. It was clear they should have known me, and they didn't... but that was where they left it.

I passed by what looked like a cleaned-out potato field and reached the edge of the tents. There were only four of them, two by two, from what I could see. Not enough room for busloads full of people, making it seem all the more necessary for the camp to be bussing out almost as many people as it was bussing in.

Along the length of the tents was a line of green and white porta-potties. For some reason, that made me breathe a little easier, as if letting people poop regularly is a sign that they're being treated fairly.

But I'd seen no people, aside from the Hutterite women... no men at all.

Who was running the colony? Who'd taken all of the men away?

"I don't know you," a voice said. A boy who'd caught up behind her. He was probably eleven or twelve. "Who are you?"

"Seffy Schmidt," I said. "I'm from Fargo. My family was brought here. Do you know if there are people in all those tents?"

The boy pointed to the far corner. "That's where they take them," he said. "Once they arrive."

"What do they do with them?"

"I don't know."

I gave him a nod. "Thanks," I said.

I walked around to the far tent.

And managed to step out in front of two armed men in combat armor.

I stopped.

I should have kept walking, to show that I was supposed to be there.

But I messed that up pretty effin quick.

"Put your hands on your head," one of the soldiers said. His automatic rifle was already pointed at my patterned green dress.

I did as he said. Bots or not bots, I wasn't immune to bullet-in-the-brain disease.

The other soldier quickly began to restrain me, pulling my hands down and behind my back and slipping on a set of plasticuffs.

There'd been no attempt to be gentle. He'd done it to be rough… he wanted me to know that he wasn't falling for whatever act I was trying to pull.

"That dress doesn't come close to fitting you properly," he said, as he turned me around to face him. "You're not fooling anybody, chicky-poo."

"This one's not infected," the other soldier said.

"Why do you say that?" I asked.

"Because I know." He lowered his rifle, letting it hang from his shoulder. "I'll take her inside, Byzzan."

He opened the door to the tent.

Opened it *for* me, like he was just expecting me to walk on through.

So I did.

The inside of the tent was wide open, like you'd see in a dining hall or wedding reception, but with only a few folding tables along the back wall.

And a hospital bed, along with what looked like a medical scanner, much like the one I'd used at the biomedical lab, sitting on a rolling cart.

"You were never infected," the soldier said as led me toward the bed. "The others all were at one point."

"The others?" I said.

"I'm assuming you know them. That would make the most sense."

"Who are you?"

"Sgt. Mike Magden," he said. "US 3rd Cavalry. Retired."

"You don't look retired."

"And you don't look Hutterite."

"I'm not," I said.

"I know."

"So you're *not* retired?"

"No, I am."

"Uh, okay."

"I'd like you to lie down on that bed, miss."

"Kinda hard with my wrists cuffed behind my back," I said.

I watched him pull a small blade out from what I thought was a pocket. He'd cut off the ties before I had time to start my panic, about the sharp knife heading toward the small of my back.

"Better?" he asked.

"Still being detained," I said.

He chuckled.

I hadn't expected a chuckle.

"On the bed, please," he said.

I sat on the bed.

"Lie down."

I saw the leather restraints... maybe they're standard, since I used them on Iris... but I don't think they are...

"You will need to be restrained," he said. "It's better for everyone."

"You need to strap me down for a scan?"

"I don't do the scans. I don't stay for that. So, please, lie down and I'll put you in the restraints."

"Okay."

I put my head back against the hard pillow.

One strap over my chest, straps for my wrists.

He moved on to a strap a few inches south of my crotch, then a couple more for my ankles.

"Thanks for making this go easy," he said.

"Thanks for not shooting me."

He gave a strange little nod and walked back out the front of the tent.

And I realized that he hadn't actually called anyone about me.

I pulled against the straps a little, for about as long as it took to realize I wasn't going to be getting out… so not very long at all.

And I waited.

I heard the chimes sound. The noon meal.

Claudia wouldn't be making it back in time.

I wondered what that would mean for her; were they keeping count at every meal? Would they know that Claudia had run off? They'd assume I'd been involved. They'd probably realize that Ruth was part of it too, even if she hadn't wanted to be.

I had a feeling that I might have just made things a whole heap worse for everyone.

Classic Seffy.

A door opened at the rear of the tent, not far from where I'd been left.

A woman walked in. Wearing scrubs. She was probably mid thirties, maybe a little older, but in an aged-well kind of way. She looked Persian, or maybe Turkish, with dark eyes, extra-thick eyebrows, and a no-nonsense expression on her face.

"I'm Dr. Jones," she said.

"Jones? I wouldn't have guessed that."

"It doesn't really matter."

"You're here to scan me."

"I'm here because Sgt. Magden is very excited about you," she said. "That you were out wandering around in the big bad world and still aren't infected."

"How does he know I'm not?"

"We'll scan you… then we'll all know."

She aimed the scanner and turned it on, the red light moving up and down, head to feet.

There was a console built into the cart, underneath the scanner itself.

She was keeping a close watch on it.

"This makes no sense," she said.

"What?"

"You have the bots… but no parasite."

"I know. It's called immunity."

"You have no trace of *t. gondii* at all," she said. "Not like the others who came in. Or at least, not quite like the others."

"The others," I said. "Can you—"

"Did you come here to find them? The Schmidts and the Kimmerns, and some random Canadian girl..."

"Yeah."

One Canadian girl. Leona? So they might not have taken Errol and Jetta...

"They've all developed immunity," Dr. Jones said.

"Yeah."

"And you're immune, too, I'm guessing."

"Right again, doctor. We found a cure. And a vaccine, too, I guess."

"*You* are the cure," she said.

"It started with me, yeah." I wasn't about to mention my sister.

"That's not good," she said.

"What are you talking about?"

"We can't have someone like you. Not here."

"So we should go, then?"

"You can't leave," she said. "Sorry."

"And so...?"

"Hold on," she said. "I'm thinking."

"Sgt. *Whoever* thought it was a good thing, didn't he?"

"Sgt. Magden doesn't know what's going on."

"Oh."

She shook her head. "I don't think I can help you," she said.

"I don't need help. I'm immune."

"They don't want that."

"Who doesn't want that?"

"I honestly don't know what to do..."

"Take off my restraints," I said.

"I can't..."

"Tell them I got loose. I'll make a run for it."

"No..."

"Are they going to kill us?" I asked her.

She didn't answer.

"Please tell me... are they?"

"I think... I think they're going to want to kill *you*, at least."

"Then you need to let me out of here," I said. "Please."

"I have to go…"

She started heading back to the door.

"No," I said. "Dr. Jones…"

She left the tent.

And I wasn't exactly equipped to run on after her.

Since any Seffy-saving cavalry would need to consist of Iris and the newly unzombified Anna Louise — and Claudia, *maybe* — I wasn't exactly expecting a rescue op. Errol and Jetta might still be out there, too, but even if they met up, shared notes… that still wouldn't be enough. There were real live soldiers standing guard outside the tent.

It's not like Errol and his welding helmet are going to do anything about that.

It made me think about chickens.

Obviously I haven't eaten a chicken in a very long time, unless you consider a chicken to be a chicken right from the moment the egg is laid. When they hatch new chickens, they end up with a whole butt-load of boy-chicks. In big operations it's still usually cheaper to just hatch those wrong-gendered balls of fluff than it is to invitro-sex them before they're come out of their shell, because the moment your chicken sexer tracks down their boy bits, they get culled — the chicks, not the sexer — "cull" being a fancy farming word for murdered.

And yes, I'm allowed to be preachy about it, even if I do eat the surviving girl-chicks' eggs. Not that I'm some animal rights diehard, but I cringe at the idea that cute little chicks are something you can just throw into a grinder.

But that's the system, and like everything else in the United States of America it's quantity over quality, bigger is better, talking versus walking.

I might need to make amends to those little baby chickens, for all the omelettes and huevos rancheros and rum-heavy egg nogs. These toolbags were about to cull me, because *I was perfectly healthy.*

The first special thing about Seffy Schmidt was the thing that was going to get me killed.

Fan-frickin-fabulous.

The front door to the tent opened.

Sgt. Magden came in. He walked over to the hospital bed.

He gave me a nod. No smile, which was probably good, since there was a higher chance than not that it would have been the wrong kind of smile. Like something you'd get from Lucas.

He stood by the bed, not speaking.

And not undoing the straps.

"Can you tell me what's going to happen to me?" I asked him.

For a moment, I thought he was going to answer. I could see his lips move.

But that was all.

"Did she get you to kill my family?" I asked. "The Schmidts?"

I waited for a reply I knew wasn't about to make an appearance.

"So... did you swear an oath to kill little girls?" I asked. "Or was it just a blanket kill-everyone kind of deal?"

"You're not a little girl," he said.

"Uh... same question."

He didn't say anything else.

I gave him a bit of a stare, all indignant, like, I don't know... that he should be ashamed of himself. I guess he should be ashamed. That *milfy* doctor with the thick eyebrows was going to get him to kill me...

The back door opened.

In walked the famous eyebrows.

"I need you to take her out to the field," the doctor said.

"There are things I won't do," Sgt. Magden said.

"I know. That's why I asked you to do it. They can't find out about her."

Doctor Jones gave me a quick look. No smile.

She looked back to Sgt. Magden. "You need to make sure they don't find out."

She walked back out of the tent.

Sgt. Magden started undoing my ankle straps. "You're going to make this smooth, right?"

"Are you going to tell me what you'll do to me?" I asked.

He gave another short nod. Then started on the leather strap over my upper thighs. "That sentry out there will expect me to walk you outside. Out to the fields."

"To kill me."

"That's what he expects. Because otherwise you'd be staying in detainment, with your family."

"I don't get the between-the-lines part here, sir," I told him.

"I'm taking you out, and I'm going to make it look like you're dead and in the pit."

"There's a pit?"

Another nod.

"So you're letting me go?"

"You can't come back here," he said. "You will put all of our lives at risk if you do. Including your family."

"I can't do this. I can't leave them here."

"It's not your decision."

"Like *hurr* it isn't."

He finished the last straps, the ones pinning my wrists to the bed.

I sat up.

He took out another set of plasticuffs.

I put my hands behind my back. At some point you just get used to feeling like a miniature schnauzer, about to be led out on another leash walk.

✍

We passed by the other sentry, who offered to take me instead. With the kind of look men give that I've learned to hate.

Sgt. Magden politely declined, giving me a shove to keep going.

He led me south, across a track of a mile road, and past a pile of old junk, old tires, old tanks and bins, and old… metal bits?

We went past a marshy slough, and past another pile of junk.

The Hutterites had a lot of junk…

Then he led me to the right, toward the wetlands and another slough.

And I saw the pit he'd been talking about.

At least thirty feet long, and it looked deep, but I could tell just how deep, since it had started filling with water.

"That idiot Byzzan took the Cat and dug a trench in a marsh," Sgt. Magden said. "What a mess."

I could see the bodies. Floating in the trench. The mass grave.

The Hutterite men, from what I could see, some still wearing their nondescript gray caps. Some bodies with their dark jackets open, patterned shirt underneath.

I wondered how the soldiers had killed them, if they'd tried to hide it from the women and children, if they hadn't used their rifles. Had Sgt. Magden been the one to do it?

He was still leading me up to it, to the ditch filled with swamp-water and dead Hutterites. He had a rifle, and that knife he'd pulled out earlier. And I had my hands cuffed behind my back.

I realized that it might have all been an act, some trick to make me think I wasn't about to be murdered and tossed in that ditch. To keep me calm, to keep me from shouting out or trying to run. Because then they would have had to shoot me. And the Hutterite women would have heard.

And known for sure what kind of camp it was.

"I'm feeling a little vulnerable here," I said. "Can you cut these cuffs off now?"

"I need to ask you some questions, Ms. Schmidt."

"I can answer questions with my hands free…"

"What did they do in Fargo?" he asked. "You were there, weren't you?"

I didn't want to answer.

I felt like he ought to already know what had happened.

"Roxana thinks they wanted to kill everyone," he said.

"Roxana? Is that your so-called doctor?"

He nodded. "I know they were infected. Most of them."

"Almost all of them," I said. "So they decided to wipe us all out, just to be safe. But there's a cure."

"I know. She told me."

"When did she do that?"

"I still can't believe they did that," he said.

"My father thinks they're trying to clean this up… keep us all quiet."

"We're not part of that, Ms. Schmidt. This is something else."

"Something else?" I said. "What kind of something else?"

"They want to take advantage of the situation," he said. "They want to refocus the infection."

"Refocus?"

"I don't think I should say anything else on that."

I felt a tiny shred of hope. That Magden didn't want to tell me too much, because I wasn't going to end up floating in that ditch.

"Can you cut me loose now?" I asked.

"Yeah."

He made with the blade, and my wrists were free.

"There's a secured area at Devils Lake," he said. "In North Dakota, three hours from here. Camp Grafton. You should go there, talk to the base commander, Colonel Magden."

"Magden?"

"My little brother. Find him and tell him what you did. The cure."

"I need to get my family out of here."

"No," he said. "That's just not happening. We can't make that happen for you. Sorry…"

"I can't leave them."

"You need to leave them," he said. "And you can't come back here."

I shook my head.

"You understand that, right? You need to leave and you can't come back."

"Yeah. Okay."

"No… you're lying to me, Ms. Schmidt. You think you can risk it. But you'll lose. And your family will lose. And it's not fair to me, and it's not fair to Roxana. *We didn't have to let you go.*"

"So I owe you for not murdering me in cold blood?" I instantly regretted saying that one out loud.

"Dr. Jones is the bottom of the ladder," he said. "She doesn't want to be here, she doesn't think this is okay. If they catch wind of that, she's dead. And so am I."

"Okay. I understand."

"You're telling me the truth."

"Yes," I said.

"Good." He let out a pretty big sigh. "Devils Lake, okay? Camp Grafton."

I nodded. It's not like I was promising him something.

"Thank you, Ms. Schmidt. There's just one more thing."

"What?"

"I need to slice an artery."

"Are you frickin kidding me?"

"In case he's suspicious," he said. "The other sentry. I need at least a little bit of blood to wipe off my boots."

"You said he dug a trench in a marsh."

"Just let me do this. Seriously… don't make me regret cutting you loose."

"You know that it'll hurt like a *sonofagoat*, right? You ever had someone slice you open?"

"Does shrapnel count?"

"You can cut my palm," I said. "Will that do?"

"Maybe…"

"Okay."

I held out my left hand.

He took his knife and made the cut.

And spent almost five minutes painting his clothes with tiny splotches of blood.

It wouldn't have fooled most people.

But maybe Magden was lucky and the other sentry was an idiot… or maybe Sgt. Magden was the idiot. Of course, there was no reason why it couldn't be all three…

But Sgt. Magden was the one with the rifle. And the military training. So I wasn't about to get him all bogged down in the petty details.

I let the man fingerpaint himself with my blood, and then I started walking south.

I'd have to loop around the long way, to get back to the place where Iris and the other two were waiting for me. Probably a good five miles, with my luck.

But I imagine it's better than spending the rest of your existence in a watery grave next to a Hutterite junk heap.

They were still waiting for me.

Iris and Anna Louise and a very anxious Hutterite woman, by the line of trees.

"What happened?" Iris asked, her new rubber necklace still out on display. "Did they figure it out?"

"That did not go well at all," I said. I looked over to Claudia. "I'm sorry."

"What does that mean?" Claudia asked.

"They knew I wasn't one of you guys. And then they strapped me down to a hospital bed and scanned me."

"Scanned you?" Iris said. "So now they know that it can be cured, right?"

"Yeah. They know and they aren't happy about it."

"That makes no sense," Anna Louise said.

"When can I go back?" Claudia asked. "Can we switch our clothing again?"

"I'm not sure you can go back," I told her.

"Because I missed the noon meal… they'll know I went missing."

"And they'll connect the dots, Claudia. I'm sorry."

She looked down at her feet. Then back up to me. "Did you… did you find out what happened to the men of our colony?"

"Ruth was right," I said.

That's all I'd needed to say.

She covered her face with her hands.

"What does that mean?" Anna Louise asked.

"What do you think it means?" Iris said. "*Frick*…"

"Why did they let you leave?" Claudia asked me. "Since they knew you weren't from our colony."

"I'm not sure what happened, exactly," I said. "The doctor told one of the sentries to let me go… to make it look like he'd taken me out to kill me."

"What about Mom and Dad?" Iris asked.

"I think they're still there, but I'm not a hundred percent on that. And I think they have Leona, but not Jetta. The doctor mentioned having one random Canadian girl."

"She's so random," Iris said.

"Is this a joke?" Anna Louise asked, glaring pretty hardcore at my sister.

"She grows on you," I said. "Potentially."

"I need to go back," Claudia said. "Take off that dress."

"You can't go back."

"Give me back my clothing."

"I'm sorry, Claudia."

"You are all insane," she said. "I was a fool to trust you. I need to go back. I need to see if my sister is alright."

She started walking toward the gravel road.

"Do we need to stop her?" Iris asked me.

"They might kill you, Claudia," I said.

"You don't know that," she replied. And kept walking.

"They killed the men," I said, making sure she could still hear me. "They dropped them in a ditch at the south edge of the colony."

"I will put my faith in the Lord," Claudia said.

"Your God let your father and brothers die," Iris said.

I shushed her.

But Claudia looked at Iris for a moment, then shook her head. "You think you've gained the world by giving up on God," she said. "But you know, deep down, that you are missing something."

"Don't go, Claudia," I said. "Please."

She kept walking.

"We need to go," Anna Louise said. "She'll probably tell them everything."

"I don't think she will," I said.

"We can't risk it," Iris said.

I nodded.

And the three of us started walking back to where we'd stashed Lucas Berg's SUV.

5

BOTHOT GIRL, INTERRUPTED

We found the SUV where we'd left it. I didn't push for us to check on Lucas Berg, to see if he'd found his way out of that basement. It would be a risk even going back into that house. And it didn't matter what happened to him, did it? If we were lucky we'd never have to see him again.

The bigger concern was that there was still no sign of Errol and Jetta, where they'd dropped us off. There was no indication that they'd ever come back. Not that I could sniff the pavement and make a note of every car that had come by.

So we decided to head toward the bed and breakfast. It was possible that Errol and Jetta had decided to do the same, not realizing what a faux-pas it is to completely abandon half your team in the middle of frickin nowhere. Not that either one of them is particularly gifted when it comes to social conventions.

Iris drove, but only after hanging Lucas' ring gag from the rear view mirror, taking the same backroads we'd taken on our way to the colony, to keep us away from any alleged FEMA buses that might be moving around the Red River Valley.

They'd tricked my father, told him his family would be safe. Or at least that's what Leona had led us to believe with her note.

Assuming that it had been Leona's note.

I doubt Jetta's particularly gifted in handwriting detection. And since I couldn't just sniff the sticky note...

For all I knew, my father and his wife and the rest had been hustled off against their will, at gunpoint, maybe... that would make more sense, wouldn't it? Then to think that Dad would be comforttable with doing nothing more than having Leona leave us a sticky note. Or more specifically, that Beth would allow him to be comforttable with that.

It had seemed so farfetched before, like Jetta had said, that FEMA would be up to something sinister — although Kellen and his ilk would probably make the case that FEMA is *literally* Hitler — instead of just evacuating people who weren't infected.

But there was no reason to believe the people running that camp had anything to do with evacuations. Not that I had any idea what they *were* up to. And why my immunity would be a bad thing, and why it would matter that I was never infected, whereas my father and the others had been.

"I'm missing part of the picture," I said. "What they're doing at that Hutterite Colony. Why they'd bother to take it over, to kill all the men…"

"That's what Lucas would have done," Anna Louise said. "If he could have."

"Hutterite women?" Iris said. "Not sure about that. A little too salt-of-the-earth, I think. Not enough spice."

"He wanted you, Persephone," Anna Louise said. "He talked about you and another girl. Not Iris, I don't think."

"Jetta," I said.

"Yeah."

"He's an ambitious young man," Iris said. "And also… I'm not at all jealous."

"Well, I doubt we've just got some smarter version of Lucas running that Hutterite Colony," I said. "They've got a buttload of buses and they've got armed men."

Iris shook her head. "Or so Lucas told us."

"No," Anna Louise said. "I told you. So unless I'm lying to you…"

"Yea, okay," Iris said. "It's the same kind of idea, isn't it? Same thing we were doing, too. Set up a home base, and start building up your control over the local area."

I shook my head, not that she wasn't busy watching the road in front of her. "We weren't doing anything like that, Iris. We wanted to cure people, remember?"

"You cured me," Anna Louise said. "So thank you for that."

"We wanted to cure *everyone*," I said. "Or vaccinate. But Iris… what about Claudia?"

"What about her?" Iris asked.

"She thought she was immune."

"She wasn't infected. That I'd have known. But she wasn't immune, either. Not if we're talking about the bots."

"How can you know that?" Anna Louise asked.

"It's hard to explain," Iris said. "When you have the bots you start to… I don't know… *sense* the other bots. Like when you were infected, did you feel like you had a connection to other people around you?"

"I wasn't around other people. Just Lucas."

"And he's never been infected," I said.

"Well, I can tell with you, Anna Louise," Iris said. "I can sense your bots, and I can sense that they're different than they would have been, back when you were infected."

"The soldier who let me go thought he could sense it, too," I said. "Not sure why he thought that."

"I don't understand," Anna Louise said. "So you're not infected, right?"

"I was infected," Iris said. "Back when Lucas first took you, I was there. Tied up in a bedroom, so I wouldn't spread the parasite. Seffy figured out a way to cure me. But I guess you've pieced that together by now…"

And then something occurred to me.

"Hold on," I said, slapping my hands against the front dash. "Claudia had mentioned that there were infected there, at the colony. She'd been in contact with them, but they hadn't tried to bite her."

"And she would have mentioned them having something strapped over their mouths," Iris said.

"So they were infected, but they weren't spreading the infection?"

"But she didn't know what she was talking about, Seffy. The woman thought she was immune, remember?"

"You'd think so, too," Anna Louise said. "If a zombie was standing next to you and not trying to chew through your neck."

"So what does this mean?" I said.

"Maybe they weren't even infected," Iris said. "Or they had something different than what I had."

"That doctor was looking for *t. gondii*. I remember her mentioning it."

"The doctor's a woman?" Iris asked.

"And that's weird?"

She looked over briefly and gave me a grin. "I just pictured a mad scientist type. Big, bushy hair…"

"Big bushy eyebrows," I said. "Does that count?"

We crossed the Buffalo River by a lonely Lutheran Church, one that we'd passed on the way out. We were a few miles east of the B&B, and a few miles south of the nearest town.

We hadn't seen a single vehicle, and not a single person.

"Are we going back to North Dakota?" Anna Louise asked. "Is this B&B place in Fargo?"

"Do you know what happened in Fargo?" I asked her.

"Not really. I'm guessing there are a lot of infected people there."

"We went to Fargo this morning," Iris said. "But it's not safe there right now. So we're staying north of the city, along the river."

"And that's safe?"

"That's safe. For now."

"Then what happened to your family? They took them, didn't they?"

"You think they'll check back where we were," I said. "The people from the camp."

"I don't know," Anna Louise said.

"Leona left a note," Iris said. "Or someone left a note. So they'll be expecting us, either at the colony or back here."

"Kellen's still there," I said.

Iris nodded. "*If* he's still there."

We crossed the empty Highway 75, which led back to Winnipeg, to where Jetta and Leona had come from, the land of ethnic food and teenage drinking. Three minutes later we were at the Red River, turning north along the gravel road.

I held my breath as Iris turned onto the driveway of Gaia's Point.

I saw the minivan.

"Is that them?" Anna Louise asked. "Your friends?"

"I effing hope so," I replied.

Iris pulled us up right behind.

We climbed out, me and my bow first, then Anna Louise and the rifle she had not idea how to hold, and followed by Iris.

We moved slowly toward the front porch.

"*Holy schmo,*" someone said. Jetta.

She ran out onto the porch.

"What's with the Hutterite dress?" she asked me. "Not that it doesn't look great on you…"

I started to cry.

She came down and gave me a hug.

"I'm sorry we left," she said. "I'm so sorry, Seffy."

"Why did you guys leave?" Iris asked.

She hadn't gone in for a hug.

But Jetta was too preoccupied to answer. She was staring at Anna Louise. "Wait…" she said.

"You're Jetta," Anna Louise said. "I think I remember you, too… somehow."

"I'm hard to forget. Even for, uh, zombies."

"Not a zombie anymore, thanks."

"So hold up," Jetta said, "she was with Lucas?"

"Lucas is still out by the Hutterite Colony."

"So it was a Hutterite Colony… the picture is starting to form in my mind's eye…"

"So why did you guys leave?" Iris asked. "Or are you not even hearing me?"

"It wasn't up to me," Jetta said. "I told Errol that we should stay put, sit tight, smoke a J…"

"Where is he?" I asked.

"He's inside."

"Is Kellen here, too?"

"Yeah."

I nodded.

And made my way inside.

I found Errol and Kellen sitting together at the kitchen table.

Sitting, not, you know, doing something useful like coming up with a rescue plan for their missing *compadres*. Just sitting, like a couple of worthless sacks of… umm… I want to use the S-word in Spanish, to keep with the theme Iris and I got going on. I think it starts with an 'M'…

Errol was fingering a tablet.

They hadn't looked up. They must have assumed it was just Jetta coming back inside. To be honest, it's a little rude to not look up. I mean, beautiful woman enters room and you look up. That's just manners, people.

"Sorry to disturb you guys," I said. "And your important… sitting…"

They finally looked up.

And Kellen audibly gasped.

Apparently the patterned forest green dress was obviously a bit of a shock to him.

"Persephone," Errol said, standing up from the table. "I'm glad you're okay."

"No thanks to your premature evacuation," I told him.

If he wanted a hug, he was barking up the wrong tree. This particular tree wanted to slap a branch across his stupid face.

"They would have spotted us," he said. "We had to go."

"You had to go, leave us behind, and never come back?"

"We were going to come back," he said.

"To identify our bodies?"

"What did you expect us to do? Barge in and rescue you?"

"We didn't need rescuing, you frickin idiot. We needed you to meet us where you were supposed to meet us."

"You weren't there. We were there, and you weren't."

"And then you left. Instead of waiting, *like you were supposed to.*"

"We didn't know what had happened to you," he said. "So I decided that we needed to come back, to get Kellen. To help us bring you home."

"We were waiting for nightfall," Kellen said.

"And you thought that would give you a leg up on the professionally trained soldiers?" I asked.

"I don't understand what you want from me, Persephone," Errol said.

I didn't know.

Maybe I was just glad there was someone there for me to be angry at, an easy target.

I knew he didn't deserve it.

But I wasn't about to apologize. Or admit that maybe I was a little bit in the wrong.

"I didn't even know there were soldiers there," Errol said. "I mean, if I'd known that—"

"We need to get them back," I said. "But I'm not sure we can stay here."

I sat down at the table, in the chair beside his.

Errol sat back down as well.

I heard the other girls come walking up the hall to the kitchen.

Iris popped her head in first, visibly annoyed at the continued exi-stence of the men of Gaia's Nest. Anna Louise and Jetta followed close behind.

"You think those people from the camp will come back for us?" Errol asked.

"We don't know," I said. "We found Anna Louise with Lucas. She saw the buses. They're shipping people in, doing something with them, and then they're apparently shipping them back out. Only they killed some people, too."

"The men at the colony," Iris said, taking the fourth and final seat at the table. "Dumped 'em in a ditch."

"Maybe more people, too. I'm not sure. I didn't see them all."

"How many?" Errol asked. "How many people, do you think? How many did they… did they kill?"

"A lot of people," I said. "That's all I know." I looked over to Jetta, who'd wandered beside me. "But I think Leona's still there, and that she's still alive."

"But they're doing something to her," Jetta said, putting both hands on the back of my chair. "Is that what you're telling me?"

I looked back to her and nodded. "But I don't know what, exactly. There's some kind of a doctor there, and maybe others."

"But not for treatment," Iris said. "They weren't happy when they found out that we had a way to stop it."

"That makes no sense," Kellen said.

"It makes sense if you look at it the right way," Anna Louise said. She'd boosted herself up onto the kitchen counter, something a girl like me would never feel confident enough to pull off.

Kellen looked at Anna Louise dismissively. I knew it wasn't some declaration that he didn't think she was hot — I mean, she's *objectively* hot — but like he didn't think she had anything important to say. So you know, like most guys look at pretty girls. Or any girls…

"And what way should I be looking at it?" Kellen asked her.

"If we know they don't want a cure—"

"We don't know that," Jetta said.

Anna Louise started over. "If we know they don't want a cure, then we can make a good guess at what they do want."

"I'm ready for those guesses," I said.

"Same thing Lucas wanted with me."

"No one would want my father for that," Iris said. "The man is

71

banned from speedo use in over a hundred countries."

"Not for sex," Anna Louise said. "But for anything else. Think about it. The cat poop parasite controlled those bots, right? Isn't that what it was? And those bots controlled us."

"I don't follow," Errol said. "You're saying they want people to stay infected?"

"I don't know…"

"By the way," Kellen said, "I think I saw your dog."

"What?" Iris and I both said, at pretty much the same microsecond.

Kellen gave a stupid shrug. "Your dog. Out in some bush by the river. I tried to call him, but he ran off."

"You weren't supposed to call him," Jetta said. "That just makes them run harder."

Kellen smirked. "Because you train a dog by ignoring it?"

Jetta groaned. "He's terrified, okay? Some strange guy he barely knows yelling at him sure as H-E-double-hockey-sticks isn't going to coax him back."

"That's true," I said. "But I don't know what will."

"He needs us to make him feel safe," Jetta said. "That means sending one of your girls out in the bush to wait for him to come to you."

"That sounds safe," Errol said. "Did you want to bring a dinner bell for summoning the local zombies."

"There are no local zombies," Anna Louise said. "They cleared them out."

"I think Fender's okay for now," Iris said. "Probably safer than the rest of us."

I knew she was right, so I didn't argue.

And no one else was in a place to question us on that, even if Jetta did seem a little disappointed.

"So what were we talking about?" Errol asked. "You're trying to infect people now?"

Kellen chuckled. It didn't seem like an overly friendly chuckle.

"We were talking about those people wanting to reprogram the infection," I said. "Actually… reprogram the bots, I guess, and allow the infection to stay under those new conditions."

"That infection was eating away at us," Iris said. "There are infected people in Fargo who are probably close to starving to death because of those mega-tapeworms. It's not sustainable, not by a long shot."

I nodded. "But what if they can adjust it? Find a way to control the infection. Find a way to control the infected…"

"So would they still need the parasites for that?" Kellen asked.

I shrugged. "I don't even know if any of this is true."

"So let's play it out," Iris said, tapping her fingers on the table. "They find a way to control people with those bots. If the parasites found a way to circumvent the bots, it's not hard to imagine that a mad scientist type couldn't just go and switch that around. Render the parasite harmless… or even just make it suggestible…"

"Then we'd be the problem," Jetta said. "If our cure is killing that parasite, we might be wrecking that whole mind-control plan."

"Now that sounds like a heap of woo," Kellen said. "Or, you know, a fallacy of many questions."

"Seffy knows this stuff," Iris said.

Kellen smirked. "That's just an appeal to authority."

"What is wrong with him?" Anna Louise asked.

"He's butthurt that we like science," Iris said. "Instead of magic unicorns."

I heard Kellen groan.

"Kellen has a point," I said. "Wholly by accident, I assume. We're jumping to conclusions. We don't know anything yet."

And Kellen groaned again. But I think part of his was enjoying the attention.

"I don't see how that's going to change," Errol said. "We can't just drop in for a fact-finding mission."

I nodded. "And I already tried that."

"What?"

"It's a long story."

"Explains the dress, I'm guessing." He smiled at me.

I smiled back, forgetting that I was pissed at him.

"You're too *bothot* to pass as a Hutterite," Jetta said. "You know that, right?"

"What's wrong with Hutterites?" I asked.

"I'm sure they're fine… just not… you know…"

"Bothot?"

"Exactamundo."

"So what the heck are we supposed to do?" Kellen asked. "Are we going out there or not?"

Everyone looked over at me.

Yes, to me, the *bothot* girl with the unchanged diarrhea-brown hair, wearing the homemade ankle-length dress and probably smelling a tiny bit like a chicken coop.

I was in way over my head.

But I guess everyone knew that already. Let's face it, being in over my head is one of my many charms.

"If we're actually onto something," I said, "that means that our cure might be a very big problem for those people. That's why they would have killed me."

"But they let you go," Iris said.

"The doctor... Roxana... she thought the people in charge would want me dead if they knew about me."

"What does that mean for Mom and Dad?"

Frick. She's not my mom. Not that I could say that.

"She didn't say anything about her bosses wanting them dead," I told her. "Just me."

"But what's the difference?" Kellen asked. "They're cured, you're cured..."

We'd used my blood.

That was the difference. I'd cured Iris with the printed injection and then I'd injected those experimental botshots. And then I'd injected her blood into mine.

Leona had gotten cured when she bit me.

And they'd packed up some the syringes before we'd left the lab, while I was on a *comacation* (like a *staycation*, you know, just... without being conscious), and it was only after we'd gotten to the first farm-house that I'd administered the doses to everyone else.

From my blood, mixed into theirs.

I had something in my blood... maybe Dad and Beth and the others didn't have it. Maybe Iris didn't have it, either.

But that didn't make sense, did it?

I'm not a frickin hematologist. Or an anything-ologist.

I'm not even a college drop-out, since I couldn't afford to waste my money on the application fee.

Everything I know about immunity tells me that active immunity — what I got by injecting the parasite from Iris — is the shizzle, and that passive immunity — which I assume was what I'd passed onto

Leona — is never as good. If that's the case, then Dad and Leona and everyone else but me would have developed their own anti-bodies, rather than taking a batch of my guys on board. Sometimes that might make them just as good carriers of the immunity as I am, if not better… but not always…

But either way, that wasn't what Dr. Roxana Jones had been talk-ing about. In her mind, I was the one they wouldn't want to know about. I was the danger.

Oppositeworld. Not nearly as tempting a place to visit as *Irisworld.*

"I think my bots have learned something that other bots haven't," I said. "They made some kind of adjustment, because they'd been introduced into an uninfected blood stream *at the same time as the infection.*"

"And you're thinking that the bots in everyone else don't know that trick," Iris said.

"Maybe…"

Maybe.

But Dr. Jones had figured it out, just by a single scan. And the sentry, Sgt. Magden… he'd known even before the scan. *How had he known?*

"That doesn't make sense," Kellen said. "Your bots injected into an infected person kills the infection. They're passing on their how-tos."

"Our bots are special," Iris said. "You and me, Seffy. They're not genocoded. They can transfer and survive long enough to pass on whatever's needed to fight the parasite… antibodies or anything else. But they're outnumbered by the existing bots in other people."

"So my bots are like 99% genocoded?" Jetta asked.

"Higher than that," I said. "So if you were to try and inject your blood — or just your bots — into someone else who was already infected, it probably wouldn't take. Those bots would be rejected outright, before they had a chance to pass on the message."

Jetta nodded. "Like a bag of money with an exploding dye pack."

"I don't know what you're talking about."

"So you and I are the new patient zeroes," Iris said. "But like… well, you know, with the cure instead of just… dying."

"But if they reduced the bot count, like we did with you…"

"They could make more of us. <u>We</u> could make more of us."

"Assuming any of this is true," Kellen said. "Seriously. You guys must be breaking some records for straw-grasping."

"It's not a good thing if it's true," I said. "That means that, assuming we can't find an easy way to kill off the majority of infected bots in people, Iris and I would have to personally pass our bots on to every infected person. There's no exponential growth with something like that."

"So what are they doing with our families?" Errol asked.

"Hopefully the same thing they're doing with all of the people who are released back into the wild," Iris said.

"We don't know that anyone's been released," I said. "All we know is what Anne Louise saw. They're loaded into buses and driven somewhere else. But this whole region is still emptying out, so it doesn't seem like people are being dropped off to wherever they were taken from."

"So it could actually be some kind of evacuation," Jetta said.

"You really believe that?" I asked her.

"I'd like to believe it. That they're diagnosing people then shipping them off to someplace that can help them."

"Then they'd want me there. They'd want the cure we've got."

She didn't have to take long to think about it. She frowned and gave me a slow nod.

"So what do we do?" Kellen asked.

"What, you believe us now?" Iris said.

"I believe that they're not good people down at the fake FEMA camp. I mean, Seffy saw those bodies, right?"

"Yeah," I said.

"Can you give us more information?" Errol asked. "The layout of the camp, how many soldiers and sentries there are?"

I shook my head. "I only know enough about it to know we're not capable of winning against them."

"Well, that's great," Kellen said. "Then we'll just give up."

"It's my family in there," I said. "Not yours. Obviously I want to get them out."

"Maybe we need to wait," Anna Louise said. "Since we know that people get taken out of there eventually…"

"We can't take on the whole camp," Errol said. "But maybe we can handle one of those buses."

"So we just hope to hit the right bus at the right moment?" I said. "Or do you think we're going to figure out some way to know exactly which bus they're on… if they make it on at all."

Errol frowned. "I don't know, Persephone. But I can't think of anything better."

"I know."

And I knew I couldn't think of anything, either.

6

MISSION: BLACKMAIL AND/OR BATHGASM

Kellen and Jetta made dinner.

Iris, Errol and I sat in the living room, Iris and me on the couch and Errol a lonely single on the loveseat. We made a count of the various weapons we've collected. We'd thrown everything out on the oakwood coffee table, not really spending any mental energy on worrying about scuffs or scratches to the finish.

At this rate of decay, Gaia's Nest B&B will become the Gaia Kappa Epsilon frat house by the end of the week.

Anna Louise wasn't doing much of anything, but I don't think any of us had a problem with that. She needed time to… probably not get over what happened… but maybe to put a little space after it.

And we didn't really need her help with basic addition.

The final count was three compound bows, two rifles, and Lucas' pistol. We had arrows and ammo, but not much of them. You can reuse arrows, sure, but not arrows you've shot into a hostile camp filled with soldiers; those arrows are pretty much single-use.

Errol's guess was that we could probably take out the two sentries I'd saw, but that if there was even one more soldier on site — or even just anyone with a little bit of hunting experience — our odds of making it out started plummeting pretty hardcore.

And taking out those two soldiers was also predicated on a pretty big assumption, that those men weren't infected and/or filled up with bots.

Sure, I can shoot my sister in the lung, but I'm not exactly skilled enough to make killer headshots with a compound bow.

"We could try and find help," Iris said. "Guys like Lucas, just… not Lucas."

"I guarantee you, Iris," I said, "if we start driving around and approaching random yardsites, we'll get ourselves killed. We were *redonkulously* lucky that Lucas didn't kill us."

Iris nodded. "But you know he wouldn't have killed us…"

"I don't understand why you didn't just kill him," Errol said. "The man is a roving liability."

I shushed him, then nodded my head toward Anna Louise, who was slowly rocking on a wooden rocking chair, staring at the ceiling.

He didn't push it any further.

"There is Camp Grafton," I said. "The commander is the brother of the man who let me go. I'd said I would go there, but obviously I didn't mean it."

"They won't come down here and rescue our people," Errol said. "We'll be lucky if they don't just lock us up or shoot us down."

"I think we need to find a way back into that camp," Iris said.

"So more Hutterite disguises," I said. "Not a great plan."

"You guys don't look like Hutterites," Errol said. "You're way too hot."

"I'm pretty sure you'd have been more than satisfied making skeevy comments at the ones we met," I said. "And I'm sure your Uncle Pat would have been positively ranking their Hutterite lady rumps on his scorecard."

"Seffy," Iris said.

"Sorry."

"Yeah," Errol said. "So what do we do?"

I saw Anna Louise get off her rocking chair.

She walked over to the couch, to where I was sitting with Iris.

She sat down in the middle, careful not to brush against either of the Schmidt girls.

She turned to face me.

"You have leverage," she said. "A way back into that camp."

"What do you mean?" I asked.

"Those people who let you escape. They're keeping you secret. Keeping the cure a secret."

"Yeah…"

"We can make a deal with them. They help us get your people out, and we don't tell anyone else there about the cure."

"That's insane," Errol said. "Seffy's not going back in there."

"Seffy can't go back in there," Iris said. "But someone else can go in. Just like she did. Get captured by the sentries, get seen by that doctor, and then deliver the message. I can do that."

"Deliver the threat," I said. "Isn't that what you mean?"

"Too many things can go wrong," Errol said. "They could shoot you on sight, Iris. You could get inspected by the wrong doctor. You know what? It's possible that all they'd get for not reporting the cure is a slap on the wrist. Maybe they just don't want to risk their Christmas bonus."

"He has a point," Anna Louise said. "It's a huge risk."

"It was your idea," Iris said.

"Doesn't mean it was a good one."

"So we have three options," I said. "We go to Camp Grafton. We send Iris in to blackmail people who could easily get us all killed. Or that third option, taking over a bus and seeing if the people on board can help us."

"I don't remember that plan making the cut," Errol said. "You sure we didn't dismiss it for incredibly legitimate reasons?"

"They people on those buses have been victimized, too. They could be sympathetic."

"They might think they're on their way to getting released," Anna Louise said. "They'll be more pissed off than grateful if you get in the way of that."

"She's right," Iris said.

"Yeah, maybe," I said.

"So what do we do?" Errol asked. Again.

"I've got to try," Iris said.

"It's too risky," I said. "They'll scan you and they'll know you're cured, too."

"I'm just as cured as Mom and Dad. And they already have the two of them."

"No, Iris. It's not the same. We talked about that. You and I have something else. Dad and Beth have been cured, but it's possible that only you and I can cure anyone else."

"But we don't actually know that. It's just a hypothesis."

"And if it's true?"

"Then they'll want to keep me a secret, too," Iris said. "So they'll try to take me out back like they did with you, but I'll refuse to go."

"Don't you understand how this will go?" Errol asked. "Either they're truly panicked about people finding out about you guys, which means they might just kill you before they take you to that ditch. Or else they'll call your bluff and hand you over. There's no real chance at success. Really… there isn't."

"We have to try," Iris said.

"No," I said. "You don't have to try. Not if the odds are this terrible."

Jetta walked into the living room.

"You and I should go, Seffy," she said. "I'll go first, deliver the message. Tell them about you, and tell them about Iris. That if anything happens to us, Iris will act accordingly. Whatever she needs to do to mess up their lives. Once they agree to a deal, we sneak you in, and we get everyone out."

"I said I'd go," Iris said.

Jetta shook her head. "You're more valuable in reserve."

"We're interchangeable," I said. "I can go, Iris, instead of you."

"I think you're a safer bet, Curlicue," Jetta said. "They've met you, they've scanned you, and they know you've got giant ladyballs."

"So why can't Seffy just go?" Anna Louise asked. "Why risk Jetta, too?"

"The other sentry," I said. "He'll know something's up if he sees me. So Jetta gets through, and then me."

"Or you stay back," Errol said. "And let Jetta handle it."

"But I'm the leverage, Errol. Without me there's no real threat to them. It needs to be both of us."

Errol sighed. "This is still a bad idea. With little to no chance of success. We go to Camp Grafton, we let the professionals handle this."

"Only they won't," I said. "You said that yourself, remember?"

"I don't want you to go," he said. "Just… don't do it."

The way he'd said that… he knew I'd go.

I hadn't even been sure of it myself.

Weird that he was the one to convince me.

It was dark before we'd even eaten, since it's really not that far off from December. Even if I'd wanted to go at night, hoping it would be a little bit sneakier, there was no way anyone else would agree to that. And they'd need to agree on a time to go, since Jetta and I wouldn't be making the trip on our own. We'd have backup, even if that backup wouldn't be coming any closer than the houses where we'd left Lucas.

And probably not anywhere near those houses, since we didn't need to have that extra bit of trouble thrown into the mix.

So we'd have to wait until morning. It made sense, to aim to get there at the same time I'd arrived before, and hour or so before the chime for the noon meal.

Hopefully the same sentries would be there, and the same doctor handling the scanner. Of course, there was no guarantee of any of that.

For all I knew they shift people around all of the frickin time. Maybe Sgt. Magden will be attending a Sunday morning church service in the Hutterite chapel. Maybe Doctor Bushybrows will be taking a day off. You don't really think of how much random chance is involved, until you have time to sit quietly and just *think*.

So to continue that train of paranoid thought, I decided to have a bath, since there was warm water and electricity from the off-the-grid-capable B&B. I guess solar panels, windmills, and ridiculously-priced battery sets are a lot more important now that the grid's down.

The water had that rusty well taste, hard enough that I'm not sure they even used a softener, but it was still the first bath I'd had since the morning I'd driven Mom in for her rTMS appointment.

I'm sure I smelled pretty effing grotty.

Not that anyone smelled any better.

I brought a book in with me, one of those historical romances where every half-naked man on the cover is surprisingly hairless considering the era. This one was about the Texas Revolution, and some woman named Henrietta who was being avidly pursued by two men.

I waited until the tub was mostly full, and then I pulled off the dirty forest green Hutterite dress. My long white — and borrowed — kneesocks were crusty enough to stand at attention.

I plopped myself down into the hot water.

And enjoyed the onrushing *bathgasm*, that moment when you first feel that perfect warmth.

Oh. Yes. Yes, yes, yes. OMFG. So amazing.

And then there was a knock on the door.

"*Occupado*," I said, putting my book down on the linoleum floor beside the tub.

"It's just me. Jetta."

"Answer still stands. Naked in a tub over here."

"Yeah," she said. "Can I come in?"

"Into the room or into the bathtub?"

"The room."

"Uh, no."

She laughed. "The tub?"

"Also no."

"I won't look," she said. "Isn't there a shower curtain?"

Yes, there was a shower curtain.

But that wasn't really the point, was it?

"No, Jetta," I said, "I think you should wait 'til I'm done."

And so, naturally, she opened the door and stepped in.

I clamped my hands over my chest like shells on a mermaid.

"Sorry," she said.

"I need you to get out," I said, trying to stay calm.

"It's not like I'm hitting on you, Seffy. I'm a girl, remember?"

I grasped for the shower curtain.

She stepped over to "help", but she was looking down at my impromptu mermaid bikini top.

I pulled the curtain closed. "Why are you here, Jetta?"

"I'm nervous," she said. "About tomorrow."

"And so pushing past my personal comfort zones is some form of therapy for you?"

"Worked last time."

I saw her pick up the book through the not-opaque-enough vinyl curtain.

"I've read this one," she said.

"No, you haven't."

"No, I haven't. But the chick's named after me. Henrietta. That's long form for Jetta, eh?"

"Or you're named after that chick," I said.

"Whose named after some guy named Henry, I guess."

"Better than Donalda." I think I was starting to forget that she'd trapped me in a bathtub.

"So," she said, "broken faucet time…"

"Can we not do this now?" I asked.

"I don't trust Errol."

"What?"

"I don't trust him, Curlicue. I'm sorry."

"What is it you think he's going to do?" I asked.

"I don't know... I just... I just get a vibe off him, you know? A bad vibe..."

"So you were fine with Lucas the rapist, but Errol is giving you a bad vibe?"

"I wasn't fine with Lucas," she said. "That wasn't my fault."

"What?"

"Do you really blame me? For what happened to that girl. To Anna Louise..."

"That's not what I meant, Jetta."

"If I hadn't decided to go with him in the first place, then maybe we would have figured out that Canadian car thing... maybe we would have driven to your father's place on our own, and then he would have never been there."

"And he would've hurt someone else," I said. "Or maybe if you'd told him just how creepy he is he would have grabbed you right there, on the Interstate. Then you'd have been in that basement instead of Anna Louise."

"That doesn't make it better, Seffy. It really doesn't."

"I just want to have my bath, Jetta. Why can't you just let me do that?"

"Because I think Errol will hurt us," she said.

"You're wrong about him. He saved us, remember?"

"I don't trust him."

"You were alone with him, Jetta. When Iris and I were out at the Hutterite Colony. Did he do anything then?"

"No..."

"So why is he a problem?"

"I don't know," she said. "A feeling I get. Like a creeped-out feeling."

"Uh, okay... so the guy who's done nothing wrong is creepy, while the girl who came in to watch me bathe is perfectly normal."

"I'm not watching you bathe!"

"Yeah, you are. And it's creepy, Jetta. Really frickin creepy."

"Whatever," she said.

She stormed out of the bathroom, leaving the door wide open, of course.

I had to make the call, if I should climb out and close the effing door, or if I should stay where I was with the curtain pulled, waiting for my next visitor.

I wasn't wanting to get out.

So I picked up the book and got back to reading, which wasn't as great with the vinyl curtain in the way, but was better than being on display.

And then I heard someone coming into the bathroom.

"You ought to close the door," Iris said. "I never knew you were such an exhibitionist, Seffy."

"Hilarious."

Iris hadn't closed the door. She probably left it open for the *lulz*.

"What's going on?" she asked me.

"Jetta's getting creepy."

Iris chuckled. "She's making her move, huh?"

"This isn't a joke."

"It has to be a joke," she said. "Almost one full week now, of the world's biggest hidden camera prank. That's gotta be it."

"She's badmouthing Errol. I don't know why she'd do that."

"Do you think she's jealous of him? Like he's some kind of rival for your affection?"

"No one's a rival for my affection," I said. "No one's going to be getting my effing affection."

"Well, Jetta's a bit… unstable, Seff." She said it quietly, most likely due to her hilarious open door policy.

"I don't think that's true."

The vinyl curtain slowly started pulling back.

Apparently Iris didn't think that was weird, since we're actually real-life sisters and everything.

At least she was making eye contact…

"I like her," Iris said. "I do. But some people are part of our lives mostly for the comic relief."

"That's a pretty terrible thing to say, Iris."

"I don't think it is."

"Well, you're an idiot," I said.

She chuckled.

"Do you think this is the right thing to do, Iris?" I asked her. "Trying to blackmail people with big guns?"

"I think it's the only thing to do. That's why I still want to be the one to do it."

"I'm the right choice this time."

She groaned. "So yeah... we need to try. Unless we want to give up on Mom and Dad."

"I lost my mom, Iris."

"I'm sorry for that. But my mother loves you, Seffy. You know that, right?"

"No, I don't, actually. But it wouldn't matter. Because she's your mom. Not mine. Just like he's your dad."

"Come on..."

"I mean, it makes more sense now, right? I always wondered why he liked you better, aside from how frickin perfect you are. I was his blood, wasn't I? And you were supposed to be his stepkid. But now... you're his precious little lovechild."

"Is that some stupid joke?"

"What?"

"You need to watch how you talk about them," Iris said. "And watch how you talk about me."

"Excuse me?"

"Look... don't let your weird little pity party get you thinking that the rest of us are perfectly fine with all the crap you've been slinging at us."

"What the *hell*, Iris?"

"Oh, so now you're mad."

"Yeah, I'm mad."

"Welcome to the club."

She had a point. It wasn't like I'd cornered the market in crappy days.

So I tried to lighten up.

"Do club members get discounts on bad haircuts?" I asked.

"It won't work. You owe me an apology. And Mom and Dad, too."

"No one's getting an apology. Not until this is over."

"You're storing them up," she said.

"I'm storing them up."

She laughed.

"What?" I said.

"I don't know," she said. "It's just so hard staying angry at an idiot."

We left in the morning at 9.

I was happy to be wearing non-Hutterite clothes, a shirt and jeans from the master bedroom of the B&B that were only a size or so too big. I even had a belt with a buckle on it, though nothing as *redonkulous* as Jetta's silver beaver or Leona's "Pistol Packin' Mama".

All of us made the trip, including Kellen and Anna Louise. We'd seen enough over the past few days to know that it wasn't the best idea to leave a skeleton crew back at the farm.

We'd stick together, aside from the suicidal offshoot mission that Jetta and I were about to launch.

After some awkward questions about the rubber ring hanging from the rear view mirror, Kellen drove us back toward the colony in the van, but instead of approaching from the northwest, he looped around and parked three miles south, which was only one mile north of Highway 10.

You can take that highway all the way in, to the Fargo bathroom stalls where I'd first met Jetta.

We all climbed out of the van.

Errol walked over to me, before I'd even put on my pack.

He reached in for a hug.

I pulled back.

"Oh," he said. "Well... take care of yourself, Persephone. You're... you're very important to me."

"Okay," I said. "You be careful, too."

And I pulled back a little more, just to make sure I was being clear enough.

I watched Kellen walk over to Jetta.

Also going in for a hug.

She let him have it.

"I think you're pretty," he said.

"Aw, thanks," she replied. "I think you're kinda pretty, too."

He kissed her on the cheek.

She blushed.

And looked over to me.

I did my best not to let out an eyeroll.

"The buses come this way," Anna Louise said. "So if you can take control of one of the buses, you can take the usual route and we'll see you coming."

"You can flash the high beams," Errol said. "We'll keep an eye out."

I nodded. "Don't come to get us," I said. "No matter what."

Errol shook his head. "We'll give you until nightfall. We won't wait longer than that."

"There won't be any point. Either we come back on our own or we're not coming back."

I put on my pack, which was basically just three plastic water bottles, arrows and a bow, and I started walking.

I hadn't said anything to Jetta; I guess I'm still a little annoyed with her for the involuntary peep show.

"Good luck," Iris said. "Don't die."

"Back at you," I replied, without looking back.

⁖

Jetta caught up to me as we walked north, but neither of us said anything. We started tacking a little to the west as we went, away from the road and into the fields.

I led her to the ditch.

I stopped at the edge for a moment, to look down at the murky water.

I didn't expect to see them, Claudia or Ruth. But I knew there was a chance, so I had to check.

All I could see were the bodies of the Hutterite men.

"This is where they would have put you," Jetta said quietly.

"Yeah."

"I'm glad they didn't."

"Uh... yeah."

We kept walking, past the first set of junk.

And then past the second pile.

"I'll need to stay back here," I said. "You'll need to send Sgt. Magden out to bring me in."

"Won't they still see you?"

"I'm hoping he'll think of something."

Jetta nodded.

She didn't bother to point out how thin all these threads were starting to become.

I was only grasping at a plan.

That's all.

She kept walking.

I sat down behind a low bush.

And waited.

There's something about Jetta, a cute kind of innocence that still works, even when she's annoying as heck. I like her, not like the way Iris seems to think she likes me, obviously, but I want to have her here, with us. I don't want her to go back to Winnipeg, and it's obviously not a surprise that I don't want her to get hurt.

And I think Jetta can hold her own. I think she's learned how to work with what she's got, a way of making sure that no one's threatened by her, and that no one would really want to hurt her.

I want to believe that, at least.

I want to tell myself that Jetta isn't just another *girl in the fridge*, fated to end up dead because I invited her along with me on all my stupid frickin adventures.

For some reason I'm not worried about what might happen to me. I don't worry that Sgt. Magden might just shoot me in the back of the head, or that Doctor Caterpillar-Brow Jones and her colleagues might strap me to an operating table and cut out my still-beating pancreas.

I worry about Jetta.

Because Jetta deserves better, no matter how annoying or creepy she might get when she opens her tiny little mouth. *She deserves better.*

And I guess… I guess I really don't.

✑

I had Jetta's little pink tablet with me, since there was no reason for her to bring it with her just to get taken away. She'd charged it up at the B&B overnight, so now there was 90% charge and still no network.

But it had a clock that told me I'd been waiting for forty-eight minutes.

That felt like too long.

It should have taken her less than five minutes to reach that tent with the two sentries. Then what, thirty seconds to get hustled inside? Maybe fifteen minutes with Dr. Jones. Maybe.

Then the big discussion. Is this weird little woman full of crap? Is big bad Seffy Schmidt really waiting in the wings to ruin their Sunday?

Someone should have come to get me.

I started walking toward the buildings and tents.

I saw movement.

Sgt. Magden.

He waved at me to get down.

Once I'd shoved Jetta's tablet in my pants pocket, I did, going down into a crouch. Making myself a smaller target wasn't going to help him shoot me.

I waited as he came closer.

Maybe Sgt. Magden didn't know about me and the great pronghorn hunt of 2021, how Dad had made sure I could shoot an arrow while crouching behind a decoy.

I could probably shoot the man lying down if I had to.

Not that I'd necessarily be able to get him in the head...

He slowed down once he'd gotten within fifty feet, at about the same time I was thinking I might want to pull out my bow. His military-grade rifle was strapped over his shoulder, pointing down to the ground.

He lifted his hands up, like I was about to take him hostage.

"Byzzan will be watching," he said. "So we need to be smart about this."

"Smart means not trusting you," I said.

"You're holding all the cards."

"You're holding the gun."

He smirked. "Listen... I don't think you're equipped to handle this kind of thing."

"And what kind of thing are we talking about?"

"Your little friend told us that your sister's got the same condition you have."

"Condition..."

"Seems insane to me. You're actually trying to blackmail us. You really think that's gonna work?"

"It'll work," I said, trying to sound like I'd convinced myself.

"I need you to surrender to me," he said.

"You're kidding, right?"

"I can't bring you in like this. You need to be disarmed and you need to be restrained."

"Won't he recognize me? Your buddy?"

"Byzzan's gonna wonder why you're not dead, yeah."

"And what are you going to tell him?"

"I'm not having this conversation with you," he said. "Just put down your pack and stand up, okay? And for god's sake, make it convincing when you surrender."

"I'm not surrendering."

"Would you just shut up and do what I asked?"

"How can I trust you?" I asked.

"You're not dead yet. I think that's all there is for you to go on."

I nodded.

My leverage hadn't changed. If it was any kind of leverage at all.

I put my pack down on the ground.

I stood up.

"Hands on your head," he said.

I did as he told me.

Soon he had my wrists cuffed behind me, all over again.

He started walking me back toward the colony.

"Story's that your friend doesn't know you," he said. "She saw you on her way in to ask for help. But you wouldn't approach, so she asked us to go out to check on you."

"That's the best you've come up with?"

"I struck you hard in the head, and you appeared to be fatally wounded. I assumed the bots couldn't repair that level of damage, but I was wrong."

"So that's it."

"That's it."

"I hope you're a convincing liar," I said.

He groaned. "I hope I get a chance to throw you in that ditch."

I think he was giving me a smirk at the end of that, not that I could be sure. Either way, it was a stupid thing to say to someone. And I guess there was no reason for him not to kill me at the end of it, considering what he and Byzzan did to the Hutterite men.

We crossed the dirt road and passed through the tree belt.

We reached the tent where I'd first been detained.

The other soldier, Byzzan, was watching us, his gun trained right on my chest.

"She's not a big risk," Magden said.

"Then how come you couldn't finish her off the first time?" Byzzan asked.

Magden sighed. "I could actually see in through the back of her skull. Saw her brain, man. Thought that was that."

"That wasn't, apparently. So why'd you bring her all the way back?"

"Thought they'd want to check her out. See if there's any brain injury left, or if she's back to a hundred percent."

"Yeah… makes sense." Byzzan started to grin. "But I'll make sure to take her out to the pit when they're done. So this doesn't get any more embarrassing for you, bud."

Magden chuckled.

Then pushed me toward the tent.

"You didn't fraternize, did you?" Byzzan asked.

Magden stopped. He turned back to face Byzzan, twisting my arms along with him.

"Did you?" Byzzan asked again.

"Copulation without conversation does not constitute fraternization," Magden said.

And then he clamped a gloved hand onto my left ass cheek.

And squeezed.

"I'll be the one taking her out to the pit next time," Byzzan said.

"You got it," Magden replied. "I'm pretty much all done with her."

It took a lot for me not to say anything. To put them both in their places.

Effing creepers.

But it would all go better if I seemed to be scared, if I was all trembling and cowed. Or if I looked like I had some traumatic brain injury worth the upcoming examination time. Clever comebacks wouldn't fit in well with either scenario.

It's truly *redonkulous.*

Like I've said before.

It's always the creeps and the rapists who are looking for a slice of Seffy Delight. It's never coming from the one or two guys out there I don't want to disembowel with an ice cream scoop.

❧

The tent was empty, aside from the bed and the rolling cart.

No Jetta and no Dr. Jones.

"She took your friend to the bathroom," Magden said.

"I don't believe that."

"Then don't believe it." He pointed to the bed. "We'll strap you back in."

"No frickin way," I said. "I'm not here to be scanned."

"And what if Byzzan walks in here? Or one of the half dozen doctors or fifteen other soldiers, who'd all have no issue with killing someone like you?"

I had a feeling he was fudging those numbers.

I shook my head. "No restraints. I'll lie on the bed, but you won't strap me in."

He nodded.

And cut my cuffs.

I walked over to the hospital bed and climbed on.

I put my head down on the pillow, positioning myself exactly like I'd be if he had strapped me down.

Knowing that if he tried to do it, that I'd have no real way of stopping him. He still had a gun, and he had at least eighty pounds on me. And I'm pretty sure a lot of my weight has settled into my thighs, as opposed to any kind of upper arm strength.

But I guess I could always bicycle kick the stupid toolbag…

The rear door opened.

Dr. Jones walked in.

"Where is she?" I asked.

"I have a lab," Dr. Jones said. "Jetta will be safe there."

"I don't believe you."

"You don't believe much," Magden said.

The doctor stared at the bed. "Why isn't she restrained?"

Magden shrugged.

"Restrain her, please," Dr. Jones said.

"Not happening," I said. "We had a deal, Sergeant."

He grabbed my left wrist.

I pulled it away.

"Don't make me sedate you," Dr. Jones said.

"Don't make me rip out your throat," I replied.

She smiled at me. "I like you, Miss Schmidt. Now just let me get this going, okay?"

"No one's restraining me."

"I can't take you to my lab without restraints."

"No."

"Hold her down, Sergeant."

Magden reached over, putting a hand down on each of my elbows. He was leaning right over me, his body against my chest, pinning me to the bed.

I watched as Dr. Jones reached into a drawer on the rolling cart.

A syringe. And a bottle.

I knew what was coming.

"We had a deal," I said.

"We haven't broken it," she said. "Though I'm pretty sure you broke the earlier incarnation…"

And she reached in and injected the needle into my neck.

"It won't last long," I heard the doctor say. "Strap her down."

I felt my body being pushed and pulled, the straps going over my wrists, my ankles, my chest and my legs.

I saw Dr. Jones smiling at me again, as my eyes got too heavy to keep open.

The bed started moving as I fell asleep.

7

THE MAD SCIENTIST'S INTERN'S LAIR

I don't think I was out for long. For one thing, I've got these fancy bots; you'd think they would shorten the effects, assuming that Jonesey didn't already take that into consideration. And also, I woke up as Magden was still rolling me down a hallway, head first. I rolled my head to the side, trying to see in front of me. I caught a glimpse of Dr. Jones walking in front of my hospital bed.

I wasn't in a tent; I was in what looked like a barn. An animal barn, without any animals, long, narrow pens on both sides of a center aisle. There were upside-down pylons hanging from the ceiling, probably feeding bins or something, but there was no sign of the former occupants, just a weathered concrete floor.

"She's awake," Magden said.

"That's fine," Dr. Jones said. "We're almost there."

I was pushed past a few more stalls and then Magden stopped.

"You can unstrap her," Dr. Jones said.

Magden undid the restraints, starting down near my feet.

I made the decision not to kick him in the face.

He offered a hand to help me up.

I didn't take it.

I almost fell off the frickin bed as I climbed down.

I steadied myself.

And looked around.

More rolling carts, and more hospital beds.

And more victims strapped to them, four in total, lined up along the aisle, just outside the closed-off livestock pens.

I recognized three of them. Jetta, Leona, and Claudia, the girl who was still wearing my clothes. The other was another young woman, unfairly blessed with what I'd call a resting derp face — at least when she was unconscious — and dressed in what looked like your standard Moorhead girl style, complete with an MSUM Dragon hoodie, the one where the dragon's in the middle of a circle, shooting out fire.

Definitely not a Hutterite.

"You strapped them down," I said. "What is wrong with you people?"

"We strapped you down, too," Dr. Jones said.

"Yeah. I remember."

"And now you're up and about… so that's progress, right?"

"So I should go unstrap all of them, too?"

"I wouldn't unstrap anyone other than your friend Jetta," she said.

"Why not?"

"Because they're test subjects, Miss Schmidt."

I looked over at Jetta.

She was lying on the bed, staring at the ceiling.

Not even looking at me.

Her eyes were open.

They hadn't given her what they'd given me. And it would have worn off quickly enough on her, too… considering how *hot and botted* she was these days.

"We can call it a new kind of muscle relaxant," Dr. Jones said. "Touchless. No injection required. And wireless, even. Not the easiest thing to work out, but I guess that's why I have the fancy degrees."

"You're pushing your luck with me," I said.

"I'm just trying to lighten the mood."

"Don't bother."

"Well, anyway… she can't move at the moment. We weren't just going to trust that she'd wait here for us."

I walked over to Jetta's side.

I reached for her hand. I thought I felt her tightening her grip, but I wasn't sure.

Her eyes didn't move. She was still staring up, at the ceiling.

I looked over to the doctor.

"I'm having a lot of trouble believing you're not a total piece of garbage," I told her.

"You're the one who's playing fast and loose with all our lives."

"Where is my family?"

"The Schmidts?"

"Yeah, the Schmidts. And the Kimmerns, while we're at it."

"I don't have them," she said. "Dr. Smith has them."

"Dr. Smith. So it's Dr. Jones and Dr. Smith. This all sounds so truthful."

"I'm not lying. Dr. Smith runs the lab. I get to select a few subjects for my research."

"And what is that research, exactly? Drugging girls up for fun and profit?"

"I already told you," she said. "I've been upfront with you, Miss Schmidt. We are researching ways of using the infection to benefit humanity."

"Now that's a *hu-u-uge* pile of crap."

"I don't agree with the approach that Dr. Smith and his team are taking. But I'm here, and I have a job to do. And I think what I'm doing has merit."

"Yeah. Looks great. All these helpless women strapped to hospital beds. Nobel prize for sure."

"My father used to hit my mother," Dr. Jones said. "And sometimes me and my brothers. And you know what was done about it?"

"No tangents, please."

"They couldn't do anything about it, because my mother was too frightened to press charges. And without her participation, there wasn't enough evidence."

"That's very sad," I said. "Doesn't justify that mass grave out back."

"I want to show you something, Miss Schmidt. Something you'll appreciate."

"Why would I appreciate anything coming from you?"

"Just hold on, okay? Stop being so damned self-righteous."

I rolled my eyes.

She pulled a small tablet out of her pocket.

And passed it over to me. I didn't mention to her that I already had one in my pocket. With a pretty pink case.

"Just wait," she said.

She walked over to a rolling cart beside Jetta. She started tapping on a console.

An image flickered onto the tablet.

Gray sheet metal. And bolts. And what looked like a yellowish orb.

"I don't get it," I said.

"Look up."

I looked up.

The ceiling. It matched the ceiling on the tablet. Almost the exact same position as I was could see, eyes straight up. But not quite.

It was like the camera was right over Jetta's bed. Over Jetta's face.

"This is some kind of simulation of what she's seeing?" I asked.

"It is what she's seeing. The bots are transmitting the data. It's a little grainy... a little compressed... but that's it."

I brought my left hand up and over Jetta's eyes.

I saw the pink shadows of my fingers and palm come over the view on the tablet.

"So you want to see what other people see?" I asked. "You ever heard of a helmet cam? Little less intrusive..."

"Big picture, Seffy." *No more Miss Schmidt, apparently.*

"You want to spy on everyone."

"I want to give the right tools to the right people. Not 'always on', Seffy. Only in emergencies. Say your sister goes missing, thrown into the trunk of some car, driven down the Interstate. What if the police can see what she's seeing?"

"The inside of a trunk? Or maybe the duct tape her kidnappers wrapped over her eyes?"

"Don't be so small-minded," she said. "Not just eyesight. Hearing. Touch. Thoughts. Any bit of information that could be used to help her. Like GPS. You remember GPS? The bots will know what to do. They'll receive the command, and they'll pass on the information they gather. Including your sister's location, of course."

"Sounds perfect," I said. "And no chance at all for abuse."

Dr. Caterpillar-brows sighed. "I'll take a little misuse over being dead in a ditch."

"So agree to disagree. And nice use of the word 'ditch'. Very sensitive to what everyone here's been going through. Do you know how many men are lying in that ditch out back?"

"I know a young woman who *isn't* lying in that ditch. Does that count?"

"What the heck is wrong with you?" I asked.

"That had nothing to do with Dr. Jones," Magden said.

I rolled my eyes. "I'm sure."

I started undoing Jetta's straps.

She still wasn't responding. It didn't feel like she was really there.

"You want to know if she can hear you," Dr. Jones said. "I can make that happen."

I didn't respond to that. She knew I wanted to know Jetta was okay, that whatever Jones had done hadn't fried her brain.

But obviously I wasn't going to admit anything to her, to someone who would experiment on other people. Uh… not that I hadn't experimented on Anna Louise back in the day. But that was different. I was doing it to help people. Real help, not whatever garbage she was trying to believe in.

"I'll turn it on," Dr. Jones said. "Listen up, Seffy."

She thumbed her tablet a little more.

For some reason I was expecting to hear Jetta's voice, like some kind of soap opera monologue. What came out instead, from the tinny speakers on the rolling cart, was a not-particularly-advanced text-to-speech voice, something that was at least female-*ish*.

"I really need you to get me out of here," the voice said.

"Not hard to guess at the sentiment," I said. "Girl strapped to a bed in the evil lab wants to leave said evil lab."

"No, Seffy. *Curlicue.* You need to get me out of here."

I looked down at Jetta. Looked into her eyes.

"What have they done to you?" I asked her.

"They're subvocalizations," Dr. Jones said. "Her internal speech. If she could speak, this is what she'd be saying."

"Just shut up," the voice in the console said.

Sgt. Magden laughed.

Dr. Jones glared at him.

"I can't move," the voice said. "I really can't."

"I know," I said. "It shouldn't last for much longer." Not that I had any actual clue.

"You need to get me out of here. We need to get as far away from here as we can."

"What about Leona?"

"I don't think we can help her," the Jetta-emulator said.

"You can help her," Dr. Jones said.

"And how's that?" I asked.

"She's not going to die, Seffy. Neither will Jetta, or anyone else."

"I saw a ditch that gives the exact opposite impression."

"We couldn't handle that many people," Sgt. Magden said. "So we had orders to reduce the numbers."

"To murder people," I said.

He nodded. "To murder people. Because that's what I signed up for."

I hadn't expected him to just come and admit that.

Most people try to dodge responsibility, don't they? They don't just step right into the confession of being pure evil.

"But it's not Roxana's fault," he said. "Dr. Jones. She didn't give the order. She didn't even know… not until it was all over."

"I don't need you to defend me," Dr. Jones said.

"They're all responsible," the tinny voice from the console said. "All of them."

"I'll own my share of it," Dr. Jones said. "They would have died anyway. All of them. Every man, woman, and child on this colony, if we hadn't stepped in to help them."

"Had to break a few eggs," I said.

"What would you have done, Seffy? Would you have let them all be infected, and then turn on each other? What's better? A ditch full of dead men or a buffet table filled with little kid soufflés?"

"What the *hell* is wrong with you? I have a cure. You know that now. You know that none of this makes any difference. None of it helps."

Dr. Jones shook her head. "You don't even understand your cure. You think you can just bite down on every person in four states?"

Four states?

I knew she had to be exaggerating. She had to be.

"Maybe you and Dr. Smith could be working on the dosage and delivery right now," I said. "Instead of playing Mengele."

"Mengele? That's pretty loaded, Seffy."

"I don't know what any of this means," the console said. "But Dr. Jones is a freaking loon."

"Let us go," I said, looking at Sgt. Magden. "Me and Jetta. We'll leave and we won't come back."

The soldier didn't reply. He looked over to Dr. Jones.

"You do need to go, Seffy," the doctor said. "Find your sister and get as far away from here as possible."

"And Jetta," I said.

"Not Jetta. Just you and your sister."

"That's not happening."

"You don't get it," she said. "You have two options right now, okay? You and your sister get gone, or Sgt. Magden will have to go out there with you. And he'll find your sister, and then I don't know what he'll have to do. I hope he won't have to kill the both of you. And that he won't have to burn your bodies, too. Because *no one* here can know about that cure."

"That doesn't make any sense," I said. "We have the cure, and you want to cover it up."

"Your cure isn't good enough."

"What? Why the frick not?"

"Look at her," Dr. Jones said, pointing her finger at Jetta. "You thought you'd cured her. But you haven't."

"She isn't a freaking zombie. I'd call that being cured."

"Not a zombie, huh?"

And then she fingered her stupid tablet again.

Nothing happened.

"So you turned off the voice?" I asked.

"I'm not going to use Jetta for this," Dr. Jones said. She looked over to the third bed. To the girl in the hoodie.

She was awake. She was trying to move, starting to pull against her restraints. She started cursing us all out.

"Unstrap her," the doctor said to Magden.

The sergeant walked over to the struggling girl.

He started pulling off her restraints.

"She wasn't drugged?" I asked.

"Just Jetta and Claudia are. And you were, too, but with something a little different, and a much smaller dose."

But like the others, like Jetta and Claudia *and Leona*, that third girl hadn't been moving. Until Dr. Jones had started in with the tablet…

The girl climbed off her bed.

She took a step back from Magden, back toward the wall. Not really toward any kind of escape route.

She was terrified.

"No one's going to hurt you," Dr. Jones told her. "Everything's going to be fine."

"Nothing's fine," the Moorhead girl said. "What did you do to me?"

The doctor looked back at me. "This young woman is infected," she said. "She's a zombie, as you seem to want to call them."

"Not scientific enough, Dr. Mengele?" I said.

"I'm not infected," the girl said.

"You're infected," Dr. Jones said.

Sgt. Magden was only three or four paces away from the girl.

If she was infected, she'd have lunged at him. Even when they act like they aren't infected, it's incredibly hard to resist the urge. It had been hard enough for Errol and his family not to bite me. And for this girl, so close to a man in combat armor, who'd meant her harm…

And those little parasites needed to spread.

"She isn't infected," I said.

"You don't think she's just fighting it?" Dr. Jones asked. "Or maybe it's because Sgt. Magden is already infected."

"Is he?"

"I don't know… is he?"

"I'm not," Sgt. Magden said.

"Prove it," I said. "Get her to bite you."

"She can't bite him," Dr. Jones said.

"What the frick are you talking about?"

"She's not in charge of what she does. And those nasty little parasites aren't in charge, either. *I am.*"

"I'm not infected," the girl said.

"Sure you're not," Dr. Jones said. She tapped her tablet again.

The girl collapsed, falling against the wall before crumpling onto the concrete floor.

I rushed over, pushing past Magden, who didn't try to stop me.

I bent down beside her.

She was breathing. Her eyes was closed.

"She's asleep," Dr. Jones said. "Like she was before. Sleep mode, I guess."

"So she doesn't even know," I said.

"She doesn't know. It doesn't hurt her, either."

"You know, she just fell down hard. That's how people get hurt, actually."

"She won't spread the infection. And we've fixed the problem with the parasites overpopulating. I think there's even a way to reduce how much energy she needs."

"Energy? You mean food and water."

"Yeah. She can live her life as she did before, only we can reduce how much she consumes, or increase it, or whatever. And we can keep her safe."

"By making her into a robot," I said. "A Stepford Wife."

"You're well-read, Seffy."

"I watch a lot of movies, actually. So I probably miss out on a lot of the underlying meaning. But I don't understand what you're doing right now."

"Of course you understand," she said. "It's pretty simple."

"You said you don't approve of what Dr. Smith is doing."

"That's right."

"So this isn't even the worst of it," I said.

She smiled. "You'd make a good scientist, Seffy. You really should go back to school."

"And you should stop acting like you know me."

She nodded. "Dr. Smith wasn't sent here to save the infected. He's here to control the infected."

"That's what you're doing," I said.

"I don't want to control anyone."

"Yeah, okay. So what is Dr. Smith trying to do?"

"He's going to spread the infection, Seffy."

"Spread it… so everyone can be controlled."

"Yes."

"And then he would be infected, too, wouldn't he? Or does he honestly think that he'll be the guy in charge at the end of it?"

"He's looking for a vaccine," she said. "To inoculate himself against it."

"And I have that vaccine."

"Yes. You do."

And she didn't want Dr. Smith to know.

"Even if you can cure one percent of people," she said. "The other ninety-nine percent will be under their control."

"And whose control is that?"

"Whoever hired us."

"And you don't want to tell me," I said.

"I don't know. Honest."

"She doesn't know," Magden said. "And neither do I."

"And I'm just going to believe you guys, then," I said, with a smirk. "Sure. Sounds perfectly reasonable."

"He's closer now," Dr. Jones said. "Now that he has your family. Your friends. He knows you're out there somewhere, Seffy."

"But you haven't killed me."

"No. We don't want to kill you."

I didn't buy that. A ditch full of bodies didn't exactly make them look like a couple of do-gooders.

There had to be another reason why Magden hadn't just dropped me in that trench. He hadn't even known about Iris at that point. I'd been the only source of the cure, as far as either of them had known.

"If you want me to do something," I said, "just tell me, alright?"

"What do you mean?" she asked.

"You want me to leave. You don't want Dr. Smith to know about the cure."

"He knows about it, Seffy. Think about it. Even if he couldn't find out from your people — which he can — he'd know from the bots themselves. He'd find traces of you in there. I'm sure he already knows exactly who you are and what you've done."

"Then we need to get her out of here," Magden said. "We need to get her to Camp Grafton." He looked over at me. "I can get you there."

"I'm not leaving my people behind," I said. "Not to mention how little I trust either of you."

"You need to trust us," Dr. Jones said. "We didn't kill you, did we? And we didn't turn you over to Dr. Smith."

"Because you don't want him to come up with a vaccine."

"Yes."

"And you really did want me to get to Camp Grafton," I said, looking over to Sgt. Magden.

"We can't stop him," Magden said. "But if you can get the cure out to there, maybe someone else can find a way."

"I don't think there is a way," Dr. Jones said. "Like I said, there's no good way to spread the cure. And the cure can't stop the repro-grammed bots. So someone would need to figure out a new vaccine."

I didn't say anything.

I was surprised she didn't know.

"But that's not the only way," she said, "is it?"

I shrugged.

"You're different for a reason, Seffy," she said. "We just don't know why. Could be your bots, or more specifically, how you got them."

"Same way the others got them," I said.

"You're lying."

I was.

"I have no reason to lie," I said. "Not if you want to stop Dr. Smith."

"My current guess is that it's a three-step process to create someone like you," she said. "First you need to disable the bots — or in your case, not have any in the first place — and then you inject the vaccine. And then the new bots."

I didn't answer.

But I could tell she knew.

That she was on the right track, that I couldn't think of a wild enough goose chance to send her own.

"But there's no way we can make that happen," she said. "Not before Smith releases his vectors."

"His vectors?" I said. "You mean people like my friends and family?"

She nodded. "We're using a sort of tag right now for the reprogrammed bots. It's called genocoding—"

"I know what it is."

"I've injected genocoded bots into Jetta and Haley. Haley's the girl in the hoodie, the one who looks perpetually confused."

"I figured."

"And I tried to inject them into you, Seffy."

"What?"

"Well, I did inject them. But you're not responding to them. I'll need to scan to be sure, but—"

"You think I'm immune to your new bots," I said.

"Maybe. And people like me and Sgt. Magden aren't immune. The sergeant has the bots, but not the infection. And obviously Jetta isn't immune, either, since she has the bots, too, so your cure didn't inoculate her against it."

"It was never meant to inoculate against mind control."

"So once Dr. Smith eliminates that genocoding — and he will, once he's found a way to inoculate himself — the new bots will spread just as fast as the others. Basically, Dr. Smith has taken control of the parasite in people like Haley, and replaced the little bugs completely in people like Jetta, who have your vaccine."

I shook my head. "You said that girl couldn't bite anyone. Haley…"

"I was keeping her from biting anyone," she said. She pulled out her tablet. "Sgt. Magden… get her back onto her bed. No need to strap her in."

"I don't need a demonstration," I said.

"It's not a demonstration. It's a test."

Sgt. Magden lifted Haley up off the floor and lowered her gently onto the hospital bed.

"Roll her bunk into a pen," Dr. Jones said.

He chose the nearest stall, pulling open the door and pushing the bed all the way to the far wall.

He seemed to know exactly what she was planning.

"Now for Claudia," the doctor said.

Magden brought Claudia into the same pen.

He undid her restraints, unprompted.

"And Leona," Dr. Jones said.

"Don't you dare," I said. Not that I had any real threat to follow up with.

"Don't worry," she said. "Leona's already infected."

"She's cured."

"No… she's still infected. With something a little different now."

I watched as Magden brought Leona into the stall with the other two girls. And as he took off her straps, too.

He walked out of the pen, closing the door behind him.

"Padlock," Dr. Jones said.

Magden walked over to the rolling cart beside Jetta.

He reached down and pulled a chain from the bottom shelf.

He wrapped it around the bars of the door and the pen, snapping a padlock closed. Locking them in.

"So I think we all understand the experiment," Dr. Jones said. "Haley is infected with the modified bots, as is Leona. Claudia is not. And Haley is also infected with the adapted form of the *t. gondii* parasite."

"I won't let you get away with any of this," I said.

"Just be glad that we're the ones who found you first."

She started tapping her tablet again.

Leona slowly sat up. "Seffy," she said. "What the heck is going on?"

I didn't even know what to tell her.

I saw Claudia beginning to stir.

Nothing from Haley. Not that I could see.

I noticed Dr. Jones still on her tablet.

"What the hell are you doing to them?" I demanded.

"I'm instructing Leona to spread the infection," Dr. Jones said.

"I'm not spreading anything," Leona said. "I'm not even infected, *stoopid*."

Dr. Jones nodded.

"What is happening?" Claudia asked, now sitting up, and looking over to Leona. She then looked over at me. "What have you done to me?"

She thought it had been me. That I'd done it to her.

"I'm sorry," I told her. "I didn't know they'd do this to you."

"I can't believe you'd do this to me," Claudia said. "After I tried to help you."

I shook my head. And tried not to cry.

I wanted to pull them out of there.

But I didn't have the key for that padlock. And the man who did was still a trained killer. With a well-rounded portfolio, made up of late of a ditch full of dead Hutterites.

"Can you feel anything?" I asked her. "These toolbags think they're controlling you."

"I... I don't know," Leona said. "And why the heck are you helping them, Seffy?"

"I'm not."

"Then help me."

"I can't."

"Come on, Persephone," she said. "Seriously. Do you understand what these people are doing to us?"

"Just tell me if you can feel it, Leona."

"*Gawd*, Seffy."

She was still sitting on the bed.

She hadn't climbed off.

She hadn't made any move toward Claudia.

"This is because of you," Dr. Jones said, looking over at me. "Your attempt at curing her."

"My attempt..."

"She's still infected, Seffy. She has our bots."

"But they're not responding."

"She's fighting them, but they're there. I just woke her up with my tablet, didn't I?"

"She's lying," Leona said. "I'm not infected. You cured me."

"I shouldn't be here," Claudia said. "I don't deserve this. Please."

"Okay," Dr. Jones said. "Enough of this."

She fingered the tablet some more.

Leona's head fell back against the bed.

She was out.

Claudia started screaming.

"Shut up," Magden told her. "Or I'll have to shut you up. Do you understand?"

Claudia tried to quiet herself. It wasn't really working.

"Take your fist and shove it in your mouth," Magden said. "So I don't have to."

Claudia started weeping. At least it was quieter.

Magden looked away from her. At me.

Like he was expecting me to try something.

"Leona has some resistance," Dr. Jones said. "That comes from your vaccine, Seffy. The reprogrammed bots don't have the same lust for rewiring connections that those pesky little parasites do."

"You're making a buttload of assumptions here."

"Watch Haley, then."

More commands on her tablet.

Haley woke up. "You did it to me again," she said. "Didn't you…" She looked over at Claudia. She hopped off the bed.

"What are you doing?" Claudia asked.

Haley shushed her.

Then leaned over her neck. No more derp face…

"No," Claudia said. "Please don't—"

Haley bit down on Claudia's throat.

I turned away as the blood came out.

"You're squeamish," Dr. Jones said.

"I'm disgusted by you," I said.

"I'm sorry," Haley said, pulling away from Claudia's body. "I'm… I'm really sorry."

She backed up to the back wall of the pen.

She slowly dropped down to the floor.

She started weeping.

"Haley doesn't have that same resistance," Dr. Jones said. "And you can see quite clearly that she would have resisted if she could."

"She'll remember what you've done," I said. "That you forced her to do that. That you made her infect another person."

I looked back at Claudia.

She'd already lost consciousness. Without the bots, she'd be dead within a another minute or so.

I was assuming that wasn't going to happen. But I wasn't sure.

"Claudia isn't infected," Dr. Jones said. "She's dying."

"What are you talking about?" I said.

"The bots in Haley were genocoded. They will not survive in Claudia's bloodstream. Which means that Claudia will not survive."

"So help her, then. Do something!"

"I can't help her, Seffy. I don't have a cure."

I looked over to Sgt. Magden. "Open the pen," I said.

He looked at Dr. Jones.

She nodded.

He jammed his key into the padlock.

I rushed over and pulled the door open.

I ran up to Claudia.

Her clothes — the clothes I'd been wearing the day before — were soaked in blood. The gash in her neck wasn't closing. There was nothing to heal her.

I could bite her thigh, maybe… her femoral artery.

But that wasn't the best way to do it. There was a way that I knew would work.

I brought my head down over her bleeding throat.

I fought my urge to turn away. And my urge to puke my effing guts out.

I bit down into the disgusting mess of blood and body.

Then I pulled away.

And I fell back.

And that was it.

I don't know what happened next. Just black.

8

WHAT WOULD BOTHOT IRIS DO?

I was lying on a hospital bed, still groggy from… fainting, I guess? The straps on my wrists were tight enough that I hadn't needed to open my eyes to know I was strapped down all over again.

I felt someone tapping on my left shoulder.

I opened my eyes and looked over.

Jetta was standing beside me.

"Take my straps off," I said.

"You did good," Jetta said. "That Hutterite girl's going to be okay."

I looked around the room.

We weren't in the livestock barn. We were back in that tent, where Magden had first taken me.

Just Jetta and me.

No sign of Leona or the other girls, and no sign of Dr. Caterpillar-brows and her murdering soldier *slash* love interest.

"The straps," I said again. "Hurry up."

"I can't, Seffy. Sorry."

"What do you mean you can't?"

"I mean I can't. I… I just can't, okay?"

"No, that's not okay. And that doesn't make sense. Take your freakishly tiny hands and undo these leather straps."

"You're going to need to leave us here," she said. "Leona and me. You need to take Iris and get to that fort."

"You mean Camp Grafton."

"Yeah."

"Not a chance, Jetta. Not without you and Leona. And everyone else."

"Everyone else? So all of the Hutterites, too?"

"Take my straps off, Jetta."

"I can't."

I turned away.

"Don't be mad at me, Curlicue," she said.

"Don't call me that."

"It's our little thing."

"It's your creepy little thing, Jetta. Nothing to do with me."

"They wanted me to talk to you," she said.

"Well, you've talked just about enough. All that's left is to tell me that you're about to undo these frickin straps."

The rear door opened.

Dr. Jones stumbled in, like a stork just learning to walk. She wasn't dressed in her scrubs. She was wearing a cocktail dress, and high heels. And a whole heap of makeup, while having done nothing about the infestation of caterpillars right above her smoky eyeliner. All of it looked about as natural on her as the forest green Hutterite dress had looked on me.

"Jetta can't unstrap you," she said. "Because I told her she can't."

"So you threatened her," I said.

"No... I used the bots."

"You talk to them now? You're some kind of bot-whisperer?"

"You can issue commands," she said.

"Oh, I can? Then let me command them to jab one of those sharp heels into your jugular."

"You know what I mean, Seffy."

"Don't call me Seffy," I said, seething.

"Don't call her Curlicue, either," Jetta said. "It seems to irk her all of the sudden."

I looked back at Jetta. "Do you get that she's controlling you?" I asked her.

"Yeah," she said. "I get it. And I can't control it. That's pretty much how it works."

"Then why aren't you angry about it? There must be something she didn't command you not to do. Spit on her eyeball."

"I don't know why I'm not pissed off about it," Jetta said. "I don't understand it, either."

"She can't be," Dr. Jones said. "That's part of the reprogramming. She can't feel anything too strongly. She feels just enough to live a normal life."

"A normal life," I said. "That is *effing redonkulous.*"

Dr. Jones grinned. "You sound like an idiot. *Effing. Redonkulous.* What the *eff*, Seff? Why can't you call me out like a grown woman?"

"You don't think I'm crass enough, is that it?"

"I don't think you're mature enough to understand the world. To get why this has to happen. You sit around in your little bubble and act like business as usual makes any kind of sense."

"Maybe I should launch into grandiose speeches," I said. "Maybe then people will think I'm *oh so smart*, too."

She smiled. "I like you, Seffy. I really do."

"Now's your chance to try for second base."

"I need you and Iris to head for Camp Grafton, like Mike told you to do."

"Mike. First name basis with the good sergeant, are we?"

"Of course we are. You heard him call me Roxana how many times?"

Jetta started making kissy noises.

"Is she always like this?" Dr. Jones asked me.

"I think it's charming," I said. "And only a little creepy."

"Do you trust us?"

"What?"

"Me and Mike. Do you trust us, Seffy?"

"Not at all."

"But will you go to Camp Grafton? Talk to Mike's brother?"

"I can't leave my people here," I said.

"You can't take Jetta or Leona. They're already infected with the new bots… I can't let them leave. And there's no way to get your father or your stepmother out of Dr. Smith's lab."

"And I can't have the Kimmerns, either, right?"

"No. Sorry."

"I can't accept that," I said. "I don't see how you could ever think I'd accept it. I mean, you're supposed to have some kind of smarts, aren't you? Are you even a real doctor?"

"You know I can't accept *that*, Seffy."

"Spell it out for me, Roxana."

"I'm sending Mike with you, bots and all."

"So he's allowed to leave?" I asked.

"They don't know he has the bots. He's not supposed to have

them."

"So if they scan him..."

"You're going to take him to Iris, and he's going to take both of you to Camp Grafton."

"What about his duties here? Doesn't he have potatoes to peel?"

"This isn't a joke," she said. "He won't be able to come back here. And really, I can't be sure this won't come back on me."

"What do you mean?"

"I mean he's basically going AWOL."

"He told me he's not in the army anymore."

"They'll kill him if he comes back," she said. "Which means that he can't come back for me."

"So you'll have to meet him at the Pizza Ranch."

"Do you think they'll let me leave?"

"I don't understand," I said. "Then just go with him now."

"If I go, they'll kill my test subjects. Dr. Smith has already made that clear."

"Then take them with you. Steal a bus and we'll all go together. I can accept that, Roxana."

"You really don't understand, do you... they won't let me take people out of here. Jetta and Leona have to stay here. We won't get ten miles down the road if we try to break out of this place. You and Mike need to go. You can walk out on foot, and I doubt anyone will follow."

"But they might," I said.

"If they do come after you, Mike will keep you safe. You and Iris."

"You said you'd kill us. Or did you forget?"

"I didn't say that," she said. "I was just trying to make you understand."

"And now you want me to trust you."

"You don't have a choice anymore. Mike's taking you with him, and that's that."

"And if I scream bloody murder?"

"Then you *will* end up in that ditch. Once Dr. Smith's done with you."

"You seem pretty darn sure about that," I said.

She nodded. "I know the man. I know what he's capable of, Seffy. He's the one who ordered the soldiers to dig that ditch."

Magden had me cuffed in the back as he led me out of the tent.

Byzzan was still there, on the outside, right by the door. You know, sentry style.

I was starting to wonder if they only had the two soldiers. Shouldn't they be rotating them out?

"My turn," Byzzan said, looking me over like a fully-cooked turkey.

"I wouldn't," Magden said, smirking. "This one has the clap."

I made the smart choice, to not slug him in his stupid face.

"You said you railed her," Byzzan said. He'd said it to Magden, but while still staring at me. "Or is he lying?" he asked me. "Did the big bad man take you out back and make you do nasty things?"

It was like it was just a joke. Like he was talking about Magden having squirted me with a water gun. It made me want to vomit. Or start hoofing crotches.

"Why don't I take you out back and jab my fingers into your eyeballs?" I said.

"I'll take her," Byzzan said, finally breaking his pervy gaze and speaking to Magden. "Back of the head doesn't work, yeah? Some other place I should shoot her?"

"Let's both take her," Magden said.

"You had your turn."

"I'm not a mechanical bull," I said.

"Shut up," Byzzan said. "Nothing you say is going to speed this up."

I knew I was shaking. I guess that was good... for the optics. You know, not wanting some gun-toting mercenary to drag me out into a field for what would be very non-consensual sex.

I don't know why they do it... I mean, I know why they do it, why men are *assholes* who rape and torture and kill. Part of me knows. But somehow it still doesn't compute. That they can see me not as a person at all, but as a series of body parts. Or maybe that's not it. Maybe it's because I'm a person that they want to do it to me. They want to know what it's like to have that ultimate power. More than just the kill. That they'd do something that might feel even worse than when they finally just got around to murdering me.

I didn't know if Magden would have done that. If that was something he'd do, if he felt he had the chance. But I could see it in Byz-zan, in the way he looked at me. That he wanted to hurt me. In every way possible.

Because he can.

"It shouldn't take too long," Magden said. "Ten or fifteen minutes and we'll be done with her."

Byzzan shook his head. "One of us needs to stay put."

"Then I guess you're staying put."

"You don't outrank me here, Mike," Byzzan said.

"Then let's just say I outclass you."

"You had your chance with her. Now it's my turn."

"It's not your turn, Jar-Jar."

Byzzan leaned in, over Magden. To challenge him. "Don't you freaking call me that."

Magden leaned in harder, all the way, bumping his chest against Byzzan, like they were a couple of silverback gorillas in camo.

Byzzan took a swing.

I watched as Magden ducked to the side.

Then made his own punch.

Which Byzzan took in his face.

And then he hit Magden. On the right temple.

Magden fell back a step.

Byzzan swung again.

And Magden didn't get a chance to dodge.

Another step back.

He almost fell into the tent.

Byzzan started grabbing for my wrists, cuffed behind my back.

I started running.

"I'll shoot you dead," he yelled out at me. He grabbed his rifle. "I swear to god, little girl. I'll shoot you right now."

I stopped.

He walked over to me.

He shoved me with his left hand. Hard against my back shoulder.

"You know where to go," he said.

I looked back at Magden.

He was just standing there, by the tent, staring back at me.

His gun still hanging from his shoulder.

He wasn't about to come and save me.

Byzzan was going to get what he wanted.

Unless I could find a way to stop him.

I walked past the first junkpile.

Byzzan was around five steps behind me, his rifle still pointed at the small of my back.

If he believed what Magden had told him, he'd know I had the bots. That shooting me in the back wouldn't kill me.

It would hurt like someone was running a rusty nail file along my spine, but it would heal. And as long as he didn't mind the mess, he could shoot me there and still do whatever else he wanted to do.

He could shoot me, then rape me, then shoot me all over again.

And more. He could do whatever he wanted to me, the kinds of things you'd see in the goriest horror movies. He could strangle me, he could stab me, he could do it all and do it all again.

He could take me away, like Lucas Berg did with Anna Louise. He could go AWOL just as well as Magden could, only he wouldn't be escorting me to Camp Grafton.

"Did he really do something to you?" he asked me. "Cuz I don't think he did."

"What does it matter?" I said.

"It matters."

"And what answer is better for me?"

He scoffed.

"He didn't do anything to me," I said.

"Because of Roxana."

I stopped walking.

He didn't give me another shove.

"What did they say to you?" he asked me. "Do you know what they're planning?"

"I don't know what you're talking about."

"I'm sorry… I didn't mean to scare you."

"What?"

"I had to make it look good," he said. "I had to convince him that I was going to do it to you."

I turned around to look at him.

His rifle was pointed down at the dirt.

"What are you going to do to me?" I asked him.

"Nothing," he said. "I just need you to tell me what happened in that tent. All of it."

"Why would I tell you anything? Assuming there's even anything to tell."

"I can help you, Seffy."

"Did they tell you my name?"

"Dr. Smith knows who you are," Byzzan said. "And he knows that Dr. Jones and Sgt. Magden can't be trusted."

"So you can't just make room in the ditch for them?"

"Are you trying to frustrate me?"

I shook my head. I'm pretty sure I let out a bit of a sigh, too. "I'm trying to understand what the heck is going on," I said.

"Tell me what they said to you. Please."

"Oh, well since you said 'please'..."

I heard him groan. "I'm sorry, did I ask for all this attitude?"

"I don't trust you," I said. "Can you give me a reason to trust you?"

"Hold out your hands."

I bent my elbows and pushed my bound wrists straight out behind me.

He stepped back behind me, pulling a knife from his belt.

I tried not to panic.

He grabbed my wrists with his gloved hand. Roughly.

I waited for him to cut off the cuffs.

But he didn't.

He just kept his grip on me.

I felt the knife blade against my arm. Moving up toward my elbow, away from the cuffs.

He was pushing hard, not enough to break the skin, but enough to scratch it and enough to hurt.

"You're looking for positive reinforcement, Seffy," he said. It was a creepy half-whisper, like the kind you get from pervy driver's ed instructors. "But I don't do positive reinforcement. I don't believe in the carrot. Just the stick. The stick up your ass. Or something else up there."

I couldn't decide between the fear, the disgust, and the instinctive urge to start openly mocking him.

I've run into creeps like him before.

Every girl on the planet has.

And when it happens, you know you need to make the call. You need to size that creeper up, figure out how best to get him away from you as fast as humanly possible.

He wants to feel that power over you.

But if I gave it to him, if I showed him that I was afraid… that wouldn't end it. But that wouldn't satisfy him, either. Not all the way. I would just egg him on.

But the same thing might happen if I hit back.

If I try to belittle him, or if I try to be angry and I lash out… that will just make it worse.

Either way it would keep happening.

Unless there was a third way.

What would Iris do?

"I want the handgun on your belt," I said. "Give me that and I'll do whatever you want me to do. I'll bring you all the way to funky-town, chief."

"What the hell are you talking about?"

"I don't want to die. And you can do better than a cold fish, *ami-rite?*"

"I didn't ask you to whore yourself out," he said. The knife was still pressed against my forearm. If anything, he was gripping my wrists tighter. "Tell me what they said to you."

I didn't know what else I could do.

Buying myself some time seemed like priority *número uno.*

"They told me that Dr. Smith would kill me if he knew I was there," I said. "Dr. Jones told Magden to take me off the colony and let me go."

He pushed my arms down.

I fell onto my knees, my bound arms held above me, pulling hard. against my shoulders.

I felt the burn as the knife cut into my skin. Just enough of a knick to hurt like a sonofabitch. "That's a lie," he said. "They wouldn't just let you go."

"I'm not lying."

Another cut.

I gritted my teeth.

"You can cut me all frickin day," I told him. "It won't change what they told me."

He sighed. "Then convince me, Seffy. Tell me why they'd let you go."

"Because they didn't think it was a good enough reason to kill me."

He cursed under his breath.

And made another jab into my arm.

I heaved.

It really hurt.

"How much blood can you lose?" he asked me. "The bots can't just make new blood."

I tried not to whimper. But I'm pretty sure I was whimpering.

"Come on, Seffy. Just tell me the truth, yeah?"

"The bots can create synthetic blood," I said. "Not as efficient, but it'll keep me alive until my blood cells boost up the old-fashioned way."

"That's not what I'm asking about. You know that."

I felt the blade push in a little. But no new cut. Not yet.

"I'm immune," I said. "My blood can act as an inoculant, vaccine or cure."

"What does that mean?"

"It means that I can cure the infection."

"And they don't want you to cure anyone."

I nodded.

He pulled the knife off my forearm.

But he was still holding my wrists up above me.

He wasn't going to let me go.

"They can't control you," he said.

"No."

"They must have tested it out. Your cure."

"Kind of."

"Did it keep the others from being controlled? Whoever you inoculated?"

"No."

"So what use is the cure? If they still get what they want."

"I don't know," I said.

He let go of my wrists.

I let them fall down behind my back, releasing the strain on my shoulders. But the ache was still there. Not dislocated, I didn't think... but really effing sore.

"I'm not going to kill you," he said.

"Are you going to let me go?"

"Yeah."

"Thank you."

"Not yet."

"What do you mean?" I asked.

He shoved my shoulder again.

Pushing me down to the ground. Planting my face in the muck.

He placed his rifle down on the ground, then knelt beside me.

He started grabbing at my pants.

I started kicking.

"Better than a cold fish," he said.

I kept fighting, but it didn't take him long to pull my pants down to my ankles.

With a heavy jerk he took the jeans right off and tossed them away. Then he started pulling on my underwear.

They tell you to fight, and they tell you not to fight.

I didn't want to give in.

But I didn't know what else I could do.

I let him strip my panties off, tossing them over to where he'd thrown my jeans.

I would need to pick my battles.

"You're going to be quiet, right?" he asked me.

"Just tell me why you're doing this," I said.

I heard him chuckle. "Because I can."

I turned my head to look back at him.

I watched as he took off his duty belt. And as he unzipped his pants.

I picked my battle.

I brought both feet up. Toward his crotch, making my best guess and squeezing my boots together.

I heard him squeal.

He fell backward.

I rolled onto my side.

I gave him another kick.

To the side of his head.

And another.

It wasn't enough.

He got up to his knees and shuffled backward, away from me.

I brought myself up on my knees, too.

But my hands were tied.

And he was closer to his rifle.

He had his gun in his hands and pointed at me long before I could get onto my feet.

So I stayed on my knees.

He shook his head at me, his jaw clenched.

His rifle aimed at my gut.

"You want me to lie back down in the mud?" I asked him, trying not to cry.

"Do you have any idea how much that hurt? You twisted my balls, bitch."

"What did you think was going to happen? That I'd just give up and let you do whatever you want with me?"

"Well, now I'm going to do *exactly* what I want with you. And I'm going to make sure it hurts when I do it."

I took a deep breath. "Then I'll just keep finding ways to make it hurt for you," I said. "Because I've got nothing to lose."

"You think so, yeah? Nothing to lose?"

"At a certain point I just get numb. At a certain point I don't feel anything."

I didn't know why he'd buy it. Or what good it would do.

But I wanted him to think he didn't have that power over me. That he couldn't make it as bad as he really could.

I didn't want to give him that.

He pushed me down onto my stomach.

I kept still on the ground, my nose to the muck.

I knew I was out of options.

After a few seconds, he grabbed my hair and yanked it back, pulling my head back.

I felt the knife blade against my throat.

I closed my eyes.

I wanted to be anywhere else.

Or at least shut everything off. Go as numb as I'd told him I would be.

I heard someone call out.

Iris, telling him to leave me alone.

He kept the knife against my throat.

"That won't kill her," Iris said. "You know that, right?"

"So I should jab it through her brainstem?" he asked.

"Put the knife away so we can talk."

I couldn't see her. She was to the south, and I was facing something close to north.

But I could tell she was coming closer, by the sound of her voice.

"You're going to shoot me with a bow and arrow?" Byzzan asked.

"I'm going to shoot you with the frickin arrow, yes," Iris said. "Unless you let my sister go."

"Put down the bow or I'll kill your sister. Unless you really think you can get me without me getting her."

"I don't want to kill you."

"Give it a try, yeah?"

"Okay," Iris said.

I didn't know what she meant.

Was she really going to take a shot?

"Smart girl," Byzzan said.

He pulled the knife away from my throat.

He stood up.

"Your fly's open," Iris said. "I can see your blue balls."

"Now put your hands behind your back," Byzzan said.

I slowly twisted my body, then turned my head to see.

Iris lowered herself onto her knees.

And put her hands behind her back.

"No," I said. "Just run, Iris. He can't hold onto the both of us."

"It'll be okay, Seffy," she said. "Just do what he says."

Byzzan started walking toward her.

And I heard the gunshot.

Byzzan fell.

Kellen climbed up out of a drainage ditch, holding a lowered hunting rifle. He looked at me, then looked quickly away.

Iris rushed over to Byzzan.

I watched as she picked up his knife from the ground beside him.

And as she drew it across his throat, slicing it open.

She looked to me.

She ran over.

"I think we might be even now," she said. She cut my hands free. "Your pants…"

"I don't know where they are," I said.

"I'll find them."

"We need to go," Kellen said. "The van's still two miles south of here."

"I told Errol to come when he hears the shot," Iris said. "He's coming."

"We need to go."

"He's right," I said. "We can't go back for Jetta yet."

"We know," Iris said. "But you need your pants. I don't see them."

I slowly sat up.

I saw the jeans. Or part of them.

Poking out from under Byzzan's body.

I stood up and walked over.

My borrowed blue jeans were covered in blood and so much else, pieces of what looked like… I don't know… it was beige and orange and dark reddish-purple. And it stunk like nothing else. Byzzan's stomach had been blown out onto my denims.

There was no way I was putting those back on.

I saw Jetta's tablet poking out of the right front pocket. If I hadn't seen it, I wouldn't have bothered looking for it.

I wiped it on the grass, to get rid of the literal blood and guts.

Iris started taking off her yoga pants.

"It's okay," I said.

"It's fine," she told me.

I squeezed into them, knowing that I wasn't nearly as covered up as I ought to be.

But I just needed to get away from there.

So we could regroup.

I gave my sister a quick hug.

I nodded gratefully to Kellen, who was still trying to pretend he wasn't really *noticing* me. While adding the supposed ignoring of Iris' newly exposed and tasteful blue panties.

"They still have Jetta," Kellen said. He shook his head. I guess it wasn't really at me. Or maybe it was. Not that it mattered.

"They do," I said, though I guess he already knew that. "She's okay. I'll explain it as soon as I get a chance." I turned back to Iris. "I'm glad you came looking for me. Even if I told you not to."

"We didn't come looking for you," Iris said. "It was Jetta."

"I don't understand."

"I can hear her," Iris said. "Talking to me. She told me you were in trouble. That the wrong sentry was walking you toward that ditch."

"Talking to you?"

"With the bots."

"Like before?"

"Not like before," she said. "This time it was Jetta, talking to me."

"Telling you to help me."

Iris nodded. "Yeah. And telling me she thinks she knows how we can get our people out of there."

"We need to go," Kellen said. "They'll be sending someone to check on the gunshot."

"They might just assume it was their guy shooting me in the face," I said.

"We can't be taking that chance," Iris said.

I shook my head. "But what about Jetta? It's not like she'll be able to talk to you if we're thirty miles away."

"We won't be thirty miles away, Seffy. And we'll come back. Don't worry."

I saw Kellen pull up his rifle, pointing it to the north.

Sgt. Magden was slowly walking toward us, his automatic rifle pointed down to the ground.

"I'm here to help," he said.

"I don't believe you," Kellen said.

"Ask Seffy."

"You didn't do anything to help me," I said. "You were going to let him rape me."

"I couldn't stop him," Magden said. "I had to let it play out."

"Let it play out?" Kellen said. "Are you being serious right now?"

Magden nodded. "This is bigger than all of us. I'm sorry, but I couldn't risk Byzzan sounding the alarm on this."

"You were going to let him do it," Iris said. "You knew he was going to, and you let it happen anyway."

"I'm sorry," Magden said. "But look, she's okay. You stopped him."

I watched as Kellen took aim and fired.

The left half of Sgt. Mike Magden's face disappeared.

"What the hell?" Iris said.

"You heard him," Kellen said. "He was going to let it happen."

"I didn't want you to do that," I told him. "I really didn't."

He gave me a nod. "I know, Seffy. But it still had to be done."

"She knows," Iris blurted out.

"No, I don't know," I said.

She shook her head. "Not you... Jetta. Jetta knows we killed him. She's frightened. I think that means the doctor will find out eventually. Jetta doesn't know what's going to happen."

"None of us know what's going to happen," Kellen said. "That's why we need to get out of here. As in, *right now*."

"This could come back on them," Iris said. "On Jetta, on the others..."

"I don't see how they'd get the blame," I said.

"I don't know... but I know that Jetta is really worried about it. And I can't seem to make it better for her... *frick*..."

Her eyes popped wide. She started doing that thing where she jams her jaw out from side to side. You don't see Iris lose her cool that often, but when she does...

I stepped over and put a hand on her shoulder.

"I can't hear her," Iris said. "She's gone."

"That doesn't mean anything specific," I said.

"I know... but I'm... I'm really worried, Seffy."

"Yeah..."

"We need to go," Kellen said. "Seriously."

Iris seemed to snap out of it right then, like she'd flicked a switch. She started moving back to the south, at a fast jog.

I followed her, with Kellen and his hunting rifle taking up the rear.

9

OPERATION TOOL-LORD OPENS
A SECOND FRONT

We hurried back to the van, to where Errol was standing by the hood with the other rifle. Anna Louise was sitting in the van, but I noticed that she had the pistol we'd taken from Lucas.

"Are you okay?" Errol asked me.

"I'm alive," I said.

He nodded.

I'd expected him to try and hug me again. I was relieved when he didn't.

I'd hugged Iris, sure, but I didn't want anyone going and touching me. Especially not him.

I just had to feel like I could own that space around me.

∽

Errol drove us back to the corner northwest of the colony, with the four houses. Anna Louise pointed out where she and Lucas had been.

"And you don't know if he's still down there," Kellen said.

"We don't know," Anna Louise said.

"So you guys wait here," Errol said. "Kellen and I will check."

"We're perfectly capable of checking, too," Iris said. "Pretty sure our ovaries aren't too big to fit through the front door."

"Just let us have this," Kellen said.

"Let those two deal with him," I said, trying to keep some kind of composure. "I think we've had enough Lucas for one lifetime."

"Keep an eye out," Errol said. "In case he's outside instead of in."

"We know, *Dad*," Iris said. Then she stuck her tongue out at him. Then she stuck it out at me.

Errol and Kellen took both rifles and walked over to the front door.

Iris held out a hand for the pistol. Anna Louise passed it over.

"I'm going to watch for him to come out the back," Iris said.

She climbed out of the van and took a few steps toward the back of the house. Enough so she'd hopefully have a good view of the rear porch.

Anna Louise smiled at me.

"I'm really glad you guys are here," she said.

I nodded.

"You did good, Persephone."

"I don't need you to make me feel better," I said.

"I just want to know you're okay."

"You don't even know me. So does it really matter?"

I realized who I was talking to. What she'd gone through.

And I felt like a scrap of garbage.

I started to cry.

"I can't tell you it doesn't stay with you," she said. "Not that I'm some kind of expert by now."

"It's not... he didn't get a chance—"

"I think the worst is that feeling you get, that you're not worth any more than what they're giving you, that it makes you something less. He took something from you. And you can't fix that."

"He didn't take anything from me," I said. "And he never will."

"Don't try to stand so straight that you snap like a twig."

"What?"

"My father used to say that," she said. "I always thought it was about being stubborn. And I resented that he would tell me that." She grinned. "Stubbornly. Like a twig that's ready to snap."

I nodded. I didn't have anything to add.

"But it's about letting things hurt you, being okay with crumpling every once in a while. And just... just letting go of *always being okay*."

I wiped some tears off my face. "I saw a girl who was... I saw a girl dead in the grass. I'm not sure of... of all that happened to her. And another man tried it with me, too. A cop, of all things." I sighed. "It's not okay that we're always the ones under attack. That we've always got these targets painted on our backs."

"That we always have to be on guard for it," Anna Louise said, nodding her head. "With strangers, with people we know."

She put her hand next to mine.

She didn't reach for me.

But she was letting me know that she wanted me to reach for her, if that's what I wanted.

So I held her hand.

"Do you trust these guys?" she asked me.

"I think so," I said. "I've known Errol since Middle School. He's always been a little off, but I've never been scared of him. Whenever he wasn't a zombie trying to bite me, I mean."

"And the other one... Kellen..."

"I don't really know him. We met when we were trying to get out of Fargo. We found him with my Dad and Stepmom. Iris' mom. The people who'd held them... they'd done some terrible things."

"Errol told me," she said. "You don't need to talk about it."

"Kellen killed two men back there. The one who attacked me, and another one who... well, I guess he was going to take us back across the river to North Dakota. To get help."

"Why did Kellen kill him?"

"Kellen said it was because that man didn't help me, because of what almost happened to me. But I'm not sure."

"What do you mean?" she asked me, giving my hand a squeeze.

I wasn't sure how to say it. What I'd been thinking about since the moment I'd watched Sgt. Magden die. But I had to start with something.

"I think Kellen killed him because he could."

Anna Louise frowned.

"I don't mean to say that he's a problem for us," I said.

"I think they're all *potential* problems for us," she said. "All men, really. And I don't think that's something that just started a week ago."

"I get what you're saying, but... it's not like they're all just waiting for a chance to hurt us. Errol would never hurt me. Or any of us."

"It's all about risk versus reward," Anna Louise said. "How much are we willing to risk by having any one of these men with us? And exactly what are we getting in return?"

"So we should just assign every guy we meet some kind of master score. Anything below fifty points we shoot. Or maybe seventy-five, to be safe."

"I know you think it's stupid. But it's really not."

"I can't live like that, Anna Louise. I can't sit around thinking that every man alive is going to hurt me, the moment he thinks it's worth taking the chance."

She pulled her hand away from me.

"Maybe that's because you haven't been raped," she said. "Maybe it's because someone was there to save you. All I saw when Lucas took me was you. Watching us go."

"You're really saying that to me? Right now?"

"You have to live with that. And I have to live with what happened to me, because you trusted Lucas to be on your team. Because you thought that the risk was worth the reward."

"There was no reward," I said. "I was scared of him. I didn't want him to hurt me. Or Jetta."

"So you let him hurt me. Seems fair."

"I didn't know he'd take you. I didn't know what he was capable of. You must know that…"

"Well now you know what every man is capable of," she said. "So tell me, Persephone… are those two guys on your team worth the risk?"

I didn't answer her.

Because I didn't know what to tell her.

I was angry with her. I was angry with me.

But on top of all that grot… I didn't know if I could trust Kellen. I wasn't even a hundred percent sure I could trust Errol. Not if I was being honest with myself.

⏳

Errol and Kellen came back after around five minutes, having swept through the house and searched for any concealed North Dakotan toolbags.

We didn't do much to set up at our new digs; all any of us wanted to do was sit down, and think things through.

So that's what we did, at a dining room table that still had place settings laid out, for a dinner that had never happened; I wondered if this was the kind of house where they lay out plates long before the meal's going to start, and since the walls of the room were papered with an immaculate French country-style wallpaper, and there was a solid oak hutch filled with the kind of porcelain artifacts you'd see in a museum of the uptight, I was pretty sure I knew the answer.

Errol sighed as he sat down along the side of the table, right beside me. "You know, there's a much more comfortable setup in the living room. Couches and everything."

"We're not supposed to be comfortable," I said. "We're supposed to be working this out."

Kellen sat at the other side of me, while Iris and Anna Louise sat across from us. I wasn't sure why I'd ended up in some kind of power position; I'd specifically avoided any head-of-the-table spot, but it had happened anyway.

I'm not the loudest or the most cocksure, and I'm definitely not the prettiest of the bunch, sitting across from two *bothot* blondes. So that makes me what, exactly?

I won't be a victim, but that doesn't make me a leader.

But they were all looking at me, expecting me to make some heavy pronouncement. As if muddling through a blind attempt to cure my sister had given me some secret knowledge of how to save the frickin world.

"I don't know what to do," I said.

Iris started laughing.

I glared at her. Then I realized that she was just as jittery as I was. That's just how she deals with it.

"I don't get what's going on," Anna Louise said.

"I still can't hear her," Iris said. "She's gone."

"We're too far away," I said. "We'd need to get in a couple miles closer, at least."

"You don't know that," Kellen said, rolling his eyes. "You guys don't know what's happening."

"They might have sedated her," Errol said.

We all looked over at him.

He gave us a little shrug.

"I think that could be it," I said. "They were passing out injections like rave candy at that place. Among other things."

"It came too quick," Iris said.

I put my hands out on the table, toward her. In case she wanted to hold one of them or something. Like Anna Louise had offered to me. "You can't be sure of that," I said, as gently as I could. "I saw things in that barn that… well, they can control her in an instant. Make her go limp. Make her lose consciousness…"

"Do you think it's only her?" Anna Louise asked.

"What are you talking about?" Errol said. Not dismissively, but not really with an encouraging tone.

I knew we were all tired. And bitchy.

But still…

"Iris," Anna Louise said, "do you have a connection to Jetta? Like, did you know her really well before?"

"I'd never met her," Iris said. "Seffy picked her up in a gas station bathroom."

"Is that a joke?" Kellen asked.

"Not this time," I said. "This *one* time."

"So if there are other people who are being experimented on," Anna Louise said, "shouldn't it be possible to communicate with one of them? Why just Jetta?"

"I think Jetta found me," Iris said. "It's not like I was expecting her call."

"So what about Leona?" I asked. "I think she was supposed to be reprogrammed, too."

"Reprogrammed…"

"Genocoded bots are being injected into their victims, infected or not, giving whoever holds the tablet or whatever something close to full control over someone."

"Why genocoded?" Iris asked.

"The big bad guy doesn't want to spread the reprogrammed bots to everyone just yet. Not until he knows he won't catch the bug."

"And you can't catch the bug," Iris said.

"Apparently not. And Leona… she's been fighting it. Fighting the instructions they're forcing on her."

"Jetta would fight it, too?" Anna Louise asked.

"She would," I said. "Dr. Jones said that came from me. That our bots were providing resistance. If they'd still been infected with the parasite, they'd be completely defenseless."

"I guess that kinda makes sense," Iris said. "Our bots are better than their bots. Non-genocoded next generation asskickers…"

I nodded. "They're fighting it out, I guess. A big ol' bot battle inside Jetta and Leona."

"So it's possible that you can reach out to Leona," Errol said.

Iris groaned. "With the magic bullhorn I'm keeping between my butt cheeks?"

"You gotta try *something*," Anna Louise said.

"Sure. Something. Just that we have no frickin idea what."

Iris leaned back in her chair. She closed her eyes and lowered her head, like she was about to say a prayer.

Which isn't really Iris. Not that I know of.

We all sat in silence for a couple of minutes.

Iris opened her eyes. "And I got nothing," she said.

"It didn't work," Kellen said. "So we find a Plan B."

"For now," I said. "But I don't believe that it can't work." I reached out a little further across the table.

Iris let me take both of her hands.

"You need to keep at it," I told her. "Just keep trying. Keep checking in. For Jetta and Leona. For anyone else."

"For your father, maybe," Errol said.

"Maybe," I said.

Iris nodded.

She didn't say anything.

Which, for Iris, is kind of a deep statement in itself.

We decided to head in closer to the colony. We didn't have the best maps, since there was no network and no one had anything more than those default satellite views, but from what we did have, we determined that we could get in to within half a mile of the colony buildings without being spotted, as long as we could keep low as we hiked along a sparse shelterbelt of poplar that came in from the north.

We took the van to a sand quarry, a mile and a half north. From there, we went on foot, following a fence line between two sections, right where you'd expect a mile road to be.

All five of us went together, in a spaced-out line; there really weren't enough of us left to be splitting up into smaller groups. Iris and I had our bows, while Errol and Kellen carried the hunting rifles, and Anna Louise held on to the pistol.

Errol had decided to wear his welding helmet, but hadn't managed to convince anyone else to do the same with the other one. I understand his logic, that the only place that we can't let them hit us is our heads, but the truth is, a mercenary with an automatic rifle would just mow us all down by aiming a little lower, than pull any headgear off in the time it took us and our bots to recover.

Of course, there's no guarantee that they have any more mercenaries, even if common sense tells me that there must have been a few more sentries or guards for the surviving Hutterites, and probably one or two to watch over the mysterious Dr. Smith's prisoners.

I could feel the tightness in my chest. I could see my hands were shaking… even my feet were. There probably wasn't a single person there who couldn't tell I was two steps away from a full-blown panic attack.

You can't call everything trauma. Not stubbing your toe, and probably not even a run-in with a skeevy cop who's looking for someone to blow him.

But there are other things that have happened now. Some things I've done, like the infected woman whose skull I'd bashed in, or the man I'd had to shoot, but who maybe… just maybe I hadn't need to shoot him that second and third time, maybe I hadn't needed to make sure he was dead.

And I could feel that what had happened *to me*, by that ditch… that was one more of those really bad things. That it was going to stay with me for a long effing time.

We followed the trees all the way to the road that ran north of the colony. From there, we couldn't see much, just more junk, cargo containers, and some grain buildings.

But we weren't there to look for anything. We were there for Iris to make contact, not that she had any idea how she would.

So we sat along the short fence, behind a thicker bank of shelter trees, and we waited in silence, as Iris closed her eyes and focused.

And we kept waiting as she got more and more frustrated.

Until she finally let out the worst tirade of cursing I'd ever heard from my sister. Or possibly from anyone outside of a Martin Scorsese film.

"I can't do it," she said. "I just can't."

"We could get in closer," Anna Louise said.

Iris groaned. "We can't get in closer. We're practically on top of these douchebags."

"Either she isn't there or this won't work," Kellen said. "We go back to Plan B and that's all there is to it."

I wanted to shut him up, but I didn't want to start an argument.

I didn't have anything to counter with, really.

Iris can't just keep trying over and over again. I mean, she should, but there was no reason to believe it'll work. We needed to do something else.

Kellen was right about that part.

"Do... do you think I need to go back in?" I asked. "One more time?" I hadn't even wanted to think it, much less say it.

"No friggin way," Errol said. "No way."

"Third time's the charm," Iris said. "This time they'll finally kill you, Seffy."

"Dr. Jones must be pretty effing terrified," I said. "Maybe... maybe if I can get in to see her, I can convince her to help us. Somehow." I knew I wasn't selling anyone one it, me least of all.

"Help us do what?" Kellen asked. "What do you think she's gonna do for us?"

I sighed. "I don't know."

"There needs to be a better plan," Errol said. "Anything would be better than risking your life again."

"We don't have any plan at all," Iris said.

"So we think of one," Anna Louise said. "We don't just send Persephone back over there and hope she'll come up with something."

"You're right," Iris said. She looked over to me.

I nodded.

And tried to keep it together. I could feel my heart pounding that much harder. I knew that even if I'd had a plan, I wouldn't be able to go back there.

I tried not to feel like I'd failed, like I'd let everyone down. I tried to convince myself that it wasn't my fear that was keeping me from figuring out a solution, that there wasn't some big mental block that was forcing me to mess it all up just so I didn't have to go back there.

But you can't convince yourself of things, not things like that.

I felt like crying.

And I was starting to feel it coming.

"We need to get out of here," I said, barely able to say the words.

Iris helped me up.

And she walked right beside me, as we made our way back toward the quarry, and our van.

The sun was already starting to set by the time we'd reached the edge of the sand pit. Maybe that would have been near-perfect timing, had Iris made contact with anyone through her magical bot transmitter; maybe, with some luck, we could have swept in under cover of darkness, grabbed our family and friends, and gotten as far away from there as humanly possible.

But Iris hadn't been able to do it. Because aside from that one moment with Jetta, which had lasted less than five minutes total, there hadn't been any indication that she could reach out and touch someone with those genocoded mind-control bots.

Maybe it was just Jetta who could do it.

And maybe Jetta was already dead.

It didn't feel like things could get much worse.

Then I heard something worse. A five- or six-second burst of gunfire. From the east, I thought, not that I could see where it would have started.

I dropped myself down into the sand, which was way less cushioned than I'd expected.

Everyone else had gone down, too, but I wasn't sure who'd wanted some kind of cover, and who might have been hit by the gunshots.

Iris was still next to me; she tapped my shoulder and started crawling toward a bulldozer.

I followed.

Looking behind me, I could see that Anna Louise was crawling along behind us, too.

But Errol and Kellen were in front.

And neither was moving.

"Errol," I called out, trying to be just as loud as I need to be. There'd been no second burst, and I knew that we weren't exactly invisible, but still… it was like I didn't want to give anything away. Maybe whoever it was had tried to sweep across our whole parade line; maybe they thought that they'd manage to hit more of us than they actually had.

Maybe they hadn't hit *any* of us.

But Errol hadn't moved, and he hadn't responded.

And Kellen hadn't done anything either.

We reached the bulldozer, and Iris led Anna Louise and me around to the far side, the large black tires sheltering us from where we all seemed to think the shooting had come from.

"They're not moving," Anna Louise said. "Oh my god."

"Errol's wearing that helmet," I said. "Even if they hit him, he isn't dead."

"He dropped his rifle," Iris said.

I looked to where he lay.

The rifle was a good two feet away from him, lying in the sand.

I couldn't see where Kellen's rifle was. Based on how he was positioned, and where we were hiding, it was possible he still had his gun.

Or he might have died the moment the shooting began.

"We need to get Errol out of there," Anna Louise said. "And Kellen, too, if we can."

"We can't," Iris said. "We need to stay covered."

"We don't need to pull Errol out," I said. "As long as he keeps that helmet on, he'll be okay. *I think.*"

"And Kellen?" Anna Louise asked.

"We can't help him," Iris said.

"Can you tell if he's hit?" I asked her.

Iris peered around the back tire. She shook her head. "I can't even see him."

"So what the heck do we do?" Anna Louise asked.

"We keep watch over Errol," I said. "Either he heals or recovers or… I don't know… if he gets enough strength or whatever to make his way to cover… that or whoever shot at us will have to come down and try to kill him. And we'll have our chance to take that person out."

"You should take the pistol, Seffy," Iris said. "I'm guessing you're the best shot out of the three of us."

Anna Louise handed me the handgun.

"That doesn't belong to you," a voice said, from behind us.

I turned around; I didn't even think to point the gun to where I'd be looking.

Come on, *Seffy.*

It was Lucas. With an automatic rifle, like the ones Magden and Byzzan had been carrying. Like the one that had shot at us from the far side of the quarry.

It wasn't like he could have managed to slip around us… was it?

"Put it down," he said. "And hands on your heads, ladies."

I placed the pistol down on the ground. And put both hands on my head, lacing my fingers.

And hoped that Errol would be smart enough to get the jump on Lucas Berg.

Anna Louise did the same with her hands, but Iris hadn't.

She was looking out to Errol.

She was close to blowing it for us.

"Someone's down there," she said. "Someone else."

"Yeah," Lucas said. "Someone else. Now put your friggin hands on your head."

I couldn't see what was happening.

But I heard a single gunshot.

"Oh my god," I said.

"Who is that?" Anna Louise asked.

She wasn't even looking toward Errol and Kellen.

I followed her gaze.

There was another person. A third person, behind Lucas.

A young woman, down on her knees.

I recognized her from the livestock barn, where she'd been strapped to a bed, and had then been forced to bite into Claudia's neck. Now she was back to having that familiarly disoriented look on her face.

Lucas had gotten his hands on Haley. From the colony.

And that was probably where he'd gotten his new assault weapons, too.

Had he been working with them the whole frickin time?

"Are you okay, Haley?" I asked.

"You know her," Lucas said. "Interesting. She was out wandering in the fields. Wouldn't tell me why."

I shook my head at him. "You don't feel an ounce of shame. You did it to Anna Louise, and now you're going to do it all over again."

"I'm doing what I need to do," he said. "To survive. Me and my new partner." He nodded his head toward the place where the last gunshot had come. From where Errol and Kellen had been lying motionless on the ground.

"This is some crazy helmet on this one," another man called out. "Not sure how to pull it off him."

"Just shoot around it," Lucas said. "Find some bit of scalp and aim for that."

I heard the second man grunt.

And then there other sounds… I couldn't place them. But I got the general gist of it.

Errol was trying to fight him off.

No new gunshot. Not yet.

"No," Iris said. "God, no…"

"What's happening?" I asked.

Lucas was moving to his left, for a better view.

I thought about going for the pistol, but he was still tracking me as he went.

Then the gunshot came.

And Lucas swore.

And then he slammed the handle of his gun against my temple.

I fell against the rubber on the tire.

I watched as Lucas picked up his old pistol from beside me, and ran around the bulldozer.

More gunshots. Automatic fire from Lucas.

I looked at Iris.

She was watching it happen, around the back of the dozer.

And then she covered her eyes.

And Lucas shot another burst.

He stepped back around the bulldozer.

I looked over at Iris.

She slowly shook her head at me. Nothing good.

"Everything's coming up Lucas," he said. "That whole arrangement I had sort of took care of itself. And both your boys are down and out, too… the one with the helmet still needs his headshot, but that'll happen soon enough." He looked over to Haley. "Stand up."

Haley slowly stood.

"Who's got some rope, or tape?" Lucas asked. "Haley needs to tie you girls up so I can shoot Seffy's boyfriend in the head."

"Just shoot us first," Iris said. "The last thing I'm interested in is being one of your little captives."

"It's not about what you want. It's about justice."

"Justice?" I said. "What the heck are you talking about?"

"You bitches left me to die," he said.

"We left you *alive*," Anna Louise said.

Haley walked over to Anna Louise. She started pulling a drawstring out of her MSUM hoodie. Once she'd torn it out, she pulled Anna Louise's wrists behind her back and started tying them with the white rope.

Haley then started pulling the leather belt out from Anna Louise's jeans. I had a good guess as to where that belt would end up.

"If that former partner of mine there had shown up to scavenge an hour earlier, he would have found me tied up like a friggin greased pig."

"Apt comparison," I said. "Right down to the foul stench."

"This is it, Seffy," he said. "The moment I finally beat you down. Make you submit."

"Seriously," Iris said. "Just shoot us now."

"I guess I could shoot Anna Louise," Lucas said. "Since I've already spent some time with her."

"Since you've already raped her multiple times," I said. "That's what you mean, right?"

"Just do what he wants," Anna Louise said. "Don't make this worse."

"How could this be any worse?" Iris asked. "The man has sweat stains on his sweat stains."

Haley came over to me, and bound my wrists behind me with the belt. I'd half-expected a loosie job, some way of her restraining me without making it so I couldn't get out. But she'd pulled the leather tautly around my skin, three loops before buckling and then tying a not, tight enough that I was worried about the circulation to my hands.

She started on my belt.

"Don't you even think of tying me up," Iris said. "I will go down fighting."

"Please don't," Haley said. "I don't want to die."

For some reason that worked, and Iris let her hands get pulled behind her back and bound with my borrowed belt.

We'd actually been fighting a battle on two fronts, but we'd been neglecting the one involving the pervy farmboy with a penchant for zombie porn. And now he had us, and his new and — from what I could tell — recently-departed friend on the other side of the quarry had managed to kill Kellen.

And Lucas Berg was about to do the same to Errol.

"What will it take?" I asked Lucas. "For you to let him go?"

"I can't let him go," he said. "He'll just keep coming back. You know that, Seffy. The idiot is in love with you, for god's sake."

I shook my head. "You're not a bad guy, Lucas. I know you're not. This isn't who you are."

"I've come to terms with who I am. With what I've done. With what I'm going to do to you and your sister."

"Please," Iris said. "You don't want to do this."

"I *definitely* want to do this," he said. "Especially with you."

He stepped over to Iris.

He wiped some strands of hair off her forehead.

"Girls like you are all I've ever wanted," he said. "But it's not like anyone cared what I want. I get it, you know? I'm not the guy you want. Not a guy any of you would ever want. And I can't blame you for that, can I?"

Iris let out a quiet sob. I couldn't tell if she was putting on an act. I wanted to believe it was an act.

"I can't get distracted, though," he said. "I've got something to take care of, you know?"

He started walking back around the bulldozer.

He was headed over to Errol. To take off the welding helmet.

"I'm sorry, Seffy," Iris said. "I'm sorry I couldn't do it."

"It wasn't up to you," I said.

"This is something you can stop," Anna Louise said to Haley. "Do you understand what's going to happen to all of us? To you?"

"He'll kill me if I don't do what he says," Haley said. "And he'll kill you, too. I can't fix this."

"You heard what Seffy said. What Lucas did to me. What he's going to do to you. Is that what you want?"

"I can't stop it."

"You're the only one who can stop it."

"I can't," Haley said, tears in her eyes.

I knew she was too terrified to help us.

In a way, I understood.

And Iris wasn't faking. That much I'd figured out. She'd gone from a quiet whimper to a full-blown fit of sobbing, the kind where you can hardly breathe.

I felt numb.

Then Iris gasped.

And Haley started running.

To where Errol was lying.

And where Lucas was heading.

"What the hell are you doing?" Lucas said.

I heard him groan. I was sure it was him.

And then I heard gasping.

"Lucas is down," she said. "Haley brought him down."

"What?" I said. "How do you know?"

"I know." She slowly moved back to the edge of the bulldozer, on her knees. She peered around. "I felt her."

She leaned against the dozer and pulled herself up. She jogged back over to me.

"Turn around," she said.

So I did. And she turned her back to me, and started working on the belt that was holding my wrists.

Soon she had me free, and I did the same for her.

"Help Anna Louise," she said.

And then she jogged around the bulldozer, toward Lucas and Errol.

I untied Anna Louise's wrists and we both followed after Iris.

Haley was back on her knees, staring at Lucas.

Lucas had blood pouring of his throat, the same way that Claudia had been bleeding, when Haley had bitten her.

"He's going to die," I said. "Her bots won't function inside of him. He'll need our bots, Iris. Or he'll bleed out."

"He needs to die," Iris said.

I looked over to Anna Louise.

"Let him bleed out," she said.

I looked at Haley.

She was staring down at the sand.

"Do you remember what happened with Claudia?" I asked her.

She nodded, without looking up.

"And you'll remember this."

She nodded again.

I kneeled down beside Lucas.

"Don't save him, Seffy," Iris said. "You know he doesn't deserve to live."

"He's dangerous," Anna Louise said. "So much risk."

I thought of that woman I'd killed, on my way back from Enderlin. How I'd bashed her head in with a cinder block, because I knew she'd bite me. She'd have infected me, and I would have lost my sister forever.

But I'd give anything now to erase what I'd done.

Anything.

I bit down into Lucas' throat.

"You didn't kill him, Haley," I said. "But you did save our lives."

Haley looked up at me.

She didn't say anything.

I'm not sure she'd even realized what I'd done for her.

I walked over to Errol, to where he and another man were lying on the hard-packed sand.

The other man was dead, his face covered in blood. Errol must have gotten the jump on him, either with the hunting rifle or the man's automatic weapon; I couldn't tell which.

Errol wasn't moving, but his helmet was still on.

I gently pulled it off.

He was unconscious, his eyes closed, but I watched as he took a breath.

There was blood in the sand, blood on his clothes... from his chest, his stomach, and one of his legs. It was impossible for me to know exactly how many times he'd been shot.

But I knew the bots could save them.

They'd done more than that before. For my father and for Beth. For Kellen.

Not that it had helped Kellen in the end.

I could see Kellen's head wound from where I was kneeling.

Not that different from the way Kellen had killed Magden.

"You should have let him die," Iris said, coming up behind me.

I didn't have any comment on that. I knew that it was something that I might have to do. Soon enough.

But not something I could have left on Haley's conscience.

"You said you felt her," I said. "Haley..."

"She told me to do it," Haley said. "And so I... I just did."

"Why?"

Haley shrugged. "Because I had to. I don't know."

"Because it's the same thing that doctor had done with Jetta," Iris said. "I told her what to do, and she did it. No special programming required."

"You overrode the bots," I said.

"Maybe."

"I still don't understand how. Or why it worked this time, and not before. Not half an hour ago."

"I don't know," Iris said. "I'm just really effing glad it did."

I gave her a hug.

"So what do we do now?" Anna Louise asked.

"We get Errol into the van," I said. "And I guess we find a way to restrain Lucas and load him up, too."

"We're bringing him with us?" Iris said. "That sounds a little too messed up, even for you, Seffy."

"I honestly think we're safer keeping an eye on him."

"So we can watch him escape and murder us?"

"Maybe it'll work on him," Haley said, looking down and watching her foot as she dragged it along in the sand.

"What do you mean?" I asked her.

She kept drawing some kind of abstract art into the quarry floor. Then she looked up at me. "If Iris can force me to do stuff, maybe she can do the same thing with Lucas."

I looked at Iris.

She shrugged, but she was still pissed.

"It's worth a try," I said.

10

GOSH DARN THE PUSHER MARM

We couldn't bury Kellen; we didn't have the equipment or the time. We didn't even have anything to cover him with.

I guess we could have taken him with us, found some way of burying him later on, but... it just didn't feel like a luxury we had. I made the call on that, so I'll be the one to live with it.

And I think I'm okay with that.

We went back to the B&B this time.

Errol needed time to recover; when Dad and Beth and... well, Kellen... when they'd been chopped up like cattle, it had taken quite a few hours to recover. And to be honest, I think growing back a tongue and your tasty femur meat is less work than what the bots had to do with Errol.

When you're shot multiple times, there are over a dozen likely ways for those gunshots to kill you: severed arteries and blood loss, straight-up shock, organs that look like they've been cheese-grated, infection, lead poisoning if those bullets managed to be left in a bad place...

I guess I've lost count on this, but seriously, there are a lot of ways that Errol could have died without those bots, assuming that the bots will be enough.

We're relying on a little biomedical miracle that maybe isn't as foolproof as we like to believe. I've never read of anyone dying after getting the botshots other than serious trauma to the brain or long term deprivation of oxygen, water, or food. But it's not like everyone had those bots before the infection came; Iris had been a special case, a one-in-a-million emergency case, that had been pushed past both the FDA experimental subject approval panel as well as Dad's insurance plan.

I wonder every so often if some random person intervened to squeak that treatment through, breaking a few rules to save the pretty girl's life; I mean, I guess no one aside from the most heartless of bureaucrats would be overly pissed that a beautiful young woman *hadn't* died on the operating table, but it's not like many other people had been given the same chance she did. The vast majority of the bots have gone to the rich, and rarely to those who were particularly sick or dying.

Maybe they were never designed to save people from multiple gunshot wounds; maybe their focus was more on rich people problems, like high-speed yachting collisions and acute caviar poisoning.

So we put Errol in a quiet bedroom and we gave him time, taking shifts keeping an eye on him.

There were four of us with him now, since Haley wasn't about to go back to the colony.

She'd tried to explain what had happened, but since no one had explained it to her, her story was mainly that she'd been unstrapped from the hospital bed and sent out the side door of the livestock barn. She'd felt the irrepressible urge to head south, toward the ditch where she'd somehow known — without being told — that there would be dead bodies, and that there might be two fallen soldiers nearby.

Her task had been to find those soldiers and verify that they were dead.

She was a living, breathing reconnaissance drone.

But she'd been captured, by Lucas, who'd known right away to restrain her. And there'd been another man with him, and they'd already stripped the dead soldiers of anything of valuable, including their automatic rifles. And by that point, any attempt by Dr. Jones to push Haley to do anything else had failed, because Lucas had made sure to keep her tied up.

The only silver lining to that was that his stupid rubber ring was still hanging from the rear view mirror in the SUV; I can't imagine how things would have gone if he'd had it to use on Haley. Probably no big bite for Lucas Berg.

I'd asked Haley if she could still feel or hear or sense those commands from Dr. Jones, whether they were just urges, or if they seemed a little more like instructions.

She'd told me she couldn't feel anything from her anymore, that the urges had gone after a few minutes.

Maybe it had been the distance, once Lucas had marched her a few miles away from the colony, not that they'd ever gone far from Dr. Jones and the source.

Or maybe Dr. Jones had decided to cut her loose, some kind of kill switch. But I didn't think there'd been a kill switch, for the simple reason that a kill switch would probably have been designed to go ahead and kill Haley, rather than simply let her go.

Or to at least disable the bots... of course, I didn't actually know if Haley still had those bots. Maybe she was just straight-up infected, not that Iris had pointed it out to us. And it's not like any of us had fresh uninfected necks left to bite.

We'd found another bedroom for Lucas, where we'd spread-eagled him to the bed in exactly the way you'd never want to see a guy like Lucas staked out, using zip ties we'd gotten out of a toolbox.

That particular toolbox had been half-filled with various pill bottles and decorated on the outside with a loving decal that read "Save a tree, burn a Republican"; it didn't seem like good business for Gaia's Point B&B, considering that Northwest Minnesota is not exactly a Democratic stronghold. Or that most Democrats would sign on to that kind of radical left-wing ick.

Of course, most Democrats would probably not be big on the sheer level of woo that still permeated the upholstery.

We didn't stuff anything in Lucas' mouth, leaving his gaping idiot hole wide open, but Iris had decided she needed it that way, because in her mind the best test of mind control over a testosterone-charged moron is to force him to say something completely out of character.

So she stood at the side of the bed and tried to push her commands onto him. To get Lucas to declare with absolute conviction that he's a pretty little unicorn.

But she couldn't get it to work.

So I decided to give her some advice.

"I don't think it'll work like this," I said. "It's not like you forced Haley to say something. And Jetta didn't force you to talk."

"Jetta wasn't trying to control me," Iris said. "And I didn't try that with Haley."

"Maybe you should be trying on Haley. For all we know, Lucas isn't even susceptible to this. He doesn't have the reprogrammed bots. He has *our* bots."

Iris sighed. "That's why it's a test, Seffy. We know I could do it to Haley."

"But we don't know the conditions required."

Iris nodded. "She's in with Errol right now."

"You could try right now, actually," I said. "Tell her to come over here."

"Yeah, okay."

She closed her eyes.

I looked over at Lucas.

"Climb aboard," he said.

I rolled my eyes at him.

"It's not working," Iris said.

"How do you know?" I asked.

"I just... I know, okay? And I can't get it to work."

"I can help," Lucas said.

"Maybe you need to be closer," I said.

Iris shrugged. "Maybe..."

"Cut me loose," Lucas said. "And then I'll start beating the unholy crap out of you two. Maybe that'll work."

"How 'bout I start beating on you?" I said to him. "Is that what you're looking for?"

"No," Iris said, "he's right."

"What?"

"Repeat the necessary conditions."

I chuckled. "So I'll just cut him loose, then."

"I was crapping bricks when it happened," she said. "My whole body was amped."

"Hormones..."

"Yeah. Maybe..."

"Adrenalin," I said. "Or Norepinephrine, really. Would definitely have helped you concentrate."

"I don't really understand this stuff," she said. "You're the bio-whiz, Seff."

"We get you back into fight-or-flight mode. Then you try to make contact."

"So cut me loose, blondie," Lucas said. "I'll choke Seffy to death while you watch."

"So what, then?" Iris said. "Steroids or something?"

"Not steroids," I said.

Iris looked down at Lucas. "At least we can wrap two rolls of duct tape over this douchebag's mouth."

I smiled. "And nose…"

"You're a riot," Lucas said.

"Caffeine might do it," I said to Iris. "If we can get enough of it in you."

"Like ten cups of coffee?" Iris asked.

"Like caffeine tablets. I think I saw some in that toolbox."

Iris grinned. "Look at you, Seffy. You've finally found your calling in life. Drug pusher."

"So very hilarious, Iris."

She nodded. "It truly is one of my gifts."

We set up at the kitchen table, a box of caffeine tablets that may or may not have been used for wavy-gravy homemade energy drinks. I guess as long as the cocoa powder is organic, you can drug it up as much as you like.

I was worried about Iris' bots, that they would counteract the caffeine somehow, but we had to give it a try. The bots hadn't stopped her from getting her rush of hormones, so maybe they wouldn't expend any energy keeping her from trying to replicate that experience.

I had Iris take three caplets, 600 mg of caffeine and three times the recommended dose. One of the great things about botshots, aside from the lack of chin zits, is that the concept of a drug overdose seems a little less daunting.

Not that there's any real evidence that the bots would protect against it, other than my clever assumption that too many prescript-tion drugs in the belly is a prime cause of death for rich toolbags, so an important thing for the bots to try and prevent.

Iris sat quietly for a few minutes, with me holding her hand.

Then she squeezed my fingers tightly, and closed her eyes.

I waited.

Iris has never been much of a coffee girl; I think that stems from the bots themselves. If your body is running at near-perfect efficiency due to the cutting edge in biomedicine, you probably never felt the same level of sheer crappiness that would force you past the taste of your first few cups of coffee.

But that hypothesis does not account for Haley's easy access to the dark mocha at Caribou Coffee… they even put a little chocolate-covered espresso bean on the lid. That was my gateway drug.

Iris was concentrating, so very hard… I could see her squinting, squeezing her palms tightly… that's not something you get much with someone like her… she always makes life look so frickin easy… no need to try so hard.

And then Haley walked into the kitchen.

And she looked over to me, and smiled.

Iris opened her eyes.

"I'd say it worked," Haley said. "Same feeling as before. It's really creepy, by the way."

"So now we can try Lucas," I said.

Iris nodded. And closed her eyes again.

And then I heard the call, from the other bedroom.

"I'm a pretty little unicorn!" Lucas bellowed.

"He's the prettiest," Iris said, laughing.

"It really worked," I said.

Iris nodded. "It really worked. And there was more, Seffy. I could feel them, too. All of them. Just… just a little further away."

"All of them?"

"Dad. Mom. Jetta. And people I'd never met before. Other in-fected."

"You're like Professor X," Haley said.

"I don't know who that is," Iris said.

"X-Men," I said. "The bald guy from *Star Trek: Generation Next*."

Iris smirked. "I think that's a Pepsi product."

"I'll bet you can make me do anything," Haley said.

"Until the hormones wear off," Iris said.

Haley slapped herself in the arm. And again.

Iris laughed. "Stop hitting yourself."

"Can we really make this work?" I asked.

"She just did," Haley said. "And she's being a bit of a dick about it."

"I mean, with the others. And for longer."

"I don't know," Iris said. "It feels... tenuous, maybe? Like I could just lose it at any point."

"I can't just keep shoving caffeine pills down your throat."

"We don't know that."

"There's no way we're risking it," I said. "Best case you don't die. Worst case it renders the whole mechanism worthless. Could even suppress your natural fight-or-flight reaction, like, even without using any stimulants to get there."

"Maybe it's like meditation," Haley said. "Like the more you practice it the more effective it gets."

Iris started laughing. Hard. "Did you really just say that?"

"I don't get it," I said.

Haley started laughing, too. "I said *meditation*. Not..."

And then I got it. Not that the other maxim would have been less true. I knew a girl in junior high who used to brag about her skills in that particular area (i.e., between the thighs). Like why would you ever think that was something to brag about?

"I don't think we have time for you to develop this somehow," I said. "Not if we want to use it to our advantage."

"So we drug me up like a racehorse," Iris said.

"I don't think that can keep working," Haley said. "Even short term."

I was surprised that she seemed so on-board with all of it. How much could Iris control her? I mean, maybe she could even read Haley's mind. Is that something anyone could be okay with?

It made me a little suspicious of Haley. Not that I could imagine an ulterior motive; it wouldn't be possible for Dr. Jones to be running some kind of long con, some genius-level scheme where she'd anticipated Iris taking control of Haley, where she'd expected that she'd be able to override Iris' mindjob at just the right moment.

I didn't think it was possible.

But I guess I wasn't sure.

And I'd have to keep that in mind. We couldn't just open up our entire lives to some random Moorhead girl from Roxana Jones' barn *slash* lab.

"I need to talk to you alone, Iris," I said.

"Yeah, I get that," Haley said. She left the kitchen.

I waited until I knew Haley was down the hall a ways. "Are you still connected to her?" I asked my sister.

"I think I can still control her. You want to try that hand in warm water trick?"

"I'm wondering if it's a two-way street."

"There's no way she can control me, Seff. No way."

"But can you hear what she's thinking? Like you did with Jetta?"

"No… I think Jetta was speaking to me."

"Out loud? I can't imagine…"

"I don't know. That thing where you talk in your head. Like a soap opera monologue."

I remembered thinking that. In the lab with Jetta. "Subvocalizations," I said. "And you did the same with Haley?"

"No… I didn't do that with Haley. It was more… I don't know… visual. Like I visualized Haley coming into the kitchen. And then I visualized Lucas declaring how pretty he is."

"So you should be able to visualize other infected doing your bidding?"

"Maybe… but I don't know enough about them," she said.

"What do you need to know, anyway? Their backstories?"

"For one thing, I couldn't see where they were. I just knew they were farther away. So maybe random infected guy number sixteen is wandering three miles from here, or maybe he's locked in a cage at that Hutterite Colony."

"You could get them to tell you," I said.

"I could visualize them telling me? I don't know…"

"Well, we can try it, can't we?"

"You mean I can try it."

I didn't see why that would bother her, but she seemed almost annoyed with me. Like I was putting some undue burden on her. Like she'd forgotten the burden of dragging her zombie rump to a research lab in downtown Fargo during an air force bombing run.

Self-absorbed, much?

She'd closed her eyes again.

I decided not to start that argument about who'd been burdening who.

She was squinting again, and squeezing her hands closed.

"Haley tells me that she's upset with you," she said. "She wishes you'd trust her after all she's done."

"She hasn't done anything," I said.

Iris opened her eyes long enough to glare at me.

I guess I was supposed to shut up and let her do her thing.

So I did.

And Iris squinted a little tighter, then kept going. "Haley thinks Dr. Jones is still trying to control her, but she's not sure."

Iris opened her eyes again.

"Thanks," I said.

She nodded.

I smiled. "So now all we need is a plan."

"Oh, that's all?" She'd smiled back at me.

Maybe I was overthinking any tension with her.

Maybe a little bitchiness is an expected side effect of loading your sister up with a buttload of caffeine.

Not that I could explain why I seemed to be feeling the same way.

It was Iris who came up with the plan. I wasn't sure I agreed with it, but I didn't have anything better to offer.

Once Errol had recovered — which seemed well on its way — we would head back to the colony all over again.

We'd send Haley back to where she'd come from, that livestock barn where I'd first seen her, Dr. Jones' impromptu lab for human experimentation and possibly snow cones.

Those experiments are definitely worse than our current batch of experiments with Iris and her mindjobs, or so I've decided, not that I'm a hundred percent on the whys or hows of it. I know it's a slippery slope, even if it hadn't seemed that way a week ago. You just want to find a solution, and you start to worry a little bit less about who might need to pay the price for it.

It wasn't even just Haley who would be paying; this was hard on Iris, too. But again, I didn't have a Plan B in mind.

So once Haley got inside, she would take out Dr. Jones any way she could, even if that meant ripping out her throat... which it probably would. Haley had assured us that she could do it, and Iris was convinced that she could push Haley past any self-doubt or common decency when the moment actually came.

Once Roxana was lying in a pool of her own blood, dying and without any bots to save her, Haley would release any other prisoners she could. Iris would override any of the protections Dr. Jones had put in place, and those prisoners would team up with Haley, to force their way to where Dr. Smith was holding the other captives, including Dad and Beth and Errol's family.

Hopefully Iris would be able to make enough of a connection with Dad, or her Mom, to get the information we needed, to try and protect our little battle squad of zombies from any remaining bad guys with guns.

I know there's a strong chance that some of those infected people will die in the attempt, because of what Iris is forcing them to do... what *Iris and I* are forcing them to do, since I'm just as much a part of it.

I obviously still haven't forgotten that infected woman outside Enderlin, and that cinder block. Sometimes we do what we need to do, because we can't think of any other way.

And as long as *I know* that I'll never get past what we're about to do, I think I can start to accept it. Accept it, but never be able to forget it, and never shake that feeling that I'm not the lily-white protagonist that I make myself out to be.

In the end, we're all selfish. We're all just varying-degrees of self-centred jerks. Iris and I are choosing our family and friends over people we don't know. That, right there, is a quick summing up of the entire disgusting run of human history.

11

THE BIG DANCE

We left at two in the morning, Iris driving the van while Errol and I kept our eyes out for any problems along the road. We'd brought Lucas along, tied hands and feet with a combination of rope, duct tape and zipties, and with a freshly laundered sock — against my vote for something spectacularly dirty — jammed and taped into his mouth. We were being a little overzealous, maybe, but Lucas had taught us that.

We parked at the quarry, using Kellen's body — still where he'd fallen — as some kind of indicator that no one had been there. The other man's body was still there, too, where Errol had shot him.

Errol climbed out of the van first, with Haley rushing out with him. She'd spent a lot of time with him as he'd recovered, and for some reason, she now apparently wanted more.

I'd noticed how she looked at him, and I didn't really understand it. But it's not like I mind; if anything, it's more of a strange curiosity to see a girl so smitten with a guy like Errol. Maybe that sounds really awful.

"And this is where I was supposed to die," Errol said.

Haley brushed up against him.

He gave her a smile.

"You were too stubborn to die," I said. "I guess that's some sort of virtue."

"Coming from the queen of stubborn," Iris said.

"Pretty sure we've got two queens here," Errol said. "Or princesses, maybe? Like the sisters from those Disney *Frozen* movies."

"I thought the 'Y' was a 'P'," Haley said. "In 'Disney'. I used to call it *Disnep* until I was, like, twelve."

Errol laughed a little too heartily.

And I did give her a little smile.

It was a very Jetta kind of comment, actually. I missed Jetta.

Obviously.

But I didn't want that to get in the way of everything. Like with Dad, too. Like thinking about them as the people we're coming for… it might muck things up, distract me from the job.

I knew it was worse for Iris. Not just because her mother was there, too, but because she was the one who'd need to pop those caffeine pills and focus her weird little mind.

We would wait there, at the quarry, while Haley made her trip in. We'd count down five minutes, at which point Iris would take her mind-control medicine and try to make contact with Haley. If she couldn't, or if it felt the least bit fuzzy or whatever, we'd move in a little closer.

Otherwise, we'd wait right there for Haley to get the job done.

And, if Haley fails — or Haley was meant to fail from the very start — we'd hopefully have time to get the heck out of there before any of the bad guys caught up to us.

"Just don't expect any miracles," Haley said, as she stared along the fenceline, toward the colony. "I'll be lucky to even get inside without getting caught."

"Don't be afraid to tell them about us," Iris said. "Could save your life. Don't give them anything too valuable, though. Maybe just focus on Seffy's roomy hips."

"Good luck, Haley," I said.

Anna Louise gave her a hug.

Which gave Errol a great opportunity to do the same.

And Haley hugged him back.

Then she started walking, and I took note of the time on Jetta's pink tablet, which had already survived a buttload more than I'd expected it could.

"She'll pull it off," Anna Louise said.

"I'm glad your random assessment agrees with what we're all hoping for," Iris said, with a friendly sort of smirk.

"I just wish we had more control over it," I said.

Iris nodded. "Because you're a control freak, Seff. I guess it's a good thing you're not the one with an unholy army of zombies."

"They're not zombies," Anna Louise said. "They're people."

"I don't mean it like an insult."

"Well that still doesn't make it a word you should throw around."

"Well, sorry, then," Iris said, not that it sounded like she was apologetic in the least.

But Anna Louise gave her a nod and a slight smile, and I wasn't about to get involved.

We were all nervous. Maybe that would help, in Iris' case.

I decided that I'd try giving her just two caplets instead of three; I didn't want the stress of what we were doing to overload her completely. We needed fight-or-flight Iris, not faint-or-heart-failure Iris.

"We shouldn't be talking so much," Errol said, his voice echoing from the inside of his welding helmet.

No one really answered him, which might have just been a sign that we all agreed.

So we waited in silence.

Once the five minutes were up, I passed two pills and a water bottle to Iris.

She swallowed both caplets.

And she didn't ask about the third.

She closed her eyes.

"I've got her," she said, after only a few seconds. "She's okay. She's already crossed the road."

Iris opened her eyes again.

"Can you still feel her?" I asked.

She nodded. "We're connected, I guess."

"And anyone else?"

"I'm focusing on her," Iris said. "I know there are other people, one or two so far, but I'm trying to ignore them… for now."

"Okay."

We waited another minute or so.

"Ask her where she is," I said.

"I know," Iris replied, in what was almost a hiss.

So I waited some more.

"She's in the barn," Iris said. "It's empty."

"Does she know where else to check?" I asked.

"I don't know… just hold on, Seffy, alright?"

"Uh, okay…"

Iris had closed her eyes again.

I wondered if she was feeling the connection weaken already. I knew she wouldn't appreciate me asking about it.

"She's going back to where she was first held," Iris said.

"Where's that?" I asked.

Iris groaned. "How the heck should I know that? *Just hold on.*"

I nodded, not that she could see me. And not that she'd want any response from me that wasn't just, you know, *holding on.*

It was killing me to have to just stand there, watching my sister stand perfectly still with her eyes shut, squinting and squeezing her fists. And not being able to help. I mean, I could squeeze my hands tight until they starting bleeding, but that wouldn't actually do anything for her.

"Okay," Iris said. "She's found some prisoners locked into stalls. Leona, maybe, a couple of Hutterite girls. She thinks she's found Jetta."

"She thinks?" I asked.

"Yeah. She can't really see that well into these stalls. The walls are high, blocking her view. Hold on."

"Holding on…"

"Shut up, Seffy. Please."

It was nearly impossible not to say *something.*

But I knew what she was trying to do, how difficult it was.

I had to do whatever she needed me to do, which at the moment was absolutely nothing.

Ugh.

"She sees someone who might be Mom," Iris said. "But she's not sure. Okay… okay."

I bit down on my hand. It was really that hard not to interrupt.

"No keys," Iris said. "She needs keys for the padlocks… on the stalls."

"Magden had the key before," I said. I had to tell her that much, right? "One key, that I saw…"

"She can't find any keys… she doesn't know how she'll get them out."

"She could bash the padlocks," Errol said. "I doubt they're that strong. A hammer, or something."

"It would be easier to bust the stall doors themselves," I said. "If she hammers at the hinges."

"Okay," Iris said, "quiet for a minute."

So we were quiet.

"She can't find anything," Iris said, after thirty seconds or so. "She doesn't know what to do."

"There's no one watching," Errol said. "I say we follow her in."

"I don't know," I said. "They should have someone watching."

"Then how did she get by?"

I looked over to Iris. She still had her eyes closed. I could hear her grinding her teeth.

Her eyes opened.

"No," she said. "It's not safe."

"What do you mean?" I asked.

"It could be a trap. We just don't know. I don't think Mom and Dad are in there. I think they're somewhere else. I sense them somewhere else."

"So it's someone else in there. Not your mom."

"I don't know. I'm going to try and find out, but it's... it's not right. I don't trust her."

"We sent her in there," Errol said. "It's our responsibility to keep her safe. That matters to me, thanks."

"She's not a child," Iris said. "She agreed to help."

"Did she?" I asked.

"What the heck is that supposed to mean? You think I brainwashed her into it?"

"No," I said. "I'm not saying that."

"I think you are."

"Girls," Errol said, "come on. Take it easy."

"Shut up, Errol," I snapped.

He muttered something under his breath. I was pretty sure it was the word "stupid", followed by a certain c-word. For a moment, I thought it was a bad joke.

But he was looking at me like he meant it.

"We regroup," Iris said. "We try something else."

"And you'll tell Haley to come back?" I said. "You think she'll just leave them there?"

"I'm not telling her to come back, Seffy. That's a bad idea."

"What are you talking about?"

"We can't sit here and wait for her," Iris said, "and hope this wasn't a trap from the start. I haven't confirmed anything she's told us. And we need to go."

"They might kill her," Errol said. "You know I can't let that happen."

"You wouldn't give a crap if she wasn't into you," Iris said.

"Watch your mouth, Iris."

"Or what?"

"Come on, guys," I said.

I felt a hand on my shoulder. Anna Louise. "We need to leave," she said. "Please."

I shook my head.

"We're going in," Errol said. "If it's just Seffy and me, that's fine. But we're not leaving anyone behind."

"We're not the frickin Marines," Iris said.

"We're going," I said. "You can come with us."

"As if you're giving me a choice."

"What do you mean?"

Iris groaned. "I can't leave you here," she said. "So I have to go with you."

"Well, I don't," Anna Louise said. "I'll be waiting right here, engine running."

"Not a chance," Iris told her. "You can stay here, but you won't be holding onto the keys to that van. Not with it just being you and Lucas."

"Fine. But I'm not coming with you."

"We don't need you anyway."

"Take it easy on her, Iris," I said.

"Whatever, Seffy," Iris said. "I really don't have time to handfeed the frickin trauma club. If you want to get us killed, then let's get down there and die. I don't give a flying piggie what happens to Anna Louise here. Hopefully Lucas won't get free and split her mostly-vacant skull wide open."

I didn't respond to that. And neither did Anna Louise.

There was really no time for any of us to keep arguing back and forth.

I started moving toward the colony. I had one of the automatic weapons now, not that I was in any way comfortable using it as anything more than a normal god-fearing rifle. It's not like you just wander into being the kind of person who happily sprays automatic gunfire into crowds.

Errol had the other military-grade rifle and his welding helmet, along with Lucas' pistol, too, which would leave Iris with Errol's old hunting rifle, while Kellen's rifle would be staying behind with Anna Louise. And with Lucas, who would hopefully stay nice and tied up until we got back.

Assuming we came back.

For a while after we'd first got out of Fargo, I'd pictured myself tromping across the Minnesota countryside with a bow and arrow, like some kind of... *Hunger Games* zombie killer, I guess. But now I just looked like a surprisingly supple jarhead, with my big ol' gun and kill 'em all attitude.

It doesn't feel good knowing that this is what's happening to me. That I'm being pushed into becoming a person I never wanted to be.

But the truth is, you just don't walk into a hostile armed camp and expect no one to get hurt. Assuming that Errol and Iris and I manage to walk back out means accepting that we may have to do our fair share of shooting at people.

"I really don't want to do this, Seff," Iris said.

I didn't answer her.

I just kept walking, knowing that my sister would feel she had no other choice than to follow me.

⟳

We were only two dozen steps closer when Iris started freaking.

"Something's wrong," she said, having stopped in her tracks. "I don't think Haley's telling me the truth."

Errol and I both stopped as well.

"What do you mean?" I asked.

"I'm not sure anyone's in that building with her. I don't sense anyone at all right now. Not even... not even Haley."

"Maybe you just don't know the people in there," Errol said. "Maybe you need to know them first."

"That's not it," she said. "We need to go back. I'm going back."

"You said you'd back me up," I said.

"I said I wouldn't leave you here. So I'll be at the van. Waiting for you to come to your frickin senses, Seff."

I looked over to Errol.

"I'm not going to abandon Haley," he said.

"Because you think she'll sleep with you," I said.

He shook his head at me.

And kept walking, right past me and toward the colony. With more muttering.

"You don't need to go with him," Iris said.

"He's right," I said. "Even if he is thinking with the wrong head. We put Haley into this."

"Haley's lying to us. She's lying to me."

"Do you know that, Iris? Like, for sure?"

She shook her head. "If I was sure, I'd have told you I was sure."

"Then I'm going with him," I said. "And we could really use your help, Iris."

"I'm not risking it, Seff. I mean, if we really have the cure... not to mention the possibility of stopping whatever they're doing to these people..."

"Errol and I have a much higher chance of getting ourselves killed without your help."

"I can't just walk into a trap," she said. "You ought to know that, Seff."

"No. I don't know that."

She shrugged.

And turned to head back.

I took a deep breath, and then I rushed to catch up to Errol.

✍

We didn't know exactly which door to take; I'd been brought there unconscious, and I'd left there after fainting. I had no way of knowing which barn it even was, aside from making some educated guess from having seen the inside.

I'd assumed it was attached to those tents where I'd first been, but when we came close to the tents, I saw that they weren't attached to anything else.

The only buildings nearby didn't match what I thought I'd seen; one too short and the other too narrow.

And those buildings stood alone; if Haley had moved on to an attached building to find the other prisoners... or even slipped out between two close-by barns.

She hadn't done it anywhere near those tents.

"They could have taken me anywhere," I said to Errol, in a whisper. "I don't know where Haley went."

"And you didn't ask Iris," he said. "That's great."

"You could have asked her."

"I guess I assumed you know what you're doing out here. Sorry for making assumptions, Persephone."

"Not helpful, Errol."

"No, I think that sums *you* up, right there. *Not helpful.*"

"Yeah, thanks."

"So what do we do?" he asked. "Boss man…"

"Seriously?"

"Your sister should have come with us."

"I know. Also not helpful, Errol."

"I swear, Persephone… if you've gotten Haley killed…"

"Let's just focus on finding her," I said. "Okay?"

He nodded. "Yeah, alright. *Okay.*" I could hear from how he was speaking that he was clenching his jaw. And holding back what he was really thinking.

I remembered back when he'd curl his lip at me. He hadn't done that since, well… I don't even know. Since a long time before Haley started batting her derpy eyes at him.

"We have time to look," I said. "It's the middle of the night and no one seems to know we're here."

"Which makes absolutely no sense."

"Yeah, I know."

"Dang it… do you think Iris was right?"

"Probably," I said.

"But I don't think Haley would do that."

I rolled my eyes at him. "First of all, you've known her for less than a day. And second, it might not be up to her. It's not like Anna Louise wanted to stay with Lucas Berg for as long as she did."

"We should split up," he said.

"Not a chance."

"They're a skeleton crew, Persephone. We killed two of their guys, and it looks like that was a serious chunk of their manpower."

"You really believe that?" I asked. "That they could murder dozens of Hutterite men and hold how many women and children captive? With just a handful of people?"

"Then where are they? I don't see anyone else. And you didn't see anyone else, either. When those two soldiers got shot, did they send more men after them? Nope… they sent Haley."

It wasn't like he wasn't making good points. Like the alternative theory — of a heavily-armed force just waiting to get the drop on us — made anything close to as much sense. It felt like we had the run of the place. Like we could check each barn, one by one, until we found our people and got them out.

But even if that was true, there was no reason to take any extra risk. There were only two of us.

"We go together," I said. "We take our time and we keep our eyes open. I still don't believe how easy this seems."

"Yeah, okay."

And he took the lead again, moving toward the closest barn.

The one that I was almost a hundred percent sure wasn't the right one.

But I didn't stop him, because I wanted to be certain.

I didn't want to risk missing our people.

We'd searched two barns, one with chickens and one with pigs, and neither with zombies or loved ones, when Errol stopped and stared at me.

"It's Iris," he said. "In my friggin head."

"Then talk to her," I told him.

He nodded, but I knew he wasn't too happy with me telling him what to do.

"She thinks we should go back," he said.

"You're joking."

"She still thinks it's a trap."

"Ask her how we find Haley," I said.

He nodded. He didn't speak, but I assumed he was posing the question.

Errol looked around the colony, left then right.

He motioned to a large set of newer buildings to the west.

"That's where she last had contact with Haley," he said. "She thinks."

"Tell her to meet us there."

He shook his head.

"What does that mean?" I asked.

"She says she's starting to lose touch with me. And can't sense anyone else."

"So she takes more pills."

"She already has. She thinks the bots are interfering. That they've gotten used to the extra hormone levels."

"I don't think it works like that," I said. Not that I knew for sure.

He sighed. "I think she's gone."

We started walking over to the big collection of barns.

I couldn't shake the feeling I had, that Iris was right about everything.

But I also knew that if she was right, if it was a trap... then it was probably already too late for Errol and me. Whoever was watching and waiting would take us out long before we could get back to that quarry.

12

THE WORST THAT COULD HAPPEN

Errol and I found Haley in the dairy barn.

Just Haley, standing at one end of a very long aisle, between open stalls, where there were still dozens — if not several hundred — black and white cows.

"A trap," I said to her.

She nodded. "I'm sorry. It's not up to me."

Errol sighed. He pointed his rifle up at her. "Please, Haley," he said. "Don't move. Don't come near us."

I stepped closer to Haley. I didn't have to worry about what she might do, unless she knew of some secret way to kill a *bothot* girl with her bare hands.

Haley held up two strips of beige cable. Plasticuffs. "They want you to put these on," she said.

"Or what?" Errol said.

"Don't get all pissy with me," she said.

I laughed at that.

"What's so funny?" Errol asked.

"I'm not sure," I said. "But it doesn't hurt to laugh once in a while. Unless you think it'll scare the cows."

Haley cocked her head at the cuffs in her hand.

Errol shook his head. "I'm not surrendering to you."

"Don't push him, bud," Haley said.

"What?"

"Dr. Smith. You don't want to force him to come down here to get you."

"No... I think I do want him to come down here. You know, maybe you should be the one wearing the cuffs."

"Please…"

"Don't," Errol said. "I'm the one with the friggin gun, okay?" His voice softened. "I really don't want to hurt you, Haley."

But he was still aiming that gun at Haley's chest. Right into the middle of her MSUM hoodie's bullseye, right at the dragon's head.

He'd been all lovey-dovey about her just a few minutes ago. Now he was close to shooting her.

I know that wouldn't have been an easy ride.

I wanted to intervene, to tell Errol to pull it back a little, that Haley wasn't really a threat, that there was no point in trying to make her pee herself. That would be messy and a little embarrassing for all involved.

But he was right; there was no reason for us to just give up and surrender to an unarmed college student. If Dr. Smith was such a daunting figure, where the heck was he?

Maybe it was just smoke and mirrors. Maybe Dr. Smith didn't have anyone left to fight his battles. Or maybe Dr. Smith didn't really exist. We would let Haley take us prisoner and walk us right back into Roxana Jones' lab, where it would just be Dr. Jones and her little tablet and some smug cat-poop-eating grin.

"Dr. Smith will need to come and get us," I said. "And I guess we'll just wait here 'til he does."

"That's a very bad decision," Haley said.

"It's a very big *oopsie*," someone else said, through speakers spaced along the line of the ceiling. I hadn't figured on Hutterite dairies having surround sound.

It was a man's voice, older but not all that old, really. But it was dripping with the kind of douchebaggery you'd get with a guy with Lucas, and with the smug attitude you'd find in a guy like… like my mother's doctor, I guess, the guy who'd talk about Mom in the third person, even when she was right there in the room.

Dr. Smith, I presumed.

"Do follow the girl's instructions, Mr. Kimmern," the voice through the speakers said. "Of course I mean Haley's instructions, not the pitter-patter of bad advice from your other girl, that self-important know-it-all with the fancy high school diploma."

I felt like he knew me, well enough to make me feel three inches tall in a matter of seconds, and all the way from another room, no less.

"Not good enough," Errol said. "I'm not really scared of some jerk's voice. Or do those wall speakers also shoot laser beams?"

The door at the far end opened.

Two soldiers walked in, automatic rifles in hand.

"Guns down, hands on your heads," one of the soldiers said.

I slowly lowered my rifle to the ground with one hand, while I brought the other hand upward, about as far from the trigger as I could keep it.

Errol hadn't done anything with his hands.

"They'll kill you," I said to him, as I carefully moved my other hand up to my head.

"We have the advantage," Errol said. "Or we did have it, until you dropped your rifle."

I saw two more soldiers coming in, behind the first couple.

"Four to one," I said. "Put it down, Errol. Please."

"No," he said.

The soldiers were coming closer, hustling as they walked, just short of a jog.

I lowered myself down to my knees.

I knew what would happen if Errol didn't lower his rifle.

"Drop the weapon," the same soldier said. "Drop or we will shoot."

"I'm not worried about that," Errol said.

"I'm pretty frickin worried about that," I said.

"I'll be okay, Persephone."

"Well, I don't want to get shot, Errol."

He didn't answer me.

The soldiers had reached up to where Haley was standing, in the aisle.

One of the men shoved her to the side.

They were clearing the path to shoot.

"Errol," I said.

He lowered his gun, pointing it at the concrete floor.

And the soldiers opened fire.

Two bursts from the two men in front.

I saw Errol hit the ground hard.

I didn't move.

One of the soldiers restrained me first, with cuffs he'd pulled from his gear, while the other kept his rifle trained on me.

The two at the rear had stayed back with Haley.

I could see that she was being restrained, too.

Once my hands were tightly cuffed behind my back, they did the same to Errol, ignoring the wounds they'd given him.

From what I could see, they'd hit him more than once. Maybe as many as four times, three around the chest and stomach, and one lower, just above his left knee.

And then I felt the blood on my neck.

At first I'd thought it had come from Errol, but it didn't take me to long to realize it was mine.

From the side of my head, most likely; I could feel the sting, just above my ear. Maybe half an inch off, from landing where the bots wouldn't have been able to clean up the mess.

They'd pulled Errol's helmet off, and I looked over to him. He was clenching his jaw from the pain, and probably trying his best not to pass out. He was losing blood fast, and I wasn't sure if the bots could close him up in time, while also working to shore up his blood with synthetics.

I knew that he might be dying.

But I still had a grotesque urge, to have him look at me, and see what had happened to me. That he'd come close to getting me killed. I caught his eye, and despite everything else he was going through, he put the effort in, and turned his head away from me.

The soldiers brought us back down the aisle, the three of us, all captives, in the middle of their procession, with Errol being dragged pretty much like a corpse, and leaving a lot of blood behind.

I guess in a normal world he would have been exactly that. A frickin corpse.

At the far end of the barn, I saw a stocky man with a part in the middle of his light brown hair. He was wearing thick black-framed glasses, and was dressed in what could best be described as "Hawaiian scrubs", green-hued and surgical, but with a ridiculous floral pattern.

He was close to forty, I'd guess, and not an unhealthy person, despite his size. He had a smug grin on his face that might as well have been a nametag.

"Stupid like a fox," Dr. Smith said. "This could have gone far better."

"They didn't need to shoot him," I said. "He'd lowered his gun."

Dr. Smith shook his head. "That wasn't compliance. That was theatre."

He gave a nod of his head, to the left, and the soldiers in front of us parted. He stepped into the gap, right up to Haley, first in our line.

But he was looking directly at me.

Hooray.

"You would have done well to not underestimate my capabilities, Persephone," he said.

"I didn't know we were on a first name basis," I said.

His perpetual smirk turned into a slightly less smirky smile. "No bravado necessary. I appreciate all you've achieved."

"And I'm horrified by everything I've heard about you."

"Your opinion of me doesn't really enter into my plans."

"And what are your plans?" I asked him. "Dr. Jones seems to think you are a very dangerous person."

"Roxana is right about me. A man of conviction is a dangerous man indeed."

"Is there any point to this?" Haley asked. "I mean, clearly you're completely full of yourself. We get that."

Dr. Smith seemed unaffected. "In different circumstances I would have loved to work with you, Persephone," he said. "You'd have made an excellent intern. But in this particular situation I'm afraid I need your body more than I need your mind."

"You should definitely rephrase that," I said.

He nodded. "You may have the cure I've been looking for. Or at the very least, the guidepost I need."

"I heard. That you want to be the only person alive who can't be controlled by those frickin bots."

"You and your sister Iris are already two of those people," he said. "And I want to join you in that special category."

"You've made it pretty clear that I'm not a long term asset."

He gave another nod. Then turned and started walking out the door, out into the darkness.

It didn't take long for the soldiers to make it clear that we were expected to follow, giving both Haley and I jabs between our shoulder blades.

So we went out of the barn, me looking back as Errol's body was dragged along behind us.

If there's a point when those bots reach some kind of hard limit, when they can't keep up the level of repair needed... I think Errol's at that point.

He'd better live.

I can't stay pissed off at him if he dies.

Dr. Smith and his quartet of soldiers led us across a gravel road, to another metal-framed building. The lights were already on when we came in, blanketing the entire space in cold fluorescents.

There were two hanging tracks, like you'd see at a dry cleaners, but instead of hangers there were... some other kinds of hangers, with a metal arrow shape within a suspended rectangle. Below that was a deep cylindrical metal trough, rolled up beside the track on the right.

And a tent, in the middle of both tracks. Like exactly what you'd need, if you wanted your fur coat to marry a three-piece suit in a quiet backyard ceremony, no matter the weather.

It ended up being the big rolling metal bin that tipped me off, eventually; I guess slaughterhouses don't always look like they do in horror movies, with bloodied slabs of concrete and a general dimness. Especially for smaller animals, and for that one my guess was chickens. It made sense, since the colony was well-known — even on the North Dakota side of the valley — for their roasters.

"Let me start over," Dr. Smith said. "I'm Isambard Kingdom Smith, and yes, I'm aware that I my full name *should be* Isambard Kingdom Brunel Smith, but that was never up to me."

"I think they have a form you can fill out for that," I said.

The soldiers lined Haley and I up in front of the deep rolling bin. The bin was empty, and cleaner than pretty much any other large metal *anything* I've seen outside a hospital room. They left us there, standing with our hands cuffed behind our backs, moving off toward the side of the building.

Dr. Smith sat himself down on a folding chair, more of a director's chair than what you'd see while camping, or watching two dry cleaning items get married.

"I appreciate the message this sends," Dr. Smith said.

The two soldiers who'd been dragging Errol had lowered him to the floor, at least twenty feet away from the bin. They'd left him there, on his back, his eyes having closed but otherwise pointed right at us and at the bin. Then they moved back against the wall, where the other two men with guns were already standing.

So all four soldiers ended up standing together, glancing back and forth between Errol's prostrate body and the two girls at the giant shiny bucket. *And waiting.*

They were waiting for Dr. Smith's order. I knew that. For him to tell them whether or not they should shoot Errol in the head and be done with him.

And whether or not to do something quite similar to both Haley and I.

"I want to tell you about myself," Dr. Smith said, looking at me rather than Haley. "Tell you about the purpose of this place."

"I already know," I said. "They made a documentary about you. *Apocalypse Now*, I think they called it."

He grinned. "I'll bet you've never seen it."

I didn't admit to that. "People think you're hear to help them. That you're really part of FEMA."

"I am part of FEMA," he said. "I'm the chief medical officer of this joint task force. Joint meaning the CDC. I trust you both know what that means."

"It means unaccountability squared," Haley said.

"You're smarter than you look," Dr. Smith said.

Haley smirked. "Must be nice to make assumptions all the time."

Dr. Smith sighed. "I tried to stop the bombing," he said. "I threatened to go public with the entire story. Not that I would."

"You knew about the cure?" I asked.

"I knew there was a chance of recovery. That the infected weren't unredeemable zombies. And I knew the bombing would be completely ineffective in stopping the spread of infection. If anything, it would accelerate the spread. I told them that."

"And yet here we are," Haley said.

"I'd prefer a more productive level of discourse, actually," Dr. Smith said.

"I'd prefer you removing these cuffs."

Dr. Smith turned to the nearest soldier.

I didn't see any motions, or hear any command.

But the soldier walked over to the bin and grabbed Haley by both shoulders. He then shoved her over to where Errol was lying on the concrete floor.

"First warning," Dr. Smith said. "You can see how difficult the healing will be for Mr. Kimmern, there. Not even sure he'll pull through."

Haley gave a slow nod.

The soldier brought her back to the bin, back on my right side.

"Anyway," Dr. Smith said. "They couldn't hold the isolation lines, even after attempting to eliminate those infected who were trying to push out."

"And you tried to stop that elimination, too," I said.

"No… I agreed to that. Bombing along the isolation lines was a necessary evil. If anything, we waited too long, relying too much on shutting down transportation."

"So much blood on your hands," Haley said.

And here I'd hoped she'd stick with shutting up.

Dr. Smith didn't seem anywhere near as surprised as I was.

"When the line along the Sheyenne River was breached by in-fected…" he said. "They were swimming, and even commandeering watercraft… I recommended pulling back to a new line, and bringing in reinforcements from nearby states. They agreed to that, but it didn't stop them from bombing the city."

"I was there," I said. "I remember all those innocent people dying, thanks."

"And I was there, too," Haley said. "And you know what? I was infected, sure… but none of us deserved to die."

"I know," Dr. Smith said. "I know it shouldn't have happened. And that's why we're here. Why we've done all this work."

"Reprogramming the bots," I said. "Instead of trying to cure people."

Dr. Smith smiled at me. "There's the difference of opinion, Per-sephone. I *am* curing people, but in a different way."

I shook my head. "You've lost me, Doc. Maybe I'm just not psy-chotic enough to follow along."

"I expect better from you, Persephone. This is important, for all of us."

"So how are you curing people? Since it won't be with me…"

"It's partly with you. But let's face it, the major component is the behavioral controls in the reprogrammed bots."

"Behavioral controls…"

"Keep an open mind, Persephone. Imagine a world without mental illness, without acts of violence."

"Says the crazy guy with the private army," Haley said.

"So you'll decide what constitutes acceptable behavior?" I asked him.

"It's not me who's deciding," he said. "It's common sense. Maximizing benefits and minimizing suffering."

"So what Errol's going through is *what now?*"

"You know it's not easy, Persephone. If it was—"

"You sound like a car salesman," I said. "You've said my name a few too many times."

"I like your name," Dr. Smith said. "And I like you."

"Enough to use me for my body, apparently."

He stood up from his canvas-backed folding chair.

He walked over to the bin.

None of the soldiers came with him.

It seemed like a really bad decision, considering Haley's state of mind. Or my general dislike of being tied up in slaughterhouses.

Haley suddenly dropped down to her knees. Dropped hard.

I knew it wasn't something she'd chosen to do. But I couldn't see any sign of some lackey issuing commands with a tablet.

But then again, I hadn't seen where Dr. Jones was stashing herself.

Dr. Smith put a hand on my shoulder.

It was about as creepy as you can imagine it would be.

"I can't control you, Persephone," he said. "I can force you to bend, *with violence*, but I don't want to do that."

"But you will if you have to," I said.

"Yes."

"How noble."

He leaned in, putting him lips a few inches away from my ear.

"I will kill them all in front of you," he said, in a whisper. "Including your sister, once she comes for you."

I tried not to buckle. "You'll kill them anyway."

He pulled back a little.

"I don't have to kill them, Persephone. Not the ones I can control. So that leaves just you and Iris. Maybe the only two others on the whole planet."

"But that's not really true," I said. "I think you and I both know exactly how to create more people like me and Iris."

"You and I know, perhaps. But it's not public knowledge. And it doesn't need to be."

"It's pretty basic stuff, actually. Something the CDC should have figured out at the start. You remember them, right? The CDC?"

"I don't want to kill you, Persephone. There's something special about you that really shouldn't go to waste."

"Not the best pickup line I've heard this week," I said.

"Haley is on her knees because I can control her."

"Then why did you cuff her?"

"Because I don't want to control her if I don't need to. And I don't need to, now that she has the latest release. It was your friend Jetta who helped with that one, by the way."

"I don't want to hear it," I said.

He nodded. "She'd managed to push the bots past their limit, when she found out what the perpetually moronic Corporal Byzzan was wanting to do to you, courtesy of the equally stupid Sergeant Magden. Her epinephrine was startlingly high, enough that we lost control of her for a few minutes. Roxana couldn't get her to respond to any commands."

"And now you've fixed her."

"Yes. She's in good health now. Fully recovered and within acceptable levels."

I looked down at Haley. She was still on her knees, looking up. I could tell she wanted to say something. That she would, if she could.

"And you fixed Haley up, too?" I asked him. "I didn't see the injection."

"No need to inject," he said. "It's handled wirelessly, just like any good tech. I just send the command, and that's all it takes. She was running the latest release before you even got here."

Was that was how he overrode Iris, planting false information in Haley's mind? His latest release? Why Jetta had gone silent? Why Iris couldn't sense more than a handful of infected? Why she'd lost touch with all of them, including Errol?

Had Dr. Smith pushed the update on Errol, too?

"I haven't updated Mr. Kimmern," he said.

"You're not on a first-name basis with him?"

"I don't like him."

"Too masculine?"

"I know that Iris has found a way to make contact with the infected," Dr. Smith said. "We saw it with Jetta, and then Haley. How did you do it, exactly?"

I didn't answer.

"My guess is a caffeine boost. And that would have worked well, until it wore off."

I glanced back down at Haley.

"This isn't about Haley," he said, squeezing my shoulder hard. "This is about you and me, Persephone."

I looked over to the soldiers against the wall. "Do you guys understand what he's going to do to you?" I asked. "Have you been listening to any of this?"

None of them replied. Or gave any indication that they were listening. Maybe they were already infected with the fancy new bots. Maybe it was too late for any last minute switching of teams.

Dr. Smith didn't say anything.

He started pushing down on my shoulder, trying to force me onto my knees.

I fought back, trying to wiggle out of his grip.

He put his other hand on me, my other shoulder. He was pushing harder.

He was stronger than me.

I felt the lock on my knees break.

I hit the floor hard and cursed like no kind of lady.

Dr. Smith laughed as he let go of my shoulders.

"So you've given up on convincing me," I said. "Is this where you kill me?"

"I can't kill you right now," he said. "You ought to have figured that out."

"Then I guess it's back to strapping me down. Because you know I won't help you willingly."

"Do you think there is anything the bots can't repair?" he asked. "Your bots, I mean."

"What are you going to do?" I didn't do a good job of hiding the fear.

"Your sister hasn't come. She needs to be persuaded."

"My sister can't sense anything about me," I said. "She can't even tell when I'm pissed off at her half the time."

"I know."

The door opened, the one they'd brought us through.

Jetta walked in, alongside Dr. Roxana Jones, who was still in her cocktail dress, her eye makeup having waterfalled down her face.

Jetta wasn't cuffed. She looked... okay.

But Dr. Jones was cuffed, just like me and Haley. And Jetta had one hand on Roxana's elbow, leading her along.

I looked over to Errol; from on my knees, I could see his head and neck, but not much more. He hadn't opened his eyes.

"Jetta can get connected to Iris," Dr. Smith said.

"I thought you fixed that," I said.

"I can unfix it, too."

Jetta brought Dr. Jones up to the bin, to my left. She pushed her down to her knees, beside me.

Jetta hadn't even glanced at me. There wasn't much of Jetta there, really. Once she'd dropped Dr. Jones off at the trough, she made her way over to Dr. Smith's director's chair, where she sat down.

"I don't see a tablet," I said to Dr. Smith. "So how do you plan to issue all your commands?"

"She knows," Dr. Smith said, nodding to Dr. Jones.

I looked over to her.

"The subvocalizations," she said. "Same way we could hear Jetta's thoughts... he can send commands."

"No tablet required," I said.

Dr. Jones nodded. "He's going to kill each one of us, unless you get Iris to come. Can you do that? Do you know how?"

"I can't," I said. "I don't have that particular superpower."

"Jetta will do it," Dr. Smith said. "Don't worry." He tapped on the metal bin. "They use long, shallow trays for the chickens. I had to improvise with something a little deeper. To store all the bits, you know? To allow for a full gamut of experimentation."

He walked away from the bin, leaving me and the other two women facing it, on our knees.

I turned to see him approaching Jetta, who was still sitting in his director's chair.

One of the soldiers had come over to Jetta, as well.

Dr. Smith leaned down and kissed Jetta on the forehead. He took a few steps back.

The soldier plasticuffed Jetta's hands behind her back. He then did the same to her ankles.

Then the soldier wrapped his arms around the small of her back and lifted her up. He turned her around, then twisted her body up and around, into a fireman's carry.

He carried Jetta over to the far side of the bin.

And dropped her in.

Jetta groaned as she hit the bottom.

"Thank you," Dr. Smith said, apparently to the soldier. Or maybe to Jetta...

I didn't know what he was planning, not specifically... but the pieces were starting to come together. And I knew it would probably be worse than I'd even be willing to imagine. Jetta in a bin, the rest of us gals bound up at the edge of it... and that creepy question about what parts of me my bots wouldn't be able to repair.

He was going to torture me, and make her watch.

Torture all of us, maybe. Whatever it took...

And that would be enough, wouldn't it? To get Jetta so pumped full of fight or flight signals that Iris would hear her, no matter what.

"All this just to bring Iris here?" I asked.

"She needs to be here, too," Dr. Smith said.

I felt Dr. Jones lean up against me. "You'd better hope she doesn't come," she said.

I wasn't sure what I wanted to happen.

I was feeling it now, the same kind of feeling I'd had when Byzzan had walked me out toward the ditch. The terror, the helplessness, and that little piece of me trying its hardest to convince myself that it wasn't really happening, that I just needed to *not be there*, and maybe then it would all be over.

But there's no way to blank out your mind, or to send yourself on some astral-projected vacation to a pricey resort gift shop in Cozumel. You just have to take it, and know that it won't last forever. And hope that it won't be the last thing that ever happens to you.

Two of the soldiers came up behind us, while the soldier who'd dropped Jetta in stayed on the far side of the trough. The fourth soldier had made his way over to Errol, who, from what I could see of him, still hadn't shown any sign of life.

Dr. Smith came back over to the bin, placing himself directly to the back of me. "I've disabled Jetta's bots," he said. "I'll bet you didn't know I could do that."

"With your mind powers," I said, my voice shaky, despite my best effort.

Dr. Smith cleared his throat. "Haley," he said.

The soldier behind Haley grabbed her shoulders and yanked her up. He folded her over the bin, her head hanging down over Jetta.

"Please," Jetta said. "You don't need to. I'm freaking terrified, okay?"

Dr. Smith took a step closer, his shoulder brushing up against my hair. The soldier to my left — behind Dr. Jones — pulled a knife from his belt and passed it to Dr. Smith.

"I'm honest-to-god pissing myself," Jetta said. "Don't hurt her." She was struggling to break the plastic ties. She started kicking her bound feet against the side of the bin.

"I don't have too many options here," Dr. Smith said. "Can't start with chopping fingers... they're stuck behind her back, you see..." He brought the knife up to Haley's left ear. "You know, when one of J. Paul Getty's grandsons was kidnapped, they sent home one of his ears as proof. Know what Getty did? He said he'd only pay the maximum amount of ransom that's tax deductible."

"Don't waste your time on Haley," I said. "Jetta doesn't even know her."

"We're building up to you, Persephone. A crescendo."

And then he drew the knife down Haley's ear, slicing into the cartilage.

Haley screamed.

The ear didn't come off.

So Dr. Smith tried to cut deeper.

I looked away. To Errol's face.

For a moment I thought I saw him move. His head, a little, his eyelids, like a flutter...

But I couldn't be sure of that.

Haley kept screaming.

I heard Jetta scream, too.

I looked back at Haley.

The ear was gone, and the left side of the head was covered in blood. She'd begun to sob. I had a feeling that Haley believed she'd gone through the worst of it, that he'd be moving on from her.

I didn't think he had.

"So Haley should regrow her ear," Dr. Smith. "You've seen something like that before, haven't you, Persephone? With other body parts? I wonder how long it will take for her?"

"It'll grow back," Jetta said, crying. "You'll be okay, Haley. You will."

"Of course," Dr. Smith said, "I can disable the bots. Any function of the bots. I disabled Jetta's emotional controls, and I've done the same with Haley... for better effect. So I can also disable the healing aspect, as well. Tell the bots to take their ball and go home."

"That won't bring Iris here," I said. "If you want to scare Jetta, you should be focused on me. Show that you're willing to kill me if she doesn't come."

He chuckled. "Good one, Persephone. Everyone knows I can't kill you yet."

"Not yet."

"You know I don't want to kill you. I don't want to kill anyone. That's how this started. Me trying to save the maximum number of lives, no matter the cost."

"So it's okay if Haley dies," I said. "And Jetta, and Dr. Jones. And obviously Errol."

"Find a way to bring Iris here. Then no one has to die. And then we'll work out the cure I need."

"Let's work out the cure right now, Doc. Let these girls go and I'll tell you everything you need to do."

He nodded. "I appreciate that, Persephone. Thank you."

He grabbed a chunk of Haley's hair, just above where he'd severed her ear.

He sliced the knife across her throat.

I saw Haley look over at me.

And heard her start to gasp.

And I heard Jetta start to squeal.

The blood was dripping down into the bin. I wasn't sitting high enough on my knees to see it hit the bottom.

I knew that Haley's blood was spilling all over Jetta.

I struggled to get up from my knees.

I felt one of the soldiers holding me down.

I looked back to Errol.

His eyes were half-open. I was sure of it.

He was alive. He was conscious.

And he'd seen it happen to Haley. But he hadn't tried to get up.

"The original *t. gondii* bots overtaxed their hosts," Dr. Smith said. "We reprogrammed the bots in an attempt to avoid this, to slow the buggers down. But that's a problem for throats getting cut, isn't it? Haley's losing an assload of blood right now. Most of it is just soaking through Jetta's clothing, to be honest. Talk about your sopping big dry-cleaning bill."

"Let me bite her," I said. "It might help."

"Your super-bots. I know. Worked well with that Hutterite girl... Claudia. But I don't really want Haley to pull through. I want Jetta to watch her die. And I want Iris to feel that, and know that Haley won't be the only one."

"There's no way I'll help you. Not if you let her die."

"I don't need your help, Persephone. I just need your bots."

"You can't do this," I said.

"It's already in motion."

I tried to pull away from the bin.

I couldn't move, with the soldier still pinning me on my knees through my shoulders, so hard that I was starting to have trouble breathing.

"He's going to kill me next," Dr. Jones said. "My god, Seffy... you need to do something."

I looked back to Haley.

She was bleeding out. She'd already lost consciousness.

I'd seen the same thing happen to Claudia. But I'd been able to bite Claudia.

They weren't going to let me save Haley.

They kept me pinned down for several minutes, as Haley bled.

The soldier who'd been holding Haley up against the bin had let go, leaving her body folded and dangling, over the side.

That soldier had made his way over to Roxana Jones, but he hadn't lifted her up from her knees just yet.

They were waiting for Haley to die. To make sure she was dead.

And they were waiting for that message to get passed on to Iris, through Jetta's complete state of panic.

Jetta wasn't crying or squealing anymore, or struggling or kicking. She'd begun to shake, violently, something you'd call a seizure if you'd never seen a real seizure before.

It was more like what you'd see when you throw a fish onto the dock, watching it squirm as it suffocated in the open air.

I've never seen anyone so terrified.

I wasn't that terrified. Even Roxana Jones wasn't that terrified, and she was clearly next on the list.

But Jetta was scared of what was happening to the rest of us. Which somehow, for her, was even worse. Scared because she knew she'd have to watch.

And she knew that only after all that would it be her turn to die, once she was swaddled in blood from every last one of us. Not just from Haley and Roxana Jones, but from me, as well; even if Dr. Smith wouldn't kill me yet, he could certainly make me bleed.

If there was any chance of Jetta making contact with Iris, it would happen, exactly as Dr. Smith was expecting it would.

And I couldn't change that.

Just like I wasn't able to stop Haley from bleeding to death beside me.

13

GIVING UP AND GIVING IN

I was forced to stay on my knees, as the process was repeated with Roxana Jones.

Folded over the bin, ear severed — right rather than left — and throat sliced open.

Blood dripped down all over Jetta's bound body.

They waited the several minutes it would take for Dr. Jones to die.

And then, a soldier — I'd lost track of which one by that point — brought me up for my turn.

"I'm sorry, Persephone," Dr. Smith said. "I was really expecting your sister to show up by now."

"Are you going to cut my throat, too?" I asked him. I knew I sounded weak and frightened. I *was* weak and frightened. I just wanted it to be over.

I wasn't sure I wanted to live past what had just happened in front of me.

Dr. Smith didn't answer.

He put the knife up to the side of my head, to where I'd already been grazed by a bullet.

I felt the shock of the pain as he sliced into my right ear.

One cut took it off, cleaner than with the other girls.

But it still hurt worse than anything else.

Worse than when Byzzan had shoved a knife into my leg.

Worse than anything I've felt so far in my life.

"Please," Jetta said. "Please don't kill her. I... I can't let you kill her."

"I need Iris to come," Dr. Smith said. "I'm sorry."

"Hold on," I said. "You disabled her bots."

"So?"

"So maybe that's why. Maybe she doesn't have the ability to reach out to Iris. You realize that, right?"

"I disabled some of the functionality, Persephone. Don't tell me you don't understand the difference."

"Could be the frickin torture," I said. "Making me watch innocent people die."

"Neither of those girls was innocent. You know Roxana was guilty as anything, not that I wanted to lose her. And Haley spread the infection to others, long before we brought her in."

"You know that wasn't her fault," I said.

"No one deserves this," Jetta said. "God, Iris… where the hell are you?"

"I hope she never comes," I said.

"I'm starting to worry about that," Dr. Smith said.

"She'll come," Jetta said. "Please. Just… just wait a while longer."

Dr. Smith stepped back from me, taking the bloody knife with him. "I'll give it more time." He walked back over to his folding chair and sat down.

Jetta thanked him.

I understood what she was feeling. That she'd do anything to keep me safe. Heck, that she'd probably give her life for me if she had to.

I remember feeling that way, too, when I'd mistakenly shot an arrow into my sister's lung.

That I'd give anything to make Iris okay.

But I knew that wasn't going to work this time. Because it wasn't just Iris I was worried about.

I was worried about Jetta.

I'd have given anything to make Jetta okay.

Not that I could think of how that could ever happen.

After five to ten minutes of waiting, me still slumped over the side of the bin, staring down at a ruined, bound, and blood-covered Jetta, Dr. Smith got up from his chair.

"It won't work," I said. "If what you've done hasn't brought Iris here, nothing will."

"Oh my god," Jetta said. She was staring up at me, tears in her eyes. "I'm so sorry, Seffy. I'm so, so sorry."

"Don't be sorry," Dr. Smith told her. "You're doing your best, Jetta."

He walked up to the bin. He grabbed Haley's legs and pushed her up over the edge. Her body fell down on top of Jetta, who let out a sound that was more of a whimper than anything else.

I felt the soldier behind me grab hard onto what was basically the outer edges of my ass cheeks, pressing me against the bin. The upside was that he was using his hands, rather than shoving his entire body up against me.

Dr. Smith looped behind me and my heavily-armed chaperone, to Roxana's body. He slowly flipped her into the bin as well, pinning Jetta under two dead women.

I could barely hear the muffled little sounds coming from Jetta.

"Be glad you're not in that bin," Dr. Smith said to me. "Be glad that you're special, and that I like and respect you, Persephone. I promise that I will spare you and Iris if you give me what I want. Do you hear that, Jetta? Make sure Iris knows."

Jetta didn't respond.

I struggled against the soldier who was still holding me.

I felt more of that soldier push against me. The crush, like you'd get from perverts on public transportation. I could feel the sharpness of his... I felt it. Jamming into my bound hands.

He'd wanted me to feel it.

I felt like I could throw up.

"Let her go," Dr. Smith said.

The soldier lingered for a moment, before stepping back.

Dr. Smith came up to me.

He pulled me back from the bin, then turned me around to face him. And gave me another one of his smug smiles.

"I don't know why you're smiling," I said. "Obviously my sister isn't stupid enough to come."

"She's already on her way here," he said.

I glanced around the room.

I couldn't see any sign of her yet.

He guided me over to his chair, feigning a kind of gentle concern as he did it.

I took the seat, since spiting him couldn't outweigh the feeling that my legs would collapse under me.

He'd killed two women in front of me. He would have killed Jetta at the same time, if he hadn't needed her to transmit that message to Iris. And he would have killed me, if he didn't find more value in keeping me alive for the time being.

I didn't sense anything from him. No guilt, but no perverse kind of jollies from it, either. Like he was just going about his workday, slicing off ears and slitting open throats. A sort of detachment, maybe?

That was more frightening to me than the worst looks I'd gotten from Lucas Berg, even more frightening than the primal leer of Corporal Byzzan.

You can understand the base level of sick you see in monsters like Lucas and Byzzan. You know the world is terrible because of them, because they put their own sick urges over everything and everyone else. For guys like them, this infection and everything falling apart is just an opportunity, a chance to take what they'd never be allowed to take in normal life.

But Doctor Isambard Kingdom Smith wasn't succumbing to urges. He wasn't the one pressing his manmeat against my backside, or getting off on knowing just how completely terrified those two girls he has left happen to be.

He wanted me and Iris for our bots and our cure. Apparently, that was it. And it sounded like he was on his way to getting exactly what he wanted.

I sat on the chair, my hands still cuffed behind me, the cut where my ear had been still hurting like a *sonofagoat*; I had no way of knowing if my little bot friends were actually working on rebuilding it, since I had no way of seeing it, and I couldn't exactly reach up to check with my bound hands. I guess I could have scraped my head against my shoulder, but that didn't sound like a particularly pain-free way to get some kind of confirmation.

And I wasn't really the one who mattered.

"You should get Jetta out of that bin," I said. "Please."

"Jetta will be fine," Dr. Smith replied, as he hovered over me.

"She's resilient, like a bamboo shoot."

"You're torturing her for no reason."

"You know I have a reason."

"Please…"

"You already said that, Persephone."

He walked back over to the bin.

He leaned over and looked inside.

"That's a lot of blood," he said. "How you holding up, Jetta?"

Still no response.

"I see you, Mr. Kimmern," Dr. Smith said, stepping around the bin. "Playing possume."

He walked up to Errol.

The soldier watching over Errol took a step away.

Dr. Smith sighed. "You couldn't save those girls. You know that, right? But maybe you can save Persephone."

Errol didn't answer.

But I could tell he was listening.

"Iris is outside," Dr. Smith said. "She needs a little push to come in. Go get her, Errol."

Errol groaned. He took a shallow breath. "Get her… get her yourself."

"So want Persephone to die?"

He turned his head to look up at Smith. "You said you wouldn't kill her. So… were you lying then, or are you lying now?"

"I see you were paying attention," Dr. Smith said.

Errol nodded slowly. "I'll kill you… if it's the last thing I do."

Dr. Smith chuckled. "I'll mark it on my calendar. Along with the other fifty-six instances of the exact same threat. I guess it's like a rite of passage for men. Birth, puberty, threatening the better man who is about to end your sad little life."

"So your word means nothing, Doc," I said. "You keep saying you don't want to kill anyone, and then you go and say the opposite."

Dr. Smith turned back to look at me. "I never promised Errol that he'd live through this. I've only promised you, Persephone. To spare you and Iris."

"And I told you not to hurt Jetta. But you don't seem to care what happens to her."

I saw Dr. Smith get pulled down to the floor.

And then Errol struggling to get up.

The soldier who'd been guarding him was only two steps away.

He threw the butt of his rifle against Errol's head.

Errol fell back. He went down hard, to the concrete. He wasn't moving.

I wanted to take my chance… but I didn't know what the heck I'd even do. So I stayed where I was.

"It's not really me who's deciding this for Mr. Kimmern," Dr. Smith said. "The man will do whatever it takes to get himself killed."

"You've left him no choice," I said.

"He could at least be a little smarter about it."

I saw movement, to my right. To the far side of the slaughter-house.

I didn't look; I didn't want to move my head or give any indication that I'd seen something. Because there was a chance I was the only one who'd noticed.

Noticed that someone had been waiting for a chance to move into position. I hoped.

"What do you really want from us?" I asked, hoping to keep him talking, keep him and his soldiers focused on me. "It doesn't seem like you want a couple of pet girls for various girl-petting activities."

That's what Jetta would have done, right? Turned the attention on… *that stuff.*

"You know why I'm doing this," he said. "It's not some perverted fantasy, Persephone. It's something far grander than that."

"Far grander? What could be grander than a threesome with two hot sisters?"

One of the soldiers chuckled. The one who'd shoved himself up against me.

Dr. Smith shot him a glare.

The soldier nodded, but I could see he was still a little… *afflicted.*

"What about Jetta?" I asked. "You have no thoughts on her? She's…" I tried to remember how I'd put it before. "She's very small and bendy."

A different soldier started laughing outright.

Which got the other three looking to either him or Dr. Smith, to see what would happen next.

There was a gunshot.

From the far side of the building.

I saw the soldier by Errol fall. He'd been the farthest target. And he'd hit the floor, and wasn't moving.

The other soldiers fell back into their training, finding cover and pulling their rifles into position. Two were clumped together behind the rolling bin, while the other hid behind the canvas tent, which was a great screen but not so great of a barrier for bullets.

But I'm not the professional, right?

Dr. Smith ran back over to my chair. And ducked behind it.

"Don't you move from that chair," he said to me.

I felt the blade of the knife poking through the canvas at my back. It took me a minute to realize that he didn't have it high enough to kill me, all things considered.

But I didn't move. I'd decided that staying still was probably a safer option than being a fast-moving blur on everyone's peripherals. Being a human shield for the bad doctor didn't enter into it.

There was gunfire from both sides, the soldiers returning that initial shot with multiple bursts, with the occasional single shot coming from the far end, from the back of the other conveyer track.

I couldn't see who it was.

But I was pretty sure it wasn't Iris. Not just because of the shot she'd had to have made, killing a soldier from across a long room, but because that wasn't how she'd play it. Not the frontal assault.

The three remaining soldiers were well-covered, from what I could see. They stopped shooting in bursts, replacing that with single shots every five seconds or so.

They were taking their time.

If whoever that was had been trying to pin them down, he hadn't really succeeded. The only reason they hadn't advanced past their positions was because they wouldn't need to.

It was just a matter of time before they either got a lucky shot, or the lone gunman ran out of ammo.

There was only one person I thought it could be, assuming this even had anything to do with rescuing the likes of me and Jetta. And I hoped it wasn't that person, because if Iris had sent Lucas in with her *bothot* mind control, it wouldn't take much for Dr. Smith to transmit that update that would disable him.

But maybe if Iris had sent him, there'd be more to the plan.

She wouldn't have expected Lucas to take out four heavily-armed mercenaries on his own, right?

I looked to the other side of the building, to where we'd come in, trying to be as subtle as I could.

I didn't see anyone. Not Iris, and not Anna Louise.

I was surprised that I felt relieved, at first. But I guess I knew deep-down that there was no good reason for Iris to risk her life to save me.

But I did see movement.

Not from the doorway.

From Errol.

He'd taken the other soldier's gun.

I watched as he fired a burst at the soldiers by the bin.

I gasped. Jetta was still in there.

Both soldiers fell.

The other soldier wheeled around for the shot.

Errol fired a second burst toward him.

And missed.

The remaining soldier returned fire.

Errol fell.

I saw the other gunman move out from behind the conveyer.

Lucas.

He took the shot.

The soldier fell.

Lucas started jogging over to the man he'd last hit.

He put a bullet in the soldier's head.

Then he moved on to the other two, and lastly to the one by Errol.

I was still in the chair.

Dr. Smith still had a knife to my back.

But I had no reason to be deftly afraid of him.

I jumped up from the chair.

He tried to stand up.

I kicked him in the chin.

He hit his head on the concrete wall behind him. Not too hard, just enough to daze him. He hadn't even dropped the knife.

"I'm not supposed to kill him," Lucas said.

I turned to see Lucas looking at me. A different kind of Lucas. Not cowed... just... passive. Under Iris' command, apparently.

But I wasn't sure just how strong that command was, or how long it would last.

Lucas Berg wasn't exactly an ally.

"Move away from him, Seffy," he said.

I did, heading back over to the bin.

I looked down, at the bodies and the blood.

I couldn't even be sure which arms and legs belonged to Jetta.

Nothing was moving.

"I need you to help me, Lucas," I said. "We need to get Jetta out of here."

"You... you need to bite them," Errol said, weakly.

I turned to see him.

I couldn't tell which wounds were fresh.

But I knew he'd been hit hard. All over again.

And he hadn't gotten up.

"He's right," Lucas said. "Bite them."

"The soldiers?" I asked.

"Haley," Errol said. "Bite Haley."

I turned back to Lucas. "Help me," I said.

"I need to keep an eye on Smith," he replied. "Sorry."

"Just help me push the bin right over."

He nodded.

We both grabbed the edge of the bin, pulling it toward us.

We couldn't flip it on its side.

Dr. Smith started to get up.

Lucas moved toward him, making sure his gun was pointed where it needed to be.

"I give up," Dr. Smith said.

"He's a liar," I said.

Lucas nodded.

I looked back in the bin. "Jetta," I said, "you really need to help me out here. We need to get these bodies off of you."

No response.

But she couldn't be dead.

There was no way, no chance... Errol had shot those soldiers, he hadn't hit the bin.

No matter what had happened, Jetta's bots should still be there, working.

I looked over at Dr. Smith.

"Yeah, they're disabled," he said. "No *healy-dealy* for Jetta. Not unless you give me a gun and send me on my way."

"I can't let that happen," Lucas said.

"Oh, I'm not done with my shopping list. Persephone comes with me."

Lucas shook his head. And took a step closer to Dr. Smith. "Not a friggin chance. How 'bout I just shoot you in the face?"

That felt like the standard Lucas.

Was Iris still in control?

"Good plan," Dr. Smith said. "I've enabled Jetta's bots. With new instructions. Now they're making sure she dies."

"Is that really something he can do?" Lucas asked me.

"I don't know," I said.

Dr. Smith smiled his stupid smile. "I can do it for Jetta, and for every other infected person in a ten-mile radius. That includes Mommy and Daddy Schmidt, the Kimmerns, and pretty little Anna Louise."

"Then help me pull the girls out," I said. "We pull them out, I bite them, and then you can have me."

"He'll just deactivate Jetta's bots all over again," Lucas said. "Don't be an idiot, Seffy."

"If he does, I'll kill him." I gave my best tough girl look to Dr. Smith. "You get me, Doc?"

Dr. Smith nodded. "I don't have a problem with Jetta walking out of here. Or anyone else, for that matter. I just want Persephone. And if she comes with me, I'll let the others live."

"And what about Iris?" Lucas asked. "You'd wanted her, too, right?"

"What are you doing, Lucas?" I asked.

"So Iris did get the message," Dr. Smith said.

"Loud and clear, douchebag," Lucas said.

"Well, okay… I wanted Iris. But I *need* Persephone. And I'm willing to compromise for the greater good."

Lucas looked over to me.

Like he was waiting on my instructions. Not an ally. More like a flunky.

It felt like a trick to me. But it wasn't like I could do anything about him "snapping out of it". If he turned on me, it wasn't like I had some kind of defense mechanism at the ready.

"Seffy," he said. "I need you to tell me what you want me to do."

"Seriously?" I said.

"Just tell me what to do."

I wondered what Iris had told him to do. I guess I knew what she'd told him, to save me.

But apparently she hadn't *ordered* him to drag me out of there, no matter what.

She might have been leaving the details up to me.

"Here's the deal," I said. "I will go with Doctor Mengele, *after* he helps me get these girls out of the bin. Take Jetta and the others out of here. And make sure Jetta is okay. Then I will help Smith develop his cure, and then *he will let me leave*."

"Or else?" Lucas said.

"Or else you guys will come back," I said. "Looks to me like he doesn't have his private army anymore."

"He could have more men."

"I don't," Dr. Smith said. "All I've got now is the bots. Which should be enough."

"This is a bad idea," Lucas said.

"It'll be okay," I said. I looked to Dr. Smith. "Help me get them out of the bin. Doc."

He nodded.

I held my wrists out behind me. Apparently entrusting my spine and spleen to the man who'd had no qualms cutting body parts right off of me.

He cut the plasticuffs off with the knife, then dropped the blade onto the floor.

Lucas kept his gun pointed, as Dr. Smith made his way over to the bin.

I grabbed what I was pretty sure were Dr. Jones' arms, while Dr. Smith found the corresponding legs.

We lifted her out and lay her on the concrete floor.

I brought my mouth down to Roxana's open throat.

She was cold. She wasn't even bleeding anymore, not like before; there was blood, but nothing left to pump it out of her. A stream of it just dribbled out. I'd never seen that.

Her brain would have suffocated to death, at least ten minutes before.

But I bit down anyway, tasting that same horrible taste of rust and terrible sushi.

She was so cold.

And that didn't change once I'd bitten her.

So I pulled back.

I needed to get Haley out of there.

But I felt sick.

My stomach was rolling.

My throat was gagging.

I took a few steps away from Roxana Jones' body.

And I puked my frickin guts out.

I tried to recover as quickly as I could.

I still felt like complete crap, but I had to get Jetta out of there. And I still needed to try it on Haley, even if biting down on Roxana had been a complete waste of time.

With Dr. Jones out of the bin, I could see Jetta's face.

Her eyes were closed.

But I thought I could see her chest moving. That Jetta was still breathing.

I grabbed Haley's arms.

Dr. Smith yanked on her legs.

We pulled her out and set her down beside Roxana's body.

I bit into Haley's lifeless neck.

And then I held down the sickness and reached in for Jetta.

"I expect you to honor this deal," Dr. Smith said, his arms crossed over his chest.

"Help me or I'll end you," I said.

He took a hold of Jetta's ankles.

And we pulled her out.

I knelt down next to her.

She *was* breathing. But she was unconscious.

I wasn't sure why, but I really wanted to believe that she'd passed out from some mix of shock and exhaustion. And I knew she still had the bots, and Dr. Smith's life depended on those little bots getting back to work.

I looked over to him. "She dies and you die," I said.

"I know."

"So how do we get them out of here?" Lucas asked me. "There's only one of me. Your boyfriend's not going to be much help."

"Don't let Iris come in here," I told him.

"As if that's up to me."

The door to the left opened. Closest to us.

Iris and Anna Louise walked in. Iris had a hunting rifle on her shoulder.

"You need to go," I said to Iris. "Go now."

"We made a deal," Dr. Smith said.

"Yeah, you made a deal," Iris said. "A crappy one, Seff, but it's a deal."

I knew she hadn't had anything better to put forward. Not unless she was willing to call the bad doctor's bluff.

I watched as they helped Errol up.

He was limping, and his wounds didn't seem to have closed, but he'd convinced himself that he could walk out of there.

Anna Louise took Jetta, throwing her up over her shoulders with an ease that I hadn't expected.

"Significant pub crawl experience," she said. She wiped away some tears from her face.

Iris tried to lift Haley, but couldn't seem to swing it.

"I don't want to leave her," she said.

"You don't need to leave her," I said. I turned back to Dr. Smith. "Tell them where the other prisoners are. My father and the rest."

"The pig barns," Dr. Smith said. "Out by the sewage lagoons, west side of the colony. With all the other infected."

"We'll go," Iris said, motioning to Anna Louise.

Anna Louise nodded.

"What about Lucas?" I asked. "Is he...?"

"Lucas is fine," Iris said. "Don't worry so much."

I saw that Errol had started limping toward Haley's body. I didn't tell him to stop.

"Take a bigger gun," Lucas said.

"This is fine," Iris said.

"I'll take one," Anna Louise said.

She walked over to one of the dead soldiers near the bin.

She picked up an automatic rifle.

"Iris," I said, "don't leave Lucas here... with a gun..."

"It's fine," Iris said. "Really."

Iris left the barn, Anna Louise following behind.

They hadn't actually waited for me to agree to the plan.

"We don't need to keep him alive," Lucas said to me, while motioning to Dr. Smith.

"No, you do," Dr. Smith replied. "Maybe I didn't make it clear. I've already sealed this deal. The infected in that pig barn will die if I don't change their instructions."

Lucas scoffed. "He's lying."

"We just stick to the deal," I said. "No need to improvise here."

I watched as Errol gently lowered himself down beside Haley. He didn't reach for her, he just stared at the blank expression on her face. Or maybe at the bloody slit across her throat.

I didn't want to think about that.

I was still kneeling next to Jetta, gripping one of her hands and trying to not start crying.

It was too much, all of it.

And while the crap wouldn't end for me, maybe we'd done something to save most of the people there.

I wanted to believe that.

I heard a moan.

It wasn't from Jetta.

I saw movement from where we'd left Roxana Jones.

"She's alive," Lucas said. "You see that?"

I hobbled over on my knees.

I put my hand on her forehead.

She was warm to the touch.

"Dr. Jones," I said. "*Roxana*. Can you hear me?"

Another moan. A little louder, maybe.

"Can you understand what I'm saying? Do you think you can open your eyes?"

And she did. Both eyes. And looked up at me.

And then she gave me a weak smile.

She started moving her right hand. She ran it over her throat, to where a scab had developed over what had been a deep gash. It had already begun to heal.

"You saved me," she said. "I didn't think you'd get to me in time."

"I didn't," I said. "You were dead."

"I've got a terrible headache. But I'm pretty sure I'm not dead."

"I didn't think it would work. I really thought your brain was too far gone."

"I can't believe it, either," she said.

"She's not healing," Errol said.

I looked over to him and Haley.

He had a hand on Haley's neck, where she'd been cut. "Why isn't she healing?"

"I don't know, Errol," I said.

"You took too long," he told me. "You should have bitten her first."

"We don't know that."

"She died first, Persephone. You should have helped her first. Instead you helped some bitch who didn't deserve to live."

Roxana didn't respond to that.

She was looking away from us, toward Dr. Smith.

"I'm sorry, Errol," I said. "She was just… just too far gone."

"This is your fault," he said, shaking his head at me. "You did this to her."

"No," Roxana said, quietly. "*He* did it to her." She was pointing her finger at Dr. Smith, who'd found his way back to the infamous director's chair.

"I know I'm going to kill *him*," Errol said. "But I swear to god… I wish I could kill you, Seffy."

I gasped.

I couldn't effing believe him.

He'd just met Haley; he'd known me for over ten years. He'd been halfway in love with me for most of them. But I was the easy target, wasn't I? The closest to strike out at, the easiest one to hurt.

And I knew there was a chance he was right. That if I'd bitten Haley first, before I'd puked my insides out, maybe she would have made it. Maybe there would have been enough brain left for the bots to repair.

Maybe… or maybe not. Maybe both she and Roxana would be dead. Would that be any better?

I made my way back to Jetta.

I ran a hand along her cheek.

"Please," I whispered. "Wake up."

I started to cry.

"It's not your fault, Seffy," Roxana said. "You did everything you could."

"She's not dead," I said. "She's breathing."

"I know."

But I knew what she was thinking. That breathing or not, that Jetta just might not wake up. That somehow or other she'd passed some point of no return. I knew she was thinking that, because I was trying so effing hard not to think it, too.

"Please, Jetta," I said, running my hand through her hair.

She opened her eyes. Just a little.

"Oh my god," I said.

"Is this where you're going to try and kiss me?" she asked.

I started laughing.

"What the hell is wrong with you?" Errol said, shouting at me. "This is all funny to you somehow?"

I didn't answer.

I couldn't worry about him.

I just had to be thankful that Jetta had woken up.

14

OH SO PRECIOUS CARGO

I was numb when I saw my father and Beth walk into the slaughterhouse, from the door at the back. Numb like I'd exhausted myself to the point where I couldn't feel anything new.

I was sitting on the floor beside Jetta, who was still lying down. Roxana was there as well, already sitting up with me.

Beth didn't get much past the door. She looked at me, smiled, then looked down at her feet.

Too much death for her. I understand that. I wish I had that kind of luxury. That kind of detachment from all of this.

Dad came over to see me.

He even smiled at Jetta.

I stood up and gave him a hug.

"Thank you, Seffy," he said. "I love you so much."

"I love you," I said.

Dad turned to look at Dr. Smith.

"Yes, I know you hate me," Dr. Smith said.

"It's gone past that," Dad replied. "I won't rest until I see you dead."

"I don't need that, Dad," I said. "I just need you to help get everyone out of here. Okay?"

He looked at me.

Then at Lucas and his big gun.

Then back at Dr. Smith.

I knew my father was fighting as hard as he could to keep from killing Smith. And probably wondering why Lucas hadn't already taken care of the task.

I had a feeling Dad didn't know about my deal.

If anyone were to tell him, Dr. Smith would have no chance of leaving that barn alive, no matter how much control he thought he could muster over my dad. If there's an ounce of fight in my father, it would be enough to end things.

"There are over a hundred infected people still locked up in that pig barn," Dad told me. "We'll need to cure them all. When you're ready, Seffy." He turned to Errol. "Did you want to bury your friend?"

Errol nodded.

And the two of them carried Haley out the far door, Beth following out behind.

I could see Dan and Pat Kimmern look in through the entryway, before following behind Errol. There were others out there, Hutterite men among them. They hadn't all been killed and dumped in a ditch.

I wondered if Claudia's father and brothers were among the survivors.

Leona came in, not long after Haley was brought out. She rushed to Jetta's side.

She gave me a nod. "Thank you, Seffy," she said.

"We need to go, Persephone," Dr. Smith said.

"What the heck?" Leona said.

"You can't go with him," Roxana said. "You know what will happen."

Dr. Smith groaned. "Forget the people in the pig barn... I can kill most of the people in this room. Jetta, Errol, the farmboy with the gun... all without speaking a word."

"I don't believe that," Leona said.

"Persephone needs to come with me. Don't make me demonstrate how this works. Don't make me kill you, Leona."

Leona scoffed. "You can try."

"I'm going with him," I said. "I'm helping him with the cure."

"It shouldn't take long," Dr. Smith said. "A few days, if fortune smiles on us."

He stood up from his folding chair.

He walked up to me and held out his hand.

I rolled my eyes at him.

He started walking toward the door to our left, not a surprising choice in direction, as it was the opposite side of where Lucas and his automatic rifle happened to be. Not to mention a very angry bunch of Kimmerns just past the door.

I followed him, as per the deal.

He led me outside — where it was still a little before sunrise — and over to a garage.

To where a black pickup truck was parked.

"My ride," he said. "Heated leather seats, and a nice big box of portable lab equipment in the back."

He led me to the passenger side door. He opened it and waved me in.

Once I'd sat down, he walked around to the back.

He pulled a series of bungee cords out, bringing them back to where I was sitting.

"You don't need to restrain me," I said. "We have a deal."

"We're not staying here," he said. "So you can understand my need for making sure you don't renege the moment my leverage has disappeared."

He wasn't really looking for my permission, obviously, but I guess I gave it by not fighting as he wrapped four bungee cords around my body, strapping me to the seat. My wrists were bound at my sides with their own little loops on one length of cord that wrapped around the back of the chair, while he used another wrapping up my ankles and pinning them back to the underside of the seat. The last two cords were more general wrapping, one wrapped tightly twice around my hips, the other wrapped one and little more loosely, directly under my breasts.

At one point he accidentally brushed up against my left nipple. He gave me a very embarrassed frown, then quietly apologized.

Once I was all strapped in, he buckled my seatbelt — probably as much for an extra layer of restraint as for safety — and made his way over to the driver's side.

He started the engine and started driving, reaching a rather hazardous speed of fifty miles per hour. I saw why, as we drove by not only the Kimmerns and my Dad, apparently futzing with a bobcat instead of just using shovels, but also a group of Hutterite women who recognized Dr. Smith as he passed, and not with anything close to friendly smiles.

"They aren't my biggest boosters," he said with a smirk.

"You killed their husbands and fathers," I said.

He nodded.

I could have been convinced, from the look on his face, that he felt a little bit of remorse, not that I cared to find it.

It didn't matter anyway; I had to focus on what would.

"So how does it work?" I asked him. "The subvocalizations."

"They only work for me," he replied. "Couple of implants in my throat. If you look closely you can see the little pockmarks. It's much pickier than you'd expect, actually. There's a reason it hasn't reached market yet." He pulled onto the mile road, heading south. He looked over at me. "You can't use it... there's no way to take it over from me."

"I didn't think so."

"I know... you had to ask."

I sighed. "I'm not going to try anything," I said. "Not unless you change your end of it."

"I need to know exactly how you did it, Persephone."

"Don't you already know? It's pretty straightforward. First you blast the bots, then you kill the parasites with the experimental treatment. Once that's done, you need something to repair the damage those little protozoans have done to the brain. So you inject some brand new bots. If that treatment went well, and those bots are good enough, they'll learn from your newly-healed body how to keep that cat-poop parasite out for good."

"That's how it went with Iris," he said. "Not you."

"Then I took the bots from Iris and stuck them in me."

"Don't lie to me."

"I'm not lying. That's what happened."

He shook his head. "If that's true, I should be cured already."

"What are you talking about?"

"I already injected myself with your blood."

"What? When?"

"Roxana had drawn some when she'd had you," he said. "When I found out that she was hiding you from me, I found the sample."

"Must have been too old, I guess."

"Bots don't just disappear, Persephone. If you're telling the truth, it should have worked."

"I bite people all the time," I said. "None of them are like Iris and me."

"How many did Iris bite?"

"I don't know."

"Then think about it for a minute," he said.

I shook my head. "That's not it, Doc. I think it's the number of bots they have already. Did you have any bots in your system?"

"No. I've never had botshots. And I was never infected."

"You'd be about the only one to go through this process. Just you and me. And it worked on me."

"You're still lying to me. We had a deal, Persephone."

He'd reached the paved highway. The one to Fargo.

He stopped the truck.

"You don't need to take my word for it," I said. "You can run tests, experiment on me…"

"I know."

"You don't need to kill me."

"Just be quiet for a moment, would you? I need to think."

I did what any helpless captive bungee corded to a truck seat would do. I shut my pretty little mouth and let the man think, because I knew that the chance of me not dying in the next few minutes would get higher if the man thought things through.

That it made sense to keep me alive.

After two to three minutes, he started driving again. He turned right, heading West. Back toward home.

"Where are we going?" I asked.

"Some kind of clean space," he said. "So we can do this properly."

"Do what properly?"

"I don't know, Persephone. Since you're lying to me. I hope I don't end up having to go all Unit 731 on you."

"What?"

"I'll strap you down to a goddamn table and vivisect you if I have to. I really thought you understood that about me."

"I'm not lying," I said.

I wasn't sure what else I could say to convince him.

I didn't know what else I could do.

At least I still had some value to him.

"I should have taken Iris," he said. "But you knew that, didn't you…"

I didn't answer.

He slammed his hand hard against the left side of my head, whipping my head against the side window.

"It won't work," he said. "I'll figure it out, Persephone. Those bots are in you, just like they're in Iris. It might take me longer, but I'll get my cure."

"I'm not trying to trick you. You need to believe me."

He glared at me. "This will go better if you don't talk."

I could see my face in the side mirror, or at least the side of my face that had lost an ear an hour or so before.

The bots had been working overtime, converting I don't know what into new cartilage. I'd read a few months ago — before all this grot happened — that bots tended to reorganize cell tissue more than grow from scratch, since growing from scratch would require exactly the kind of intensive input that had made the original infection overwhelm its human host. Maybe the bots were taking it from my stomach fat; I still had more of that then I wanted to preserve for posterity.

So far, my ear looked terrible, maybe a quarter of its regular size and exactly like what you'd get if you had Pablo Picasso paint a cubist block of cheese, but at least I knew it would come back all the way, in time.

Maybe just in time for an angry Dr. Smith to slice it off all again.

He turned off the highway to Fargo just before the edge of the bedroom town of Dilworth, heading north on County 11.

I didn't know of any places up County 11, not that I'm that well-acquainted with anything on this side of the river. Minnesotans come to North Dakota because they have to, for work and shopping, or just to reach I-29. The only time I ever go to Minnesota is if I'm heading to Mall of America or to a concert in downtown Minneapolis; and let's face it, I never do either.

I guess the only time I'm ever in Minnesota is to be plasticuffed and threatened and strapped to truck seats with bungee cords.

Not really anything you'll see on the tourism billboards. Not unless they've started to appeal to a much more niche type of demographic.

"There's a church up here," Dr. Smith told me. I wasn't sure why he'd felt the urge to do that. Evil villains usually like to keep a little bit of mystery in the air, don't they?

"You're taking me to a church?" I asked. "That's your 'clean space'?"

"I just need a clean kitchen. And Lutheran churches tend to have off-the-grid power because of that churchy environmental campaign they had a few years back."

"You sound like you know a lot about it."

"I grew up Lutheran," he said.

"Before switching to Satan?"

He chuckled. Apparently he wasn't angry anymore.

The way he'd switched that rage on and off again was probably the scariest thing about him. It left me feeling that it had all been calculated, like he was pushing me toward something.

Grooming me to do what he needed.

"I think I've figured it out," he said.

"How to lower your water bill?"

"I've got the bots."

"I know," I said. "You'd said you injected yourself with Seffy blood."

"No... I had bots before that. A low-level infection, I'm thinking. Not enough to turn me, but enough to mess with the cure."

"I don't think that's it."

I had no idea, really, but I felt like I ought to discourage him either way. Even at the risk of another shove into the passenger-side window.

"You had no bots, Persephone. Before you injected those experimental ones. Is that correct?"

"Yeah. No bots. But you'd think the new and improved bots would override the old ones if they could."

"But they weren't meant for subjects with existing bots," he said.

Subjects. Calling patients "subjects" says a lot about a man.

"If you had the bots," I said, "you should have been infected. That's pretty much how it works, Doc."

"If I was bitten or injected."

"Either or, yeah."

"What about other forms of transmission?"

"Other forms? Like toilet seats?"

"Don't try and be cute, Persephone. You know what I mean."

"Not really," I said. "Maybe just come out and say it. Don't be shy."

"I had sex with an infected woman," he said.

"And I'm sure it was a hundred percent consensual. Like all your experiments."

"I told you to stop being cute."

"Screw you, Doc."

"You want me to hit you again?"

Not really.

So I took a breath and tried to be civil. To the man who'd wrapped me in bungee cords, some of which were really starting to hurt at the ends, scratching against the skin on my wrists.

"Was it unprotected sex?" I asked him.

"Yes."

"What kind of sex?"

"Excuse me?"

"Different parasites are transmitted in different ways," I said.

"And you would know all about the transmission of this particular mutated parasite?"

"We both know *t. gondii* doesn't transmit from human to human. But this bot-loving form of it does."

"Because of the bots," he said. "Obviously I know that."

"I know you know that. You're a real doctor and everything."

He raised an eyebrow at me. "I wonder if unprotected sex with you would help."

"I honestly see no reason to help you at all," I said. "You tied me up, you hit me, and now you're threatening to rape me."

"I was trying to be cute."

I groaned. "I really hope you die soon."

⊷

We reached the church, a somewhat odd mix of a squat stone-fronted workshed-style thing, in front of the more traditional wooden steeple that adjoined it. There was a good-sized cemetery around the church, looking out on the trees that clumped along the Buffalo River. We'd passed by a church along the Buffalo a few days before, but this wasn't it.

Dr. Smith pulled onto the gravel drive and backed in diagonally to park, facing both the road and the entrance to the church.

"You can't see the back of the church," I said. "Whoever you're worried about could sneak up that way."

"We're meeting someone," he said. "I'm not scared of anyone."

I rolled my eyes. "Don't be cute."

It was starting to be our little thing, he and I. Our go-to expression of mutual distrust.

"Can you at least untie me?" I asked. "I mean, if we're just going to be sitting here…"

"It could be a while. Just power through it, Persephone."

"At least loosen these things up a little."

He smirked. "Don't be a princess about it."

He was tapping his hands on the steering wheel, about as cloyingly annoying a sound as a person could make without a nearby chalkboard.

"If you're waiting for someone to bring the keys for the front door," I said, "I can just go out and find us a big rock."

He sighed. "I really wish you'd take a step back and just think about things."

"I'm willing to pay the church for a new window."

"You ever think about what happens when you pass out?"

"Like from peach schnapps, or from douchebag doctors shoving drugs into your arm?"

"Your body keeps on," he said. "Your heart keeps pumping, your lungs keep breathing… if you were in a coma, and a man climbed on top of you, you could get pregnant and even deliver the child without waking up. Of course, we'd probably use some drugs to induce labor and loosen up your muscles…"

"What the *eff* are you talking about? Is this some lame attempt to shock me?"

"I'm trying to illustrate a point."

"Try harder, because all you're doing is sounding like a frickin psychopath."

"All I want to do is supplement those autonomic functions. When you think about it that way—"

"I don't think about it that way," I said.

He leaned in to me. To *illustrate*, I guess. "A misunderstood teen's body could keep her from becoming so depressed that she'd attempt suicide. An abusive man's body could prevent him from assaulting his wife, whenever he loses his temper. The president's body could keep him from starting another unjust war."

"Not bodies, Doc. It would be your mind control that did all that. The world would just be you and eight billion robots."

"You're on the wrong side of this, Persephone. I wish you'd just think about that."

"One of your soldiers was going to rape me," I said. "And I wasn't even in a coma, which, apparently, is your preference. But that's not as bad as all of the men your mercenaries murdered and dumped in a ditch, *on your orders*. Or the young woman you butchered in front of me, just so you could place a personal call at work. So maybe it would be easier for me to stop and think about your pompous and self-serving idea if you didn't have so much blood on your hands."

He nodded. "It's not an easy concept to understand."

I shook my head. That was about all the movement I could muster.

"No, it's a pretty simple concept," I told him. "You've just gone about it in the worst possible way. Even if I agreed with you, I'd still want you to fail."

He chuckled.

I hadn't wanted to make him chuckle.

The tapping on the steering wheel got louder and more frenzied as the time dragged on. Over an hour of sitting outside the church. Listening to the constant noise and, of course, being strapped to the seat. It made me wish my little bots had given my body some kind of self-destruct mechanism.

Dr. Smith had started darting his head around like an owl, trying to see from all directions. He really was nervous about something.

And then I found out what he was nervous about.

A van, coming up the mile road, from the east. I knew the van, since there weren't many vehicles that were still able to operate at all.

"Was there any point in running from them in the first place?" I asked. "Since you've now told them where we are."

"Just shut up and let me handle this."

That felt like the opening preliminaries for another whack.

So I shut up. Because I was still strapped in tight with bungee cords, like you would to a piece of gently-used furniture from an estate sale.

And they don't get more gently-used than a girl like me.

The van pulled into the parking lot.

Errol was driving.

He parked right next to us, with maybe ten feet between the doors.

"He came because of you," Dr. Smith said. "Not that you appreciate the loyalty. You barely notice he exists most of the time."

"How is that your business?" I asked him.

"Do you think he still blames you for Haley?"

"He blames *you* for Haley. I remember him saying he was going to kill you."

"It's really hard for me to keep track," he said.

"Why did you bring him here?"

"Because I knew I'd need to know more about how you were cured."

"I thought I was supposed to tell you that," I said.

"We both know you don't want me to succeed."

"And Errol does?"

"Mr. Kimmern knows what will happen to you if I don't. And that apparently matters to him much more than it matters to you."

I looked out my window. Errol was staring at us. At Dr. Smith more than me.

He hadn't gotten out of the van.

"Oh," Dr. Smith said. "Just a tick. I've got something to handle."

It wasn't long before Errol opened the van door and climbed out.

"You just sent him some kind of command for that?" I said. "To get out of the frickin van?"

"No time for standoffs."

"It's not a standoff if you're in complete control."

He grinned. "I know, right?"

Errol walked to the back of the van.

I saw Dr. Smith's eyes widen.

"Maybe it's not all under your control," I said.

"Seriously. Just shut up."

Errol opened the back door.

He started pulling on something.

Dr. Roxana Jones fell out the back of the van, landing roughly on the gravel. I could see from the duct tape wrapped around her body — her wrists bound, her arms pinned to her torn cocktail dress, her feet taped together into a one giant silver bootie — that she hadn't had much of a chance to brace herself, assuming she was even conscious; I wasn't sure if she'd been knocked out somehow. It wouldn't have been hard to find some knock-out drugs in the barnyard lab of horrors.

I heard Dr. Smith exhale.

He opened his door and hopped out.

"I didn't tell you to bring her," Dr. Smith said.

"I thought you'd want to finish her off," Errol said. "And I'm pretty sure no one else wants to keep her around."

I wanted to shout out to Errol, about what a complete prick he was being, about how the slim chance of me overlooking his considerable failings as a person was now officially dead.

But that wouldn't do anything for me, or for Dr. Roxana Jones. Maybe I ought to hate her as much as Errol seems to, for being a part of the experiments, for treating me and my friends like lab rats, for letting Byzzan get a hold of me...

I think the difference between me and people who spend their time hating is that I still remember how to pity the many declawed toolbags of the world, to remember that the worst punishment they can have, for all they've done, is to continue being themselves.

Once Dr. Smith is brought down a couple hundred pegs, I won't sit around hating him, either. But I do think it's best if he's lying dead in a water-logged ditch somewhere at the end of it. Or a deep metal bin in a Hutterite slaughterhouse.

Errol walked over to the passenger door of the truck.

He opened my door.

"Are you okay?" he asked me. I could hear the concern, but there was more there, not anger, but... *begrudgingness*? Is that even a word?

"I'm okay," I said.

"I'm going to get you out of here."

"Like right now? Like you can take off these stupid bungee cords?"

He nodded.

And started by undoing the seatbelt.

He kept glancing up at me as he bent in and unwrapped the cords.

I waited until he'd freed my hands before I said anything.

"What is it?" I asked.

"You haven't said 'thank you'," he said.

"Uh, okay…"

"I'm serious."

"Is this really the time or place, Errol?"

"I'm risking my life for you," he said.

"Can you be mad at me later?"

He sighed and shook his head.

He then looked down at the bulge in the pocket of my latest stolen pair of pants.

He reached in.

"What do you think you're doing?" I asked him, with about as much hate as I could stuff into the words.

"This doesn't belong to you," he said as he took Jetta's pink tablet out of my pocket.

He stuffed it into his pants, with no apparent sense of irony.

Then he pulled a roll of duct tape out of his pocket.

"That's not happening," I said.

"It has to."

"I'm not kidding, Errol."

He grabbed my right hand.

I pulled it away.

I'm not sure I'd have been able to that normally; I assumed he was still weak from being shot up at the slaughterhouse. You know, twice.

"I'll tape your hands in front of you," he said. "It won't be that bad."

"No, Errol."

I saw Dr. Smith coming up fast in the side mirror. "We will hold you down, Persephone," he said. "You *will* be restrained. For everyone's safety."

"Please," Errol whispered to me.

I put both of my hands in front of me.

He wrapped several layers of tape around them.

And then he stepped away from the truck.

He hadn't offered me his hand to get out, so I slowly climbed out on my own.

By the time I'd done that, Errol had already gone back to where he'd left Roxana lying on the gravel.

Dr. Smith was still standing by the truck, waiting for me.

"So what's stopping me from just running away?" I asked him.

"Because I left my gun in the truck," he said.

"Yeah."

I thought about making a grab for it.

But something held me back.

Nothing like subvocalized commands from a jerkoff... just my duct taped wrists, along with a sense that it wouldn't be the smartest idea.

I knew it wasn't a good plan to underestimate the man in the Hawaiian scrubs. He hadn't won Iris back at the slaughterhouse, but he had managed to get away from the colony with me as his prisoner. It was all at the cost of four mercenaries, six if you counted Magden and Byzzan.

And now he was out here with me and Errol and Dr. Jones. And Errol seemed to be under his control, at least for the parts that counted; I'm pretty sure the brooding disgust Errol was throwing at me was perfectly sincere... you know, from the heart.

Dr. Smith wouldn't need us once he'd found a way to inoculate himself. He'd get rid of me, for sure, and Iris if he could, and then he'd just hide out in his own little prairie kingdom, waiting for the infection to spread to every person who ever wronged him.

And then he'd call all the shots, and he'd tell himself it's best for everyone, when what he really means is that it's best for him.

And he probably won't ever feel bad for the people he killed.

Or his glaring lack of succession planning.

It's that part that worried me the most, not the succession planning, but the general lack of remorse, because I've been alive just long enough to know that people like Isambard Kingdom Smith are *exactly* the people who win out in the end.

Errol would give him precisely what he wanted, all in the name of saving me, because even if he was as angry as he'd ever been with me, he'd still convinced himself that he was in love with me, no matter what... and all that because I was the first girl who'd spent any time with him.

Not "love" for any real reason.

Maybe it wouldn't all suck so much if Errol wasn't just fooling himself into giving up the whole planet to save me. Letting Dr. Smith win because I gave him a Valentine's Day card in grade eight, just like

I gave to everyone else in Mr. Simon's homeroom.

There was no way I could let that be the reason for the end of human civilization. All because I'd gone to Dollar Tree for a cheap chocolate bar in early February of 2020 and bought a pack of V-Day cards on a whim.

But I wasn't sure how I could stop Dr. Smith.

I wasn't sure it was something I had the power to do.

I knew the answer — the real cure — he was looking for was probably somewhere inside me, a way for him to harden himself against other bots, his or anyone else's. Even if I'd had a cyanide capsule hidden in my tooth and/or butt crack, that wouldn't have stopped Dr. Smith from getting my bots. Heck, he already had some of my bots. If that was all he needed, then I was just a possible shortcut, a tool to get him to that answer a little bit faster.

I started to wonder if this had been his plan from the start, to have his soldiers dealt with by outside forces, to feign interest in Iris so he could convince everyone to let him take me.

But maybe I was giving him too much credit.

I honestly didn't know.

While I'd quietly pondered my middle school missteps, Errol had helped a slowly rousing Roxana up from the ground, not really in a gentle or friendly way, and then he'd abruptly shoved her in the general direction of the front door to the church.

She fell once, still half-dazed.

He didn't help her up for a second time, so she slowly lifted herself up to her feet and kept stumbling toward the church.

I could tell he was planning the same kind of treatment for me.

"Don't touch me," I said. "Don't you frickin dare."

He waved his hand toward the church. "Then just get in there, alright?"

I shook my head at him, like I was such a tough opponent... but then I started walking to the front door.

15

SPREADING THE HATE

There was a kitchen in the basement of the church, separated by a long half-wall from the large empty space beside it, a space that could be used for a dining hall or a small gymnasium, depending on the audience.

For Dr. Isambard Kingdom Smith and Errol Kimmern, it was the perfect place to stow two duct taped women, Errol affixing us both to our own metal chair, while Dr. Smith was busy in the kitchen, unloading his large plastic crate of medical supplies that he'd lifted out from the back of his truck.

Roxana was still winning the contest for who had more duct tape, her legs and feet not far off from a shiny mermaid tail, but by the time Errol was done taping me, I knew I wouldn't be working my way free in the short term. My hands were still taped in front, but since they were now wrapped tightly against my chest with at least a half dozen layers of the silver stuff, I'd once again been rendered completely unable to scratch my nose.

So naturally, I could feel it beginning to itch.

Once he'd secured us, Errol took a third chair and sat down beside me.

Dr. Smith rolled a large whiteboard out to face us.

There was a cute drawing in blue marker on it, of an Easter Bunny and what was probably the Baby Jesus. He grabbed the eraser and started clearing it.

"I think that's a thousand years' bad luck," I said.

He turned and gave me a frown. I preferred it, compared to his near-constant smirk. "I need you to be honest with me, Persephone. About the cure."

"You don't honestly still think I'm lying…"

"It doesn't make sense," he said.

"Then you should have kept it in your pants."

"What are you talking about?" Roxana asked.

"We're debating whether or not I had pre-existing bots," Dr. Smith said. "When I injected her blood."

Roxanna sighed. "You've already explained it, Smith."

"Enlighten me."

"You injected Seffy's blood. Not her bots."

"There are bots in her blood," he said. "Are you forgetting that? When you wanted to hide that from me?"

"A vial of blood with some bots inside is a far cry from a pure botshot."

"But Persephone was injected with Iris' blood," Errol said.

"You don't need to help," I told him.

"Is that true?" Dr. Smith asked me. "That it was her blood and not her bots?"

I didn't give an answer.

He walked up to me.

I looked over at Errol.

He was still sitting comfortably in his chair, no duct tape required.

"You'd better answer me," Dr. Smith said.

"Or what?" I asked.

I knew he didn't have an answer.

Sure, he could cut my ear off again; I had already started to expect that it would happen again at some point, because it wasn't like it had been a particularly lucky day for me so far. Or he could torture me in other ways, or he could torture Roxana and make me watch.

But just threatening me wouldn't make it happen.

He'd have to take the time and effort to actually do something. And there was no guarantee that the answers he'd get would be anything close to the truth.

He looked over to Errol.

"I already told you," Errol said. "Iris' blood was enough for Persephone. She never injected the bots into herself directly. I was there when she found the vial."

"So it worked for her," Dr. Smith said, "but it hasn't worked for me."

"Then try again," Roxana said.

I didn't understand what Roxana was doing, why she seemed to be trying to help him. Did she honestly think he was going to cut her free after he was done? She was almost as big a roadblock for him as Iris and I happened to be. There was no way he'd risk her running off and passing on what she knew, or what she'd seen him do.

Maybe she was trying to string him along... but that seemed to me like a waste of time. She'd probably be taped to that chair until her last breath, and after that happened, it wasn't like I'd be getting a second chance to bring her back. Because there was a strong chance I'd die taped to my chair, too.

Dr. Smith walked over to the kitchen. He came back after a few seconds with a large clump of plastic bags, each filled with various translucent bits.

"Blood donor kits," he said. "FEMA always has a crapload of these things on hand."

He walked over to me and my chair.

"Too much tape," he said.

He went back to the kitchen, returning with a pair of scissors.

He cut some of the tape away from my arms, opening up almost all of the skin between my wrists and elbows.

He knelt down beside me and started opening the first baggie.

He started with the needle.

"Make a fist," he said. "I'm hoping this will hurt."

The smirk was back, in full bloom.

I made the fist, because I didn't like the alternative.

He stuck the needle into the pit of my elbow.

"You should have taken Iris," Roxana said. "She's the source of the cure."

"Iris isn't some magical elixir," Dr. Smith said, as he attached the tube and collection bag to the syringe in my arm. "Maybe she was more efficient, but maybe it's just that the injection site on Iris still had a higher concentration of bots. They hadn't had time to spread out. I'm starting to believe that I can give myself enough of Persephone's blood to inoculate myself."

"Like old-fashioned blood doping. Is that safe?"

"Should be safe for me," Dr. Smith said.

"And what about Seffy?"

"I'll take two units to start. She should recover almost immediately from that."

Two units. I was pretty sure that was twice the recommended donation amount. But he was right, it probably wouldn't be too dangerous for a *bothot* girl like me.

"You have four kits there," Roxana said. "Enough for four units."

"I'll be taking more to store. Gradually."

"Four units could kill her," Roxana said, looking at Errol.

Errol stood up from his chair.

"Sit back down," Dr. Smith said.

Errol didn't at first, but then he did.

Probably another subvocal command.

I wondered if he'd even chosen to come there at all. After what had happened to Haley, I hadn't expected him to want to spend a lot of time with me.

Not that he'd want to watch me die.

There's something unsettling about having a buttload of blood drawn from your body. It's uncomfortable, but only a little, and you don't feel like you're losing a lot, not as long as you're still just sitting in that chair. And since I was still wrapped in multiple layers of duct tape, getting up too quick didn't seem like a particular worry for me.

Roxana and Errol were both just sitting there, watching me, dumb looks on their faces. I thought it might be nice to pass the time by playing a little mental game, trying to decide which one I now disliked more.

I mean, Roxana was guilty of some pretty awful crimes against humanity, illegal experimentation, those giant bushy eyebrows… but I felt more anger toward Errol.

I knew that probably wasn't fair, if you looked at it rationally, since he'd come there to try and save me. But still, he'd helped Dr. Smith, given him a lead that could bring on the cure.

If that was how it worked. The theory made sense; you inject ten thousand or so magic bots into someone, then grab blood from that same site minutes later, and inject it into someone else, you'll likely a much higher concentration than some bad guy trying the same thing a week later. So he just needed a lot more blood.

But maybe that wasn't it.

I hoped it wasn't.

Not that I could think of another explanation.

It was tempting to think that it was because Iris and I were half-sisters, that it boosted those bots, but that didn't make sense to me. If anything, blood transfusions between blood relatives are riskier than between strangers, and the bots had no genocoding that would have prefered Iris' sister to anyone else.

Unless Iris' bots — and my bots — had developed some kind of inherent genocoding, some... I don't know... some genetic algorithm, the kind that tries to mimic natural selection. Iris has always loved that notion, that there'd be a way to one day have robots who evolved and radiated and differed from each other over time, drifting into becoming some kind of mechanical individuals.

But that was far-fetched.

Too far-fetched.

There wouldn't be some surprise twist in the end, where Dr. Smith discovers that the bots won't flourish without the gift of friendship or true love.

He'd milk me for my blood for a year if he had to, if he felt it was making a difference. I'd be his little blood bank, maybe even duct taped to this chair until I finally became so rank that he'd be forced to find a way to hose me down.

And what would Errol be doing while it happened? Would he just sit in that chair beside me? Would he be the one in charge of force feeding me and changing my adult diaper?

I looked over at him.

He was reading a frickin magazine. Something about Lutherans.

What the hurr *was that about?*

I was being drained out like a hunk of kosher beef cattle, and Errol was checking in on the latest news on the Lutheran World Federation.

Had he forgotten that I was here against my will? That he'd duct taped me to a frickin chair?

Piece of grot.

Frickin toolbag.

Errol Kimmern, you worthless sack of crap.

He looked at me.

And I heard him.

He hadn't spoken, not out loud, but I could hear him.

Like… like Iris had heard Jetta.

All he'd "said" was that he was sorry.

Then show me, Errol. Get up right now and kill him. Kill Dr. Smith.

He didn't answer me.

Or maybe I'd lost that little bit of connection I'd had.

He put the magazine done, slowly and quietly.

He was watching Dr. Smith, who had made his way back into the kitchen, to dig out some equipment from his crate.

I noticed Roxana was watching Errol.

She looked over at me.

I gave her a nod, like you would a co-conspirator. Hoping she'd go along with it, that she wouldn't give us up to her former boss. She'd have to trust us, not just that we'd be capable of pulling something off, but that we didn't hate her enough to just kill her ourselves.

Errol was the one who'd kidnapped her in the first place.

She stared at me for a good ten seconds before returning my nod.

Errol got up off the chair.

He walked toward the kitchen. He didn't have a weapon on him, as far as I knew, not even a knife.

I could see a knife block in the kitchen, black-handled knives poking out the slanted top.

Hopefully he'd have the element of surprise…

Dr. Smith turned around and saw Errol, before he'd even passed through the open doorway. Dr. Smith stepped back, putting some distance between them.

That meant the knife block was now closer to Errol.

I could tell Dr. Smith was trying his best to send out a command, to make Errol go back to his naughty chair.

I tried to do the same, closing my eyes to concentrate… I couldn't *feel* him. Or anyone else. I was just some weird girl with her eyes shut.

So I opened them up again.

In time to see Errol run for the knives.

Dr. Smith was shocked by that, for maybe half a second. He then pulled his own knife from his pocket. The knife he'd used in the slaughterhouse, to slit Haley and Roxana's throats. And to slice off my perfectly good ear.

I hadn't realized he still had it.

Errol had grabbed the thickest handle from the block. A chef's knife. I had no idea if that was any good for hand-to-hand combat, but it was certainly bigger than Dr. Smith's.

"So what, Mr. Kimmern," Dr. Smith said, "we're going to try and swordfight with kitchen utensils?"

"I'll win," Errol said.

Dr. Smith smiled. "I'll make you a deal, Mr. Kimmern. *Errol.* We can share the blood. You can even go first."

"I'm not hungry, thanks."

"A day or two, and we'll have enough for both of us. If won't hurt Persephone. I promise."

"She'll lose too much blood," Roxana called out. "He doesn't care what happens to her, Errol."

"I'm not sure I care," Errol said.

"No," Roxana said. "You care... I know you care about her. So save her life, Errol. Save *your* life, too."

"She thinks you'll let her live," Dr. Smith said. "And maybe you will. It'll be up to you, Errol. You can decide what happens to both of them, to the rest of the world."

"And how would that work, exactly?" Errol asked. "You get the world and stick me with Australia?"

Dr. Smith chuckled. "Like I'm General Zod, and you're Lex Luthor. *Superman II.*"

"Didn't end well for either of them," Roxana said. "You're just delaying the inevitable knife fight. Or Metropolis street brawl."

I had no idea what they were talking about. I'd only seen one Superman movie, Part Two of *Justice League.* I ended up with a crush on Wonder Woman somehow, but that's all I remembered of it.

Errol lunged forward, swiping with the chef's knife.

And Dr. Smith dodged to the left.

The knife struck his shoulder.

Dr. Smith struck back, jabbing the knife into Errol's side, just below his rib cage.

Errol stepped backward, dropping his larger blade, as Dr. Smith pulled his knife out of Errol's body.

Dr. Smith jabbed again, hitting Errol straight on in the gut. He kept jabbing.

"Wait," I said. "We still have a second vial of bots. From the clinic."

"Not true," Dr. Smith said.

Errol grabbed the handle of the knife lodged in his stomach, wrestling with Dr. Smith.

"Bite him," Roxana said.

I wasn't sure Errol had heard her.

But it was a good idea.

"Bite him!" I screamed.

And Errol did, throwing his teeth into Dr. Smith's neck.

Dr. Smith fell against the kitchen counter.

Errol had gotten full control of the knife that had been dicing up his stomach, and he stabbed it hard into Dr. Smith's chest, likely getting him right in the heart.

Errol pushed the bad doctor down to the floor.

He walked back out of the kitchen, bracing his stomach, his face covered in Dr. Smith's blood, and the rest of him dripping with his own.

"So he'll bleed out and die, right?" he asked me.

"I think so," I said.

"Good."

He walked up to Roxana.

I checked to be sure; there was no knife in his hand.

"Don't hurt her," I said.

"I'm not going to hurt her," he said.

He stepped over to me.

He brushed a little tuft of hair away from my forehead.

Then he knelt down and gave it a kiss. The forehead, not the hair.

He walked back to the kitchen.

I waited patiently, all things considered, while he patched himself up from a first aid kit, apparently not content to wait for his bots to handle things.

He came back over to me once he was done.

"Are you going to untie me now?" I asked.

"Bag's almost full," he said, nodding to the collection bag sitting on the floor. "How do I change it?"

"You don't need to change it," I said. "Just cut the tape off me and I'll take the needle out."

"Okay… I can figure this out on my own."

"What?"

He knelt down beside me.

He opened another blood donation kit.

"You've made your point, Errol," I said. "I don't appreciate you like I should. Now cut the frickin tape off me, alright? We'll go for gelato."

"We're going to see this through," he said. "See if it works."

"I don't want to see if it works."

"He's right," Roxana said. "We've gotten this far."

"No," I said. "I don't want to do this."

"It's okay," Errol said. "We'll just try it with the two units of blood. It won't hurt you."

"I said no, Errol." I started pulling on my arm, seeing if I could loosen the needle, but Dr. Smith had taped it in well.

"Don't struggle like that, Seffy," Roxana said. "You don't want to hurt yourself."

"I really don't want you to hurt yourself, Persephone," Errol said.

"Then cut me loose!" I screamed.

He didn't answer me. He was still crouched down on the floor beside me, staring at the catheter and the two collection bags.

Roxana and I both watched as he gingerly swapped out the bag.

"Good job," Roxana said.

Errol nodded as he stood up.

"You know," Roxana continued, "I could help you get your needle in. We could start right now."

"You know I don't trust you," Errol said.

"There's no reason for me to try and hurt you, Errol. You and Seffy are my best chance of getting to Camp Grafton. And we need to get Seffy there, at least. I want to help with that."

He looked over at me.

"I trust her," I said.

I did. For real.

Like her or not, she probably did save my life when she let me leave the colony, and when she'd hidden the news of the cure from Dr. Smith. I guess she'd probably helped save Dad and Jetta and everyone else, too.

And she hadn't wanted Haley to die. I knew she was as upset as the rest of us by that. She was nothing like the outgoing Dr. Smith.

Errol gave me a nod.

Then he started cutting Roxana free of her duct tape.

"You know I'll kill you if you're lying," he said.

"I know," she said. "Thank you."

Errol took a seat back on his old chair.

I watched — because I was still taped and unable to do anything else — as Roxana prepared Errol for his transfusion, retrieving another syringe from the donor kits, and then swabbing his elbow pit.

"Once the blood's getting pushed in," Errol said, "I'll need you to go and sit along the far wall."

"That won't work," Roxana said, standing over him. "I need to hold up the blood bag, and monitor the transfusion. You need to trust me, Errol."

He looked over at me. "Do you really trust her, Seffy?"

"What do you think she's going to do?" I asked him.

"Maybe what I just did to that other guy?"

I tried to shrug, but it was harder than you'd think with all the tape wrapped around my arms.

"I give you my word," Roxana said. "As a doctor."

"Are you even a real doctor?" Errol asked her.

"I was an MD, yes. Before any of this happened." She put her hand on his shoulder. "I'll do whatever you need me to do. As long as you guys will take me with you. Just… don't leave me behind. Please."

Errol gave me yet another glance.

"I think she needs us more than we need her," I said.

Errol looked back to Roxana. "Let's give this a shot," he said.

Roxana nodded.

And soon she'd injected the needle into Errol's arm, and attached the catheter to the blood bag, which she then lifted a little higher than his head.

"I'm not sure how we can test this," Roxana said. "How we'll know if it worked."

"Smith never mentioned anything?" Errol asked.

"That wasn't something I was involved in."

"We'll need Iris," I said. "Iris can test it."

"I think you can test it," Errol told me. "It worked before."

"I don't know…"

"You can control the bots?" Roxana asked me.

"I don't think so," I said. "Not like Iris can."

"It'll be enough," Errol said. "Enough for me to know."

"We'll be going back to get Iris, anyway."

"Yeah."

A couple minutes later, Roxana passed the blood bag over for Errol to hold, and came over to take out my needle.

"Loosen the tape a little for me," I said. "I can do the rest."

"We'll worry about that in a few minutes," Errol said. "Let's just focus on one thing at a time, okay?"

Roxana taped a cotton ball over my little puncture hole, then took my collection bag and walked back over to Errol and his original bag of my ill-gotten blood.

Once that first bag had been drained empty, Roxana switched over to the second.

"I should warn you," she told him, "there is always a chance of heart attack or stroke it the blood becomes too thick."

"Is two units too thick?"

She shook her head. "I doubt it. Especially considering how much blood you lost."

"The bots have probably been working to create a substitute for that lost blood," I said. "So in theory, more blood into the system should get your bots to undo some of the work they just did."

"And *your* bots," Errol said. "Since they're joining the pool party."

"But I will say that we shouldn't go past two units," Roxana said.

Errol seemed confused by that. "We don't have any more blood," he said.

"I mean, when you meet back with Iris. You don't want to be doing the same thing with her. You should wait at least a few days, better if it's a week to ten days."

Errol nodded.

And we all waited as the contents of the second bag emptied into his vein.

My butt was starting to chafe. And I wasn't big on the idea that I'd probably spent as much time tied or taped up as not over the past couple of days.

I still felt a little simmer of anger toward Errol, even if it seemed to have passed with Roxana. I'm sure there's some kind of misandry there, an ingrained wariness of men, even a guy I'd known for ten years. And nothing over the past week had convinced me that it was a bad idea to have serious misgivings when it comes to the grottier sex.

I waited for Errol to be unplugged and standing before I asked him again. "Can you please get me out of this chair?"

"Just hold on," he said. "One last thing."

"We should test it out," Roxana said. "Try to reach him, Seffy."

"Someone needs to let me go," I said. "I'm serious, here."

"Test it out," Errol said. "Then I'll let you go."

"Are you joking?"

He smirked. "I'm serious, here."

"I don't need to be pissed at you for it to work," I said. "Just get me out of this frickin chair. *Prick*."

And then I felt him. And I knew he could feel me.

And then I heard what he was thinking. Just what he wanted to do to me. And what he was going to do to Roxana.

And what he wanted to do to Iris... what was that? About Iris?

He'd broken the connection. That's what it felt like. Something he'd done to push me away.

"Roxana," I said. "Get me loose. Hurry."

She just looked at me.

"He's going to kill you," I told her.

Errol grabbed onto the hair at the back of Roxana's head.

He yanked her backward, throwing her down to the floor.

She tried to get up, so he kicked her in the head.

I rocked the chair forward, trying to get onto my feet. If I could get it just right...

I saw Errol running over to the kitchen.

And then I rocked my chair too hard, flipping myself hard onto the floor, my knees and my face slamming against the linoleum-covered concrete.

I tried to get up, but ended up twisting onto my side. The duct tape was still holding my wrists and upper body against the back of the chair. I wasn't going to be able to work myself free. Not in time.

Errol came back out from the kitchen, holding a new knife from the wood block.

But Roxana was on her feet by then.

She'd hesitated for a moment, looking down at the twisted mess of duct taped Seffy, before making a run for the stairs up to the main floor.

Errol chased after her, both of them sprinting up the stairwell.

I thought I could hear the front doors open.

I was hoping she'd made it out.

But my focus was on trying to get my hands free.

The fall had loosened the tape, enough that I could start wriggling, slowly adding some slack to tape around my wrists.

I knew I could work my way out of it. Eventually.

I heard footsteps coming down the stairs.

It was Errol.

I couldn't see Roxana.

I didn't know if she'd made it out.

I didn't think she did.

Errol walked over to me.

I couldn't see the knife, either.

He grabbed my chair and lifted it — and me — back into place.

"You've almost worked your way free," he said.

"Are you going to kill me, too?" I asked him.

"I didn't kill her. She got away."

"I don't believe you."

"Doesn't matter," he said.

"I don't want to die, Errol."

He sighed. "If you were anyone else…"

He sat down on the chair to my right, where he'd been sitting before. He reached down and picked up the magazine, and started flipping through it.

Like he had all the time in the world, for whatever it was we were doing. Maybe he was thinking it over.

"I get it for the articles," he said, not looking up at me.

Maybe there was still a chance he'd come to his senses and cut me free. If he was telling the truth about Roxana, that he hadn't killed her…

I couldn't read him. I couldn't hear his thoughts at all anymore.

"Say it," he said.

"What?"

"Just say it, Persephone."

I just stared at him.

And he stared back at me.

And then I realized what he was waiting for.

"Thank you, Errol," I said. "Thanks for coming to save me."

"You're welcome, Persephone. Not so hard, was it?"

"I want to go now, Errol. I want to find Iris."

"You should go and find Roxana. She won't last long on her own."

"I think she's stronger than you give her credit for."

"Maybe…"

"Can you help me get out of this tape?" I asked.

"You're doing fine, Persephone. Keep at it."

"Errol…"

"I'll dig those truck keys off of Smith for you," he told me. "Once you're free, you can take his pickup and find your family."

"What about your family?"

"You can find them, too. I'm not telling you not to. I doubt they're all that happy with me for ditching 'em."

He stood up, dropping the magazine to the floor.

"No, Errol," I said. "I mean you should come back with us. With me."

For a minute, I saw it.

He curled his lip at me.

But then his face changed.

And he shook his head at me.

"I can barely even look at you now," he said. "I just… I don't want to look at you anymore. So uh… this is going to seem really misplaced."

He pulled Jetta's tablet out of his pocket.

And took my picture.

"I thought you didn't want to look at me anymore," I said.

"It's not for me."

He walked over to the kitchen.

First he came back out with the plastic crate, taking it over to the edge of the stairs and dropping it off. Then he went back into the kitchen.

He bent down, to where I couldn't see him through the half wall.

He was getting those truck keys.

He came out from the kitchen, walking right back over to me.

He threw the truck keys onto the floor, just in front of me.

"I don't know if I was in love with you," he told me. "Or if I just loved you like a best friend… for all these years. I really have no clue what the difference is. I really don't. But you know, that's done with, Persephone. I'm done with whatever this was."

"Nothing's changed, Errol. The infection is still out there. You can't just strike out on your own."

He leaned in and kissed me, on the lips.

At first I was surprised. For a guy who apparently hated my *bothot* guts and never wanted to see me again. Mixed signals, much?

I didn't know if I should respond… and then I kissed him back.

Not because I felt it… I don't. Believe me, I don't.

But because I was hoping he'd change his mind. That he'd come back with me. Because… well, I don't know why. For his father and his uncle? Certainly not for me…

He turned away from me, and started walking toward the stairs.

I thought about telling him that I'm in love with him. But he'd know I was lying. And I honestly didn't know why I'd want him to stay with us.

I just sat quietly, and watched him take the large plastic crate and go. And once he was up the stairs, I went back to freeing my hands.

Once I'd managed to break free of all that frickin tape, I grabbed a knife for the kitchen block and made my way upstairs. I didn't expect Errol to still be there, and I could see out the front door that the van was gone.

And the black truck was still there.

And I saw Roxana, standing beside it.

I rushed out to her.

"Are you okay?" I asked.

"He let me go," she said.

"He said you got away."

"No… once I was outside he just turned around and went back into the church."

"Oh."

"I guess he didn't really want to kill me," she said. "I guess you got your wires crossed."

I'd been sure of it.

He'd wanted her dead.

Maybe he'd just been worried I'd get away. But he ended up letting me go anyway, in the end.

Maybe he just wanted to keep me taped up until I said *thank you*.

Now that is more than messed up.

Even more than wanting to kill another human being.

I wasn't about to waste time trying to convince Roxana that no, no really, that guy really had wanted to murder her, so I climbed into the driver's seat of the truck.

Roxana took the passenger side. She hadn't waited for an official invitation; she'd just assumed I'd be okay with it.

Which I guess I was.

I put on my seatbelt and started the engine.

"He says it's the second one," Roxana said.

I looked over to her. "What are you talking about?"

"Errol..."

"He's talking to you?"

"I... I can hear him," she said.

"What's he telling you to do?"

"He isn't telling me what to do. And... I think he's gone now." She reached over and put her hand on my knee. "What does he mean? The second one?"

"That he isn't in love with me... *wasn't* in love with me," I said. "Uh... thank god. I mean, really..."

"Yeah."

I saw dust in the distance, on the gravel road, to the east.

At first, I thought it was Errol in the van, but the cloud of dust was moving toward us.

"I don't think it's him," Roxana said.

I nodded.

I didn't know who it was. I could hope that it was one of our people, that there weren't many other vehicles out there these days.

But I didn't want to be disappointed. Or careless.

"We should keep down," I said. "In case they're the wrong kind of people. If they aren't looking for us, they might not bother stopping to check out the truck."

I looked to the small back row of the cab. The automatic rifle was gone.

As the cloud of dust came closer, I could see it was coming from another pickup truck. It was red, and pretty heavy duty. A farm truck.

It started slowing down as it neared the church.

"They saw the truck," I said.

All I had was a kitchen knife.

The red pickup pulled into the parking lot.

And right up beside us.

A woman driver.

A Hutterite woman.

And Pat Kimmern, riding shotgun.

I sat up.

He hopped out and rushed over to my side of Dr. Smith's pickup.

"Seffy," he said, "thank Christ. We've been looking everywhere for you, sweetheart."

"I'm okay," I said. "And Roxana's okay... and Errol's... okay, too. But he's gone."

"What?"

"I don't really know, Uncle Pat. He left in the van."

"Is Iris with him?"

I felt my heart sink.

I didn't want to ask.

"Seffy," he said, "did Errol take Iris with him? Do you know where she is?"

I started heaving.

Errol had taken her. That's what he hadn't wanted me to know. Why he needed to make sure I didn't find my way out of that basement before he'd taken the van. Iris had been out there, knocked out or tied up in the back, just like Roxana had been. And he'd driven away with her.

He'd picked Iris instead of me. And taken her away from us.

All because he couldn't stand the sight of me anymore.

16

BRINGING FENDER HOME

We've spent four days looking.

A search grid that spreads out over almost two thousand square miles. We have fourteen teams of two, rotating the seven vehicles — the black truck and six more that the Hutterites have that still run — as they travel every mile road and check every driveway, in search for any sign of the van, of Iris, or of Errol.

Every able-bodied person has been more than willing to pitch in, even Lucas, not that we can risk letting him out of our sight now that Iris isn't there to control him.

He's doing his best to convince us that he knows his place, that he's turned over a new leaf. And all that's convinced me of is that he's planning to screw us the first chance he gets.

But the Hutterites won't let us kill him, not if we want their help and expect to share their home. So Lucas will live for the time being, at least until we leave the colony for good.

And I don't think we'll go anywhere else, not until we've found Iris.

You know I don't want to admit it. You know what I won't accept.

So we'll keep looking for now, for the foreseeable future, because I have an over-indulgent father, and friends to match.

But first I'm going back to the B&B, to see if I can get our dog back.

Dad had told me how Fender had gone missing; he'd been outside, just doing whatever dogs do, peeing on stuff, peeing on more stuff... when the bus showed up. It was noisy, there were two soldiers with guns, and Fender ran away.

I'm glad he did. That little dog wouldn't have done us any good getting himself shot.

And, of course, Kellen had spotted him once, but running out and calling for him had managed to push Fender ever farther away, because it was like our little pup had given up on ever coming home and being a normal dog.

I don't want you to think that I haven't been thinking of him, even with everything else that's been going on. Sometimes that's the easiest friend to miss, the one who you know is always supposed to want to be with you, no matter what.

But now he didn't seem to want to come back to us at all.

Jetta had come up with the idea a while back, based on what a dog rescue organization in Manitoba had been doing, but Iris and I had made it clear that we had to wait on trying anything.

From what she'd heard — and described at length, Jetta style — the fight or flight in Fender hadn't caused him to connect to loads of nearby infected people, but had made him revert to a feral mentality, so that he needed to hide from people, because people are dangerous. That even people like me and Iris are dangerous, because he's so terrified he doesn't even recognize us anymore.

So what the rescuers had come up with was a rather odd but simple technique. Whoever was most bonded to that dog was supposed to sit out on a chair not far from the last sighting — but not too close — and just read out loud from a favorite book. Not loudly, not overly quiet, just reading like you would if people could hear your thoughts, which, as we all know, is a surprisingly common thing nowadays.

Dad thought the idea was a waste of time, and considering that his preferred daughter is still missing, I can understand that.

I think Iris is the one Fender has bonded with the most, anyway. And probably her mother, Beth, is in second place.

But Beth asked me to do it; she wasn't comfortable leaving the colony, she'd said, which I'd thought was unusual considering that she'd spent all of her previous time there locked up in a stall in a pig barn.

So I went out with Errol's father and Jetta, back to the B&B, and I set myself up just off the road, me and a lawn chair and a book, while Jetta and Dad waited nearby at the house.

There could only be one person there, Jetta had told me. More than that would definitely scare Fender away.

Iris couldn't be there, so I chose one of her books to read. It wasn't her book, I guess, since her copy was still left behind in Cass County, North Dakota, but it was a slightly-less-dogeared edition of her favourite book, *A Confederacy of Dunces*. If you don't know that one, it's written by a guy who killed himself long before it was ever published. And apparently it's a comedy, too.

After about five minutes of reading I started to regret not bringing a backup book. Because whatever it is, masterwork or not, I wasn't finding it to be that much of a kneeslapper.

But I'd committed to the plan, so I read out loud, following along with the story of a completely unsympathetic fat guy who does his best to get an innocent old man arrested in his place. I know it's the guy's magnum opus… I mean, it's his only work… but I should have grabbed something a little more my style.

I kept at it for three hours, rationing my one bottle of water as my throat dried up like the badlands.

And then I saw something.

Just a flash of brown, and definitely not a deer.

And hopefully not a hungry, hungry coyote.

I kept reading. About Darlene and her bird and a possible new career path for me and one of the surviving Hutterite chickens: Seffy Schmidt and her Exotic Hen Dance. You know a man is smitten with you if he sits through the whole act.

And then there was another flash.

I was getting excited, but I knew I had to keep my voice level. I couldn't show that anxiety, because god knows Fender would sense it even quicker than me.

I read about tube socks.

And Fender came bounding right up to me.

He jumped up on my lap, like he was under the impression that he was a Pekingese, and not a forty pound hunting dog.

He licked my face like a good — *and also terrible* — first date. I clicked the leash onto his collar and then I lead him back to the house.

❧

Dad was glad to see Fender, not that he got up from the table to greet him; it was Jetta who made much of his return, and Fender was ready and willing to take it, the heavy petting and the babytalk, and most importantly, another pale and pretty palette for his affectionate Fender slobber.

"Thank you, Jetta," I said. "I'm still amazed that it worked."

"I'm just glad he's back," she said.

I walked over and gave her a hug.

And I tried to ignore the general disapproval of my father. Like in all other parts of my life.

Jetta kissed me, on the cheek.

For a brief moment... I don't know, two or three seconds, I considered it. I really did.

I like Jetta. A lot. And she's pretty, and fun, and... sexy, in a way that you appreciate that someone else might be attractive to people who are attracted to them... *gah*.

It's not me. And I almost wish it was, that I could give her what I'm pretty sure she wants from me.

I want that, too, a beautiful person who loves me.

But it's not the same. I want Jetta to be here, with me... but not like that. So I delicately broke off what was still a hug, and gave her a smile.

"You look worn out," she said.

"Thanks."

"I'll make you something." And she headed toward the cabinets without waiting for my answer.

I sat down at the table with Dad.

"You did great, kiddo," he said.

"Yeah, I know," I said, not even sure myself if I was ribbing him, or just feeling pissy.

"We'll get her back."

"I know, Dad."

He nodded. He knew it was just some platitude, some mantra of false hope that you throw around because… because I guess the real hope just isn't there.

We haven't found Iris.

I don't even understand how Errol could have taken her, without her finding some way to stop him.

Roxana had said she remembered Errol coming up behind her, while she and Iris were working in the pig barn to cure the infected, and then he'd planted a needle into her neck about as meatily as someone could, as far from not-a-doctor as you could get.

But it worked, and she didn't die; of course, that could have come from some help from her bots. Roxana figured that she was his test case, that once he could be he'd gotten the dose about right, he'd moved onto Iris.

He'd been lucky, that Iris hadn't seen what he'd done to Roxana, and she hadn't had a chance to warn anyone of what was happening.

And by the time Iris had regained consciousness, and I was assuming she had, she'd been too far away to send anyone a call for help.

But if Iris had that power over the infected, and I'd seen it… she should be able to use it again. Errol could tie her down, wrap her in a tarp, lock her in a walk-in freezer… she'd be able to get in touch with anyone within so many miles, anyone who'd been infected.

Maybe she would find her way home, as long as she knew where home happened to be.

"We need to keep someone at the B&B," I said. "In case she comes back here, instead of the colony."

"We can leave a note," Dad said. "You know we can't defend two far-flung locations."

"No, Dad. A note isn't good enough."

"It has to be, Seffy." He finally stood up from his chair and walked over to where I was sitting. He put a hand on my shoulder and squeezed. "I can't risk losing you, too."

"I'm staying here," I said.

"I can stay, too," Jetta said, as she rinsed out a french press coffeepot with some of the water she'd boiled. "Like the world's most depressing sleepover." She bit her bottom lip.

I nodded. "We can stay up all night and talk about Norwegians."

She laughed.

"You're not staying here alone," Dad said.

"You're going to chaperone?" I asked him.

"I'll head back to the colony. Send someone back here. Someone who knows how to shoot."

I rolled my eyes. "I know how to shoot."

"I want someone out here with you," he said.

Jetta looked at me with a frown. She seemed a little offended.

"The more the merrier," I said. "Just… not Uncle Pat."

Dad chuckled. "You know there's no way I'd ever send Uncle Pat."

He gave me a kiss on the cheek — the same cheek as Jetta, not that I think he realized — and walked out of the kitchen.

Then came back in when he noticed that he'd left the keys behind.

Not long after Dad had left *for realzy*, Jetta served me my special drink.

"Here's your coffee, dollface," she said as she poured it.

I thanked her and took the mug in both hands, trying not to notice the silhouette of Che Guevara on it. I don't think Che was ever really about kicking back with a cup of joe.

But I never met the man.

I took my first sip.

It was *redonkulous*.

"This is amazing, Jetta," I said. "What is it?"

"It's coffee," she said. "They grind up beans and put it in a little bag, and then I mix hot water with it."

I shook my head. "No… how does it taste so frickin good?"

"Now that's the big secret, Curlicue. Maybe if you'd been paying attention when I made it…"

I looked over to the counter.

A bag of coffee, an oversized electric kettle, and an assortment of cans and bottles that hadn't been out on the countertop before.

"Hazelnut liquer, creme de cacao, and dulce de leche," Jetta said. "In just the right amounts. I think it's call the strangled Irish monk or something. My mom taught me."

"You have an important skill," I said.

"I have all sorts of skills. Mostly just ways to mix drinks, actually." She sat down beside me.

"I want to be an honorary sister," she said.

"We already made you an honorary sister."

"We were just screwing around with that. I don't think you guys were serious."

"I *think* we were serious," I said. I guess I wasn't sure. "But what about Leona?"

"Leona can figure that out for herself."

I nodded. "So you want to be one of the *bothot* Greek Goddesses."

"I'm *bothot* enough, aren't I?"

"Yes, you are." I reached over and took her hand, to squeeze.

"I know it's a crappy time for this, Seffy. But... I want to be here. With you. And with Iris, when she comes home."

When she comes home. It didn't sound like a platitude, coming from her.

That made me a lot happier than I would have expected.

"Jetta is still not a goddess name," I said. "You'll need something better."

"You're telling me to change my name? Are you kidding me?"

"Your goddess name, idiot. Like how I'm known in Olympian circles as Persephone, but my real name is apparently Curlicue."

She giggled.

"Galatea," I said.

"A sea nymph," she said.

"I thought she was a statue."

"I guess she's both. I took an Ancient Myths class once. You're an underworld goddess, Iris is Olympian, and now I'm a scurvy sea dog."

"I was just trying to come up with something close to Jetta."

"I like it," Jetta said. "I don't *love it*, yet, but it'll grow on me."

"Hard to scream out in bed."

She laughed. "So what do we do in the meantime?" she asked me. "Do we just sit here and drink hard coffee?"

"I can teach you to shoot with a bow," I said.

"Not sure I have the right blood for zombie-fixin'."

"You can scratch some bots off of me, Jetta." I started laughing. *Finally feeling like I could, like it was still okay to laugh.* "You can scratch bots off of me anytime."

∾∾∾

BOOK THREE

GALATEA: EMPRESS OF THE LAST-DITCH EFFORT

COMING SPRING 2015

ABOUT THE AUTHOR

Regan lives in Winnipeg, Canada with his wife, two children, and, for some reason, there is still a cat living there, as well.

You can find out more about Regan at his website:
www.reganwolfrom.com